Beneath Montana Skies

Vivian Belle

STERLING RIDGE PRESS LLC

Cover designed by Sterling Ridge Press LLC

Published by: Sterling Ridge Press, LLC www.sterlingridgepress.com

ISBN: 978-1-966093-20-6
Printed in the United States of America

First Edition: March 2025

For permissions, contact: support@vivianbelle.com or visit www.vivianbelle.com

Dedication

To the dreamers who find themselves between two worlds,
the artists who see beneath the surface,
and the hearts brave enough to cross vast plains for love.
May you discover, like Lydia and Joseph,
that the most beautiful landscapes are not just those
we capture on paper, but those we create together
when we have the courage to lay down our burdens.
For all who have found their home in unexpected places
and their purpose in unexpected faces—
this story is yours.
Vivian Belle

About The Author

Vivian Belle is a talented author known for her sweeping **Historical Christian Romance** novels set against the untamed beauty of the American frontier. With a deep love for history and storytelling, she brings to life **resilient heroines, steadfast heroes, and faith-filled journeys** in the vast, rugged landscapes of the past.

Nestled in the **majestic mountains of northern West Virginia,** Vivian finds endless inspiration in the rolling hills, winding rivers, and boundless sky that mirror the spirit of her stories. When she's not writing, she enjoys **kayaking on tranquil waters, hiking through breathtaking mountain trails, and, of course, getting lost in a good book.**

Vivian's novels capture the heart of **faith, love, and perseverance**—where strong women and honorable men overcome life's trials to find hope, home, and happily-ever-after. Whether she's exploring the great outdoors or crafting her next frontier romance, Vivian's passion for adventure and storytelling shines through in every word she writes.

You can find out more about Vivian and her latest releases at www.vivianbelle.com or follow her on social media for updates and behind-the-scenes glimpses of her writing process. Stay connected—you won't want to miss the heartfelt stories of love and family she has in store!

Also by Vivian Belle

Where the Heart Finds Home
Faith on the Frontier
Love in Hopewell Creek
Abigail's Promise
Beneath Montana Skies

Contents

Chapter 1

The stagecoach lurched to a violent halt, throwing Lydia Hayes forward against the opposite seat. Her gloved hands shot out to brace herself, preventing a most undignified collision with the elderly gentleman who had nodded off across from her. Outside, the driver's shouts to the horses mixed with the grinding of iron-rimmed wheels against packed dirt.

"Bozeman! End of the line, folks! Bozeman!"

Lydia steadied herself, smoothing the wrinkles from her traveling suit, a handsome blue-gray affair that had been pristine when she'd boarded in St. Louis but now bore the marks of five days' hard travel. She gathered her reticule and small leather-bound sketchbook, heart fluttering with nervous anticipation. After months of planning, countless letters, and particularly tense conversation with her parents, she had arrived.

The door swung open, flooding the coach interior with blinding afternoon light and a cloud of dust that immediately caught in her throat. The elderly gentleman roused himself with a snort and blinked owlishly at the brightness.

"Ladies and gentlemen, welcome to Bozeman, Montana Territory," the driver announced, extending a weather-beaten hand to assist Lydia's descent.

She stepped down, her boots meeting not the wooden platform she expected, but simply packed earth. The impact jolted through her legs, stiff from confinement. Drawing a steadying breath that immediately filled her lungs with dust, Lydia took her first real look at her surroundings.

Bozeman was nothing like the artist's renderings she'd pored over in Harper's Weekly. The illustrations had suggested a charming, if rustic, frontier town nestled beneath majestic mountains. The reality before her was considerably more... primitive.

A wide street stretched before her, lined with a haphazard collection of wooden structures in various stages of completion. Some were properly constructed buildings, others little more than shacks with canvas awnings. Men in worn work clothes moved with purpose between establishments, while horses and wagons kicked up clouds of dust that hung in the still air. No cobblestone streets here, no gas lamps, no sense of orderly development that characterized Eastern towns.

But beyond the rough settlement, the mountains rose exactly as she had imagined—breathtaking peaks, their jagged grandeur seeming to mock the tiny human settlement at their feet. Lydia's fingers itched for her charcoals.

"First time in Montana, miss?" The driver interrupted her thoughts as he hauled her trunk down from the coach roof.

"Is it so obvious?" Lydia asked, self-consciously adjusting her hat pin.

The driver chuckled. "Ma'am, your clothes practically scream you're from the east. But don't you worry, Bozeman's growing fast. We got most everything a person needs, even if it ain't fancy."

A man approached from the direction of the stables, wiping his hands on a rag. "This all for the hotel, Walt?" he asked the driver, eyeing Lydia's trunk and matching valises.

"Yep. Miss here's staying with Martha."

The baggage handler looked Lydia up and down with undisguised curiosity. "Visiting family, ma'am?"

"No," Lydia replied, straightening her shoulders slightly. "I'm here on commission from National Geographic. I'll be documenting the Montana landscape and the frontier communities."

Both men exchanged glances that Lydia couldn't quite interpret, something between amusement and skepticism.

"Will you be needin' directions to the hotel, miss?" the driver asked.

Lydia glanced down the dusty thoroughfare. "I believe I can manage. Is that it there?" She pointed toward the largest structure on the street, a two-story wooden building with "BOZEMAN HOTEL" painted in large, if slightly uneven, letters across its face.

"That's the one. Martha runs a good place. Clean beds, decent food." The driver tipped his hat. "Good luck with your... documenting."

Lydia nodded her thanks, gathered her skirt to avoid the worst of the street dust, and made her way toward the hotel. As she walked, she became acutely aware of the stares from the townspeople. A woman in a store doorway ceased her sweeping to watch Lydia pass. Two men loading barrels outside what appeared to be a mercantile paused in their work, one nudging the other and nodding in her direction.

Lord, grant me strength and wisdom in this strange new place, she prayed silently. *Help me see this land and its people through Your eyes, not just my own.*

The boardwalk in front of the hotel offered blessed relief from the street dust. Lydia paused at the entrance, removing a handkerchief to dab at her face, wishing desperately for a mirror. She must look a fright after the journey.

Drawing a deep breath, she pushed open the door and stepped inside.

The hotel's main room served as both the reception area and dining hall, with a long wooden counter separating the entrance from what must be the kitchen behind. A large stone fireplace dominated one wall, though it sat cold and empty. Several rough-hewn tables with mismatched chairs filled the space, most unoccupied at this hour.

At the counter stood a woman, her graying hair pulled back in a severe bun. She wore a practical brown dress with an apron that had seen better days, and her hands were red and chapped from work. She looked up at Lydia's entrance, assessing her with sharp eyes.

"You'll be Miss Hayes, I reckon," the woman said without preamble. "I'm Martha Tipton. This is my establishment."

Lydia moved forward, extending her hand. "Yes, Lydia Hayes. How did you know?"

Martha's handshake was firm and brief. "Got a telegram from the stage company. Plus, you're the only city lady booked for a room this week." A ghost of a smile crossed her weathered face. "Room's ready. Hot water for washing up will cost you extra, but I suspect you'll want it."

"Yes, please," Lydia said fervently.

Martha nodded. "Your guide stopped by earlier. Said he'd return at supper time to discuss your departure."

"My guide? Mr. Calloway, you mean?"

"That's right. Joseph Calloway." Martha busied herself with a ledger, pushing it toward Lydia to sign. "Best rancher in the territory. Knows the land better than most born to it."

Lydia's spirits lifted at this unexpected endorsement. In her correspondence with the Montana agent who'd arranged her commission, Mr. Calloway had been described merely as "experienced and available." If he truly knew the territory so well, perhaps he could show her the authentic West she sought to capture—the noble cowboys, the unspoiled wilderness, the spirit of this vast frontier that had so captivated her imagination through paintings and stories.

"He sounds perfect," Lydia said, signing the ledger with a flourish. "I'm most eager to begin my work. I hope to capture the very heart of Montana... the vanishing frontier in all its wild beauty and romance."

Martha looked up from the ledger, her expression unreadable. "Montana ain't much for romance, Miss Hayes. It's beautiful, sure enough, but it's a hard beauty. Takes as much as it gives." She closed the ledger with a snap. "Room's upstairs, last door on the right. I'll send up water for washing. Supper's at six."

As if on cue, the baggage handler from the stage stop entered, struggling under the weight of Lydia's trunk and valises. Martha pointed him upstairs, then turned back to Lydia.

"Word of advice, Miss Hayes. Montana doesn't much care for being captured, by a camera or a paintbrush. Folks who do best here are those who come to understand it, not just look at it."

Before Lydia could respond to this cryptic counsel, Martha disappeared through the doorway behind the counter, leaving Lydia standing alone with her reticule and sketchbook.

Chapter 2

The small room at the end of the upstairs hallway proved to be clean, if sparse. A narrow iron bedstead with a surprisingly plump mattress stood against one wall. A washstand with a bowl and pitcher occupied another corner, beside a small, unvarnished dresser and a writing desk. A single window looked out over the main street, offering a view of the distant mountains beyond the town's rough buildings.

Lydia set her sketchbook on the bed and moved to the window, drinking in the sight of those magnificent peaks. This was why she had come to document this untamed landscape before civilization tamed it completely. The West was changing rapidly; railroads were pushing farther each day, settlements expanding, the great buffalo herds dwindling. She would capture this moment of transition, preserving it through her art for generations to come.

Her thoughts were interrupted by a knock at the door. A young girl, perhaps twelve or thirteen, entered with a steaming bucket of water, which she poured into the washbasin without a word before departing.

Grateful for the opportunity to refresh herself, Lydia removed her traveling jacket and loosened her collar. The warm water felt heavenly against her dust-streaked skin. She changed into a fresh shirt waist, one of her simpler ones, though still finer than anything she'd seen on the local women, and a skirt of practical navy blue. She re-braided her chestnut hair and secured it at the nape of her neck, a few stubborn tendrils escaping to frame her face.

Once presentable, she retrieved her sketchbook and moved back to the window. The lowering sun cast long shadows across the street, giving the rough buildings a certain dignity. Lydia opened to a fresh page and began to sketch rapidly, capturing the interplay of light and shadow, the silhouettes of mountains beyond the settlement's edge.

She lost herself in the work, as she often did, the familiar movements of her hand across the paper soothing her travel-frayed nerves. This was what she understood, translating what she saw into line and form, finding the essence beneath the surface.

The light was fading when another knock came at her door. The same girl as before stood in the hallway.

"Ma says supper's ready," the child announced flatly. "And there's a man asking for you downstairs."

Lydia glanced at the small clock on the dresser. Six o'clock already? "Thank you. Please tell Mrs. Tipton I'll be right down."

The girl gave a half-hearted nod and disappeared down the hallway.

Lydia closed her sketchbook and tucked a stray lock of hair behind her ear. This would be her first meeting with Mr. Calloway, the man who would be her guide through the Montana wilderness. She sent up a quick prayer that he would be amenable to her artistic purpose, someone who could help her find the true spirit of the West she had traveled so far to capture.

***

The dining room was more populated now, with what appeared to be local businessmen and a few travelers seated at the long tables. Conversation quieted briefly as Lydia descended the stairs, then resumed with a few curious glances her way.

Martha stood by the counter, exchanging words with a man whose back was to Lydia. Even from behind, he presented a striking figure, tall and broad-shouldered, with dark hair cut short at the nape of his neck. He wore a simple cotton shirt; the sleeves rolled to expose forearms browned by the sun, and dark trousers tucked into worn boots. A wide-brimmed hat rested on the counter beside him.

Martha nodded toward the stairs, and the man turned. Lydia's steps faltered slightly.

Joseph Calloway was not what she had expected.

The face that turned toward her was all hard angles, high cheekbones, a strong jaw dark with stubble, a nose that might once have been broken at one time. But it was his eyes that caught her, gray as storm clouds and just as turbulent, set beneath heavy brows that seemed permanently drawn together. His expression was impassive, assessing, giving nothing away.

This was no dime-novel cowboy with rakish charm and a ready smile. This man looked as unyielding as the mountains themselves.

Lydia approached, extending her hand with what she hoped was a confident smile. "Mr. Calloway? I'm Lydia Hayes. It's a pleasure to meet you."

Joseph regarded her outstretched hand for a moment before taking it in a brief, impersonal grip. His palm was rough with calluses, his fingers strong and weather-worn. A working man's hand, so different from the smooth, manicured hands of the gentlemen in her social circle.

"Miss Hayes." His voice matched his appearance, deep and slightly rough, with no attempt at social niceties. "You ready to head out tomorrow?"

"Yes, if that suits your schedule," Lydia replied, trying to maintain her poise despite his curt manner. "I'm eager to begin my commission. I understand from Mrs. Tipton that you know the territory exceptionally well."

Something flickered across his face, annoyance, perhaps, or wariness. "I know it well enough. Been ranching here eight years."

Martha interjected, gesturing toward an empty table. "Why don't you two discuss the particulars over supper? The stew's hot, and there's fresh bread."

Joseph nodded curtly and moved toward the indicated table without waiting to see if Lydia followed. She glanced at Martha, who merely raised an eyebrow as if to say, What did you expect?

Gathering her composure, Lydia followed Joseph to the table. He remained standing until she was seated, at least, before taking the chair opposite her. A small courtesy, but it gave her hope that there might be some civility beneath his rough exterior.

Martha brought over two bowls of stew, thick with chunks of beef and vegetables, accompanied by slices of brown bread still warm from the oven. Lydia murmured her thanks, suddenly aware of her hunger after the long day's travel.

They ate in silence for several minutes. Lydia used the time to study her guide further. Despite his worn clothing and unpolished manner, there was a quiet dignity about Joseph Calloway. He ate with the efficiency of a man accustomed to regarding food as fuel rather than pleasure, his movements economical and controlled.

"Your letter mentioned a two-month commission," he said, breaking the silence. "That's a long time. You sure you're up for it?"

The question held a challenge, as if he already knew the answer. Lydia straightened her spine.

"I assure you, Mr. Calloway, I am quite determined. National Geographic has entrusted me with documenting the vanishing frontier. It's important work."

"Vanishing frontier," he repeated, the words flat. "Seems to me people have been coming out here to 'document' us for years. Painters, photographers, writers. All of them thinking they're capturing something before it disappears."

Lydia set down her spoon. "Because it is disappearing, Mr. Calloway. The railroads coming, the settlements are growing, the decline of the great buffalo herds... the West is changing rapidly. I hope to preserve something of its spirit through my art before it's gone entirely."

Joseph's expression darkened at the mention of buffalo, though he covered it quickly. "And what do you know about the 'spirit' of the West, Miss Hayes? What makes you think you can capture it with your fancy Eastern education and your sketchbooks?"

Lydia felt heat rise to her cheeks at his dismissive tone. "I may not have lived here, Mr. Calloway, but I've studied the work of those who have documented the frontier so far. I've read firsthand accounts. I have a deep appreciation for—"

"Appreciation." He cut her off with a sound that wasn't quite a laugh. "The West isn't something to 'appreciate,' Miss Hayes. It's not a painting to hang on your wall or a story to tell at dinner parties back East. It's life and death. It's struggle and survival."

Lydia pressed her lips together, refusing to be baited into anger. "I understand that my experience is limited, which is precisely why you've been hired you as my guide. I hope you'll help me see beyond the surface, to understand this place as it truly is."

Joseph studied her for a long moment, his gray eyes unreadable. "Two months is a long time," he repeated. "We'll be covering rough country. Sleeping under the stars more often than not. No hot baths, no fancy meals, no conveniences. The weather changes fast in the mountains. It could be sunshine one minute, and snow the next."

"I'm prepared for hardship, Mr. Calloway."

His gaze dropped pointedly to her hands, visible on the table beside her bowl. They were unmistakably a lady's hands, slender and unblemished by hard labor.

"Are you?" he asked quietly.

Lydia resisted the urge to hide her hands in her lap. Instead, she met his gaze directly. "I may not have your experience or your physical strength, Mr. Calloway, but I assure you I have determination and purpose. I won't be a burden to you."

Something that might have been respect flickered in his eyes, though his expression remained guarded. "We'll see," was all he said.

They finished their meal in silence, the air between them heavy with unspoken judgments. When the bowls were empty, Joseph pushed back his chair.

"We leave at dawn. We'll take a wagon to my ranch. It's about a half-day drive. You'll have a room there. I'll stay in the barn," he said, standing. "I hope you've brought sturdy clothes and practical shoes. I'll provide you with a saddlebag to pack lightly for each of our journeys. I'll provide the horses and camping equipment." He reached for his hat on the nearby peg. "Any questions?"

Lydia had dozens, but his stance made it clear he was not inviting an extended conversation. "No, Mr. Calloway. I'll be ready."

He settled his hat on his head with a nod. "Good evening, then, Miss Hayes." He turned to go, then paused. "One more thing. Montana doesn't care much for romantic notions. Neither do I. You'll do better to leave those behind with your fancy dresses."

Before she could formulate a response, he was striding toward the door, his movements as purposeful as everything else about him. The door swung shut behind him with a decisive click.

Martha appeared at Lydia's elbow, collecting the empty bowls. "Well?" she asked, a hint of amusement in her voice. "What do you think of your guide?"

Lydia gathered her composure. "He seems... competent."

Martha's laugh was short but genuine. "That he is. Joseph Calloway knows every ridge and valley from here to the Dakota Territory. If anyone can keep you safe out there, it's him."

"He doesn't seem particularly pleased with the arrangement," Lydia observed.

Martha regarded Lydia thoughtfully. "Joseph's not much for strangers, especially city folk. Had some hard years before he settled into ranching. But he's a man of his word. He'll do right by you."

Lydia nodded, grateful for the reassurance, however qualified. "You've known him long?"

"Long enough." Martha's expression softened slightly. "He helped my late husband with our first cattle drive. Worked from sunup to sundown without complaint. Wouldn't take more than a meal as payment." She shook her head. "Don't let the rough exterior fool you. There's quality there."

With that cryptic endorsement, Martha turned back toward the kitchen, leaving Lydia alone with her thoughts.

Quality, perhaps. But warmth, understanding, and enthusiasm? Those seemed in decidedly short supply. Joseph Calloway clearly viewed her as just another naïve Easterner playing at frontier life, someone to be tolerated rather than respected.

Lydia sighed, running a finger along the edge of the rough wooden table. This journey was not beginning as she had imagined. Where were the colorful frontier people she'd envisioned? The sense of adventure and possibility?

Instead, she had dust and discomfort, curious stares from townspeople, and a guide who clearly thought her incapable and her mission frivolous.

Lord, this is not what I expected, she prayed silently. *Give me strength to persevere, wisdom to learn, and patience with those who doubt me. Help me see beyond my expectations to whatever You would show me in this place.*

Chapter 3

L ydia flung her trunk open with more force than necessary, the heavy lid banging against the wall of her small hotel room. She winced at the noise, hoping Mrs. Tipton wouldn't come marching upstairs to investigate. The woman seemed kind enough beneath her somewhat gruff exterior, but Lydia had no desire to test her patience.

With a methodical precision that belied her inner turmoil, she began sorting through her belongings. Two months in the wilderness. What had seemed so romantic and adventurous to her in the comfort of her New York home now loomed before her as a daunting reality, made all the more challenging by her less-than-enthusiastic guide.

"Pack light," he'd said, as if she were some frivolous socialite who'd brought a dozen ball gowns to the Montana Territory. Lydia snorted softly as she lifted out a sensible wool riding skirt. She'd planned her wardrobe carefully, researching what frontier women wore for practicality. True, she'd included a few nicer items. A woman had to maintain some standards, but nothing extravagant.

Yet, Mr. Calloway had looked at her as if she were made of porcelain, likely to crack at the first sign of discomfort. Those stormy-gray eyes had assessed her and found her wanting.

"He has no idea what I'm capable of," she muttered, extracting a pair of sturdy boots from their protective wrapping. The leather was well-oiled and broken in. She'd at least had the foresight to break them in before coming here.

A floorboard creaked outside her door, followed by shuffling footsteps moving along the hallway. The hotel had filled up since her arrival, with various travelers stopping for the night before continuing their journeys. Martha's establishment might be plain, but it seemed to be a popular accommodation in Bozeman.

Lydia moved to the small desk beneath the window and lit the oil lamp, casting a warm glow over her meager quarters. Night had fallen completely now, the darkness outside her window absolute except for a few scattered lights from the buildings across the street. No gaslights here, no steady glow of city life. She pressed her palm against the cool glass, peering into the darkness where she knew the mountains stood like silent sentinels, invisible now.

"What am I doing here?" she whispered to her reflection.

The question wasn't new. It had followed her from New York, through every city and whistle-stop on her westward journey. It had been there in her father's study when she'd announced her commission, his face flushing with indignation.

"A lady artist, traipsing about the wilderness? Absolutely not, Lydia. I forbid it."

She could still hear his voice, the way it rose on "forbid," a word he'd used far too often throughout her twenty-four years. Forbid her from studying art seriously. Forbid her from submitting work to exhibitions under her own name. Forbid her from considering the teaching position at the ladies' academy.

Lydia had respected his wishes then, finding small ways to pursue her passion while maintaining the appearance of the dutiful daughter. But the National Geographic commission had been too significant to reject. A chance to document the vanishing frontier, to be published alongside respected male artists and photographers. It was everything she'd worked toward.

"There comes a time, Father, when even a daughter must follow her own path," she'd told him that final day, standing straight-backed before his mahogany desk.

"Then follow it without my blessing," he'd replied, turning away from her.

She'd left the next morning before dawn, her mother pressing a small Bible into her hands at the door, tears shining in her eyes.

"Be safe, Lydia. Remember who you are."

The memory stung freshly now, standing alone in this strange place, so far from everything familiar. Perhaps Mr. Calloway was right to doubt her. Perhaps this venture was folly, a willful daughter's rebellion rather than a true artistic calling.

Lydia shook her head sharply, dispelling the thought. No. She had earned this commission on the merit of her work. Her sketches of urban transformation in New York had impressed the Geographic's editor enough to offer her this opportunity. She belonged here as much as anyone.

With renewed determination, she returned to her trunk, extracting her art supplies and arranging them carefully on the small desk. Her prized watercolors nestled in their wooden case, brushes wrapped in protective cloth, sketchbooks of varying sizes, pencils, and charcoals—these were her tools, as essential to her as Mr. Calloway's rope and saddle were to him.

She needed to be practical about what she could carry with her on each journey. A small sketchbook would remain in her pocket at all times, along with a tin of pencils. She selected two medium-sized books for her saddlebags, along with a carefully curated selection of watercolors and charcoals for when they made camp.

Lydia sat back on her heels, surveying the arrangement with satisfaction. Whatever Mr. Joseph Calloway might think of her, she was prepared. She would prove her worth, not through words, but through her art and her conduct. She would capture the essence of this wild place, its beauty and harshness both. And she would do it without being a burden to her reluctant guide.

Resolved, she moved to the washstand and splashed cool water on her face, then reached for her writing case. No matter her father's disapproval, she owed her parents a letter confirming her safe arrival.

Settling at the small desk, Lydia smoothed a sheet of cream stationery and dipped her pen in ink, choosing her words with care.

April 15, 1863

Bozeman, Montana Territory

Dearest Mother and Father,

I have arrived safely in Montana after an uneventful journey. The stage line was efficient, if not particularly comfortable, and I found no cause for concern traveling as a lady alone. Mother's advice about bringing extra handkerchiefs proved prescient, as the dust of travel is considerable.

Bozeman is a modest but growing settlement, with all the necessities but few of the comforts of home. My accommodation is clean and respectable, run by a widow named Martha Tipton.

*I have met my guide, Mr. Joseph Calloway, who comes highly recom-
mended for his knowledge of the territory. He appears competent and
experienced, if somewhat reserved in manner. We depart tomorrow at
dawn to begin our circuit of the region.*

*You need not worry for my safety. Mr. Calloway's reputation as
a guide is excellent, and I have prepared thoroughly for the rigors of
the journey. My supplies are in order, and my determination remains
steadfast.*

Lydia paused, tapping the pen against her chin. Should she mention
her guide's evident disdain? Her own momentary doubts? No. Her
father would seize upon any sign of weakness as justification for his
opposition.

*I understand your concerns about this endeavor, but I ask you to trust
that I have not undertaken it lightly. The opportunity to document this
rapidly changing frontier is of genuine historical and artistic importance. I hope that when you see the results of my work, you will better
understand my purpose here.*

*Please give my love to Edward and Victoria, and assure them their
sister remains in good health and spirits. I shall write again when
opportunity allows.*

Your loving daughter,

Lydia

She read over the letter twice, ensuring it conveyed reassurance
without revealing the full measure of the challenges ahead. It was
truthful, if selective. Her parents need not know how rough the ac-

commodations truly were, or how thoroughly her guide had dismissed her abilities.

Setting the letter aside to dry, Lydia pulled out a fresh sheet for a more candid communication. If she couldn't be entirely honest with her parents, she could at least unburden herself to her dearest friend.

My darling Constance,

How I wish you could see me now, perched at a tiny desk in a frontier hotel that would make your father's hunting lodge seem positively palatial by comparison! The journey here was every bit as dusty and jarring as I anticipated, but oh, Constance. The moment I stepped down from that stagecoach and saw the mountains rising beyond this rough little town, I knew I had made the right decision.

Bozeman itself is hardly the romantic frontier outpost of dime novels. It is dusty and crude, with more saloons than churches and a decidedly utilitarian approach to architecture. The streets are not streets at all, but simply wide paths of dirt that probably turn to mud at the slightest rain, I imagine. Yet, there is something compelling in its rawness, a sense of possibility and becoming.

The hotel where I am staying is run by a remarkable woman named Martha Tipton, who manages to maintain standards of cleanliness that would satisfy even your mother's exacting requirements, despite the primitive conditions. My room is small but adequate, with a view of those magnificent mountains that leaves me breathless each time I look out.

But I must tell you about my guide, for he is nothing like the charming frontiersmen of our shared literary adventures! Mr. Joseph Calloway is tall and imposing, with the most penetrating gray eyes I have ever encountered. He regards me with the wariness one might reserve for a dangerous animal or, perhaps more accurately, an unwelcome oblig-

ation. He clearly believes I am utterly unsuited to this expedition and makes little effort to hide his misgivings.

Lydia paused, remembering the brief, assessing handshake, the cool appraisal in those storm-cloud eyes. She dipped her pen again.

He is not incorrect that I am unaccustomed to wilderness living. We both know my outdoor experiences have been limited to garden parties and the occasional picnic in Central Park. But his immediate dismissal of my capabilities based solely on my appearance and background is both frustrating and, I admit, somewhat hurtful.

Yet Martha speaks highly of him, describing him as a man of quality despite his rough exterior. There is something intriguing beneath his gruff manner, a depth of experience, perhaps, or an untold story. His hands, Constance! They are nothing like the soft, manicured hands of the gentlemen who frequent your mother's drawing room. They are strong and weathered, marked by years of hard work, and I suspect, hardship.

We depart at dawn tomorrow for what will be two months of traveling through the Montana wilderness. Imagine it, Constance! No chaperones, no calling cards, no social niceties, just the vast landscape, my art, and a guide who clearly wishes he were elsewhere.

I confess to moments of doubt. The enormity of what I've undertaken strikes me anew each time I look out at this strange, beautiful land. But I am determined to prove my worth, both as an artist and as a woman capable of more than society permits us to be.

I shall write when I can, though posting letters will be infrequent once we leave civilization behind, I imagine. Keep me in your prayers, dearest friend, as I shall keep you in mine.

With all my affection,

Lydia

P.S. I will wear the practical split riding skirt you helped me commission! I have not yet had occasion to unveil it, but I anticipate Mr. Calloway's expression will be worth every penny of the seamstress's fee when he realizes I came prepared for actual riding. Not merely perching side-saddle like a hothouse flower!

Lydia smiled as she signed the letter, imagining Constance's delight at receiving news from the frontier. Her friend had always been the more conventional of the two, content with the path laid out for women of their class, but she never failed to champion Lydia's more unconventional ambitions.

She sealed both letters with wax, addressing them carefully. She would post them in the morning before they departed, ensuring they caught the next eastbound stage.

The small clock on her dresser showed nearly ten. Stifling a yawn, Lydia stood and stretched, her back protesting. Dawn would come early, and she needed to be well-rested to face whatever challenges tomorrow would bring.

She changed into her nightgown, a practical cotton garment with modest embroidery at the collar, one of her few concessions to feminine vanity on this journey. After washing her face and hands and braiding her hair for sleep, she paused, eyeing her mother's parting gift resting atop her neatly folded clothes.

The small leather Bible was well worn, its pages marked with her mother's neat annotations. Lydia had read from it each day of her journey west, finding comfort in the familiar words even as the landscape outside her window grew increasingly foreign.

She took it now, settling on the edge of the bed and opening to where she had placed a ribbon marker. The Book of James, with its practical exhortations, seemed particularly fitting for her current circumstances.

"Consider it pure joy, my brothers, and sisters, whenever you face trials of many kinds," she read softly, "because you know that the testing of your faith produces perseverance. Let perseverance finish its work so that you may be mature and complete, not lacking anything."

Perseverance. The very quality Mr. Calloway doubted she possessed. The quality her father believed existed only in men of business and action, never in artistic daughters with inappropriate ambitions.

Lydia traced the words with her fingertip, letting them settle into her heart. Perseverance wasn't about physical strength, though that would certainly be tested in the weeks ahead. It was about steadfastness of purpose, about maintaining faith and determination when the path grew difficult.

"Let perseverance finish its work," she whispered, closing the Bible and holding it against her chest. "Lord, help me persevere, not for my pride, but to complete the work You've set before me. Help me see this land through Your eyes and give me the strength to endure whatever challenges await."

She placed the Bible on the small table beside her bed and extinguished the lamp. In the darkness, she could hear the muffled sounds of the hotel settling for the night, footsteps in the hallway, the distant murmur of voices from downstairs, the creak of wooden floors.

Tomorrow, she would begin her real journey into the heart of Montana. With Joseph Calloway as her reluctant guide, she would venture into the wilderness she had traveled so far to see. Whether he believed in her capabilities or not, she would prove herself equal to the task.

Chapter 4

The wagon wheel struck a rut with bone-jarring force, sending Lydia lurching sideways. She clutched the wooden seat with both hands; her knuckles whitening as the vehicle rocked precariously before settling back into its jolting rhythm. Dawn had barely broken when they'd departed Bozeman, the streets still quiet save for a few early risers. Now, three hours into their journey, the sun climbed steadily higher, and Lydia's initial excitement had given way to the stark reality of frontier travel.

"Hold tight," Joseph advised, his first words in nearly an hour. He guided the team of horses around another deep rut in the crude trail, his large hands steady on the reins. "Road gets worse before it gets better."

Lydia straightened her spine, determined not to complain despite the ache already settling into her lower back. "I'm perfectly fine, Mr. Calloway."

He made a noncommittal sound, his attention focused on the trail ahead. The wagon, a sturdy, open vehicle with iron-rimmed wheels and a canvas cover stretched over wooden hoops, carried her trunk and valises secured in the back. It was practical and utilitarian, like everything else about Joseph Calloway.

The man himself sat beside her on the narrow driver's seat, maintaining a careful distance that preserved propriety while making it clear he had no interest in unnecessary conversation. His profile was stern in the morning light, jaw set beneath the shadow of his hat brim, eyes constantly scanning the terrain ahead and around them.

Despite her discomfort, Lydia couldn't help but be captivated by the landscape unfolding before them. They had left Bozeman behind, venturing into a country that seemed to grow more magnificent with each mile. Rolling grasslands stretched toward distant mountains, whose snow-capped peaks stood sharp against the clear blue sky. The immensity of it stole her breath—the sheer scale unlike anything she had known in the East.

"It's so vast," she murmured, almost to herself. "Like an ocean of grass and stone."

Joseph's eyes flicked briefly toward her before returning to the trail. "Montana's big country. What you're seeing now is just the beginning."

Lydia reached for the small sketchbook in her pocket, desperate to capture some impression of the landscape before they moved on. Her pencil moved swiftly across the page, creating rapid outlines of the mountains, the sweeping lines of the prairie.

"We won't be stopping yet," Joseph said, noting her activity. "Still four hours to the ranch, at least."

"I don't need to stop," Lydia replied, continuing to sketch as the wagon bumped along. "I'm just making quick notes. For later reference."

He glanced at her work, something like surprise crossing his features, before his expression returned to its usual impassivity. "Suit yourself."

The wagon hit another rut, jostling Lydia's hand and sending a jagged line across her sketch. She bit back a sound of frustration, tucking the pencil between the pages and returning the book to her pocket.

"The spring rains cut up the trail," Joseph offered unexpectedly. "Another few weeks, and it'll dry out properly."

"Is now the best time to travel here? Before the weather changes?"

He nodded. "Late Spring and early to mid-summer are best for seeing the territory. Everything's green, rivers are running high from snowmelt, wildlife's moving. Mid to late summer gets dry, autumn comes quick, and winter..." He shook his head. "Winter in Montana's not for outsiders."

Lydia considered this, grateful for even this small piece of information. "What will we see on our journeys? I mean, specifically, what areas do you think would be most important to document?"

Joseph was quiet for so long, she thought he might ignore the question entirely. Finally, he spoke, his voice measured.

"Depends what you're looking for. If it's pretty pictures for Eastern magazines, there's plenty of mountain vistas, meadows full of wildflowers, that sort of thing." His tone made it clear what he thought of such endeavors.

"I'm interested in more than just 'pretty pictures,' Mr. Calloway," Lydia said, unable to keep a hint of sharpness from her voice. "I want to document the real Montana, as it exists now, in this moment of transition."

His hands tightened on the reins. "Transition," he repeated, the word flat. "That's a polite way of putting it."

"Putting what?"

"The end of things." He gestured with his chin toward the open country around them. "Ten years ago, you wouldn't see a fence for a hundred miles. Buffalo herds so big they'd take days to pass. Indian hunting parties following the seasonal patterns, same as they had for hundreds of years." He fell silent again, his jaw working. "Now it's all changing. Settlers putting up fence posts, marking boundaries, claiming land that was never meant to be owned."

The bitterness in his voice surprised her. "You don't approve of settlement?"

"Didn't say that." He adjusted his grip on the reins. "Change isn't good or bad on its own. It just is. But there's ways of changing that respect what came before, and ways that don't."

Lydia studied his profile, seeing something beneath the stoicism that intrigued her. "Is that why you became a rancher? A way of living with the land rather than simply taking from it?"

Joseph shot her a sharp look, as if surprised by her insight or perhaps uncomfortable with her perception. "Ranching's a living. Nothing more philosophical than that."

The wagon rolled on, silence falling between them. Lydia turned her attention back to the landscape, watching as a hawk circled lazily overhead, riding thermals in the warming day.

After another hour, Joseph guided the team off the trail toward a small creek lined with cottonwoods. "Need to water the horses," he explained, bringing the wagon to a halt in the dappled shade. "You can stretch your legs if you need to. We'll stop for twenty minutes, no more."

Grateful for the respite, Lydia accepted his outstretched hand to help her down from the high wagon seat. The gesture was impersonal, efficient, withdrawn the moment her feet touched solid ground. Still, she caught a glimpse of his face without the shadow of his hat brim, those storm-gray eyes more expressive than he perhaps realized.

Her legs protested as she took a few tentative steps, stiff from hours of sitting on the hard seat. Joseph was already unhitching the team, leading them to the creek with practiced movements. The horses, a sturdy matched pair of bays, lowered their heads to drink, flanks quivering slightly in the cool shade.

Lydia moved a short-distance away, finding a fallen log near the creek bank. She removed her hat, fanning herself with it as she observed Joseph checking the horses' hooves and harnesses, his movements sure and economical.

She opened her sketchbook again, pencil flowing across the page as she captured the scene, the cottonwoods reflected in the creek's surface, the horses drinking, Joseph's tall figure attending to them. The composition pleased her, the interplay of light and shadow beneath the trees offering depth and contrast.

"You always draw everything you see?" Joseph's voice startled her. He stood a few paces away, observing her work with an unreadable expression.

"Not everything," Lydia replied, continuing her sketch. "But I try to record impressions, moments that capture something essential about a place or person."

He moved closer, glancing down at her sketchbook. His nearness made her suddenly aware of his height, the breadth of his shoulders blocking the dappled light.

"You've got the horses' stance right," he observed, surprising her again. "Most city folk draw them like statues."

The unexpected compliment, if it was indeed a compliment, warmed her more than it should have. "I spent summers at my grandfather's estate in Connecticut. He raised horses. I used to sketch them for hours."

Joseph nodded slightly before moving away to check the wagon wheels. Lydia finished her sketch, adding a few quick notations about the light, the colors, the sound of water over stones. Such details would help when she developed more complete works later.

All too soon, Joseph was hitching the team back to the wagon. "Time to move on," he called.

Lydia tucked away her sketchbook and approached the wagon, where Joseph stood waiting with impassive courtesy to help her back up to the seat. His hands were strong and sure as they gripped her waist, lifting her with surprising ease before he stepped up beside her.

With a flick of the reins, they were moving again. The creek and its sheltering cottonwoods soon left behind. The sun climbed higher, the heat of the day settling around them despite the occasional breeze that stirred the sea of grass.

"Tell me about your ranch, Mr. Calloway," Lydia ventured, breaking another long silence. "How long have you had it?"

Joseph's shoulders seemed to tense slightly at the personal question. "Eight years. Bought it from a man heading back east. He couldn't make a go of it."

"And you could?"

A ghost of something that might have been pride crossed his features. "Takes time to understand this country. What it needs, what it'll give if you work with it instead of against it."

"That sounds like philosophy to me, Mr. Calloway," Lydia remarked, unable to resist the gentle prod.

He shot her a sidelong glance that wasn't quite irritation. "Just practical experience."

"How many cattle do you run?"

"About two hundred head. Small operation compared to some, but it's enough. Good breeding stock, strong calves."

"And you manage it alone?"

"Have a hand who helps with the bigger jobs—branding, roundup. Neighbor pitches in sometimes. I do the same for him. Way things work out here."

Lydia nodded, filing away this glimpse into the cooperative nature of ranch life. "Is that what brought you to Montana? The opportunity to have your own ranch?"

His jaw tightened, and she knew immediately she had ventured onto dangerous ground. "Had my reasons," was all he said, tone making it clear the subject was closed.

They fell silent again, the creak of wagon wheels and jingle of harness filling the void. Lydia turned her attention back to the landscape, which was gradually changing as they traveled. The flat grasslands gave way to more varied terrain—rolling hills, stands of pine and aspen, rocky outcroppings that broke the smooth lines of the horizon.

"Untouched wilderness," she said appreciatively, gazing at a particularly striking vista of mountains framed by foreground trees.

Joseph made a sound that might have been a scoff. "Nothing untouched about it. This land's been used and lived on for generations. Just because there's no buildings or paved streets doesn't make it empty."

Lydia felt her cheeks warm at the rebuke. "I didn't mean—"

"People see what they expect to see," he continued, cutting her off. "Easterners come West expecting empty land waiting to be claimed, wilderness that's never felt a human footprint. It's a convenient story, makes it easier to take what isn't yours to take."

The bitterness in his voice was unmistakable now. Lydia chose her next words carefully. "You're right, of course. I spoke thoughtlessly.

The Blackfoot and other tribes have lived here for centuries, haven't they?"

Joseph glanced at her, perhaps surprised by her ready acknowledgment. "Yes. And before them, others. Land has history, even when you can't see it written down in books."

"I would very much like to learn that history, Mr. Calloway," Lydia said sincerely. "That's part of why I'm here, not just to draw pretty pictures, but to understand and document this place as it really is."

He studied her for a moment before returning his attention to the trail. "We'll see," was all he said, but his tone had lost some of its edge.

The wagon rolled on through the changing landscape, climbing gradual inclines that opened to breathtaking views across the territory. In the distance, a herd of pronghorn antelope moved like fluid shadows across the grassland, their speed and grace mesmerizing.

"Pronghorn," Joseph identified them without being asked. "Fastest animals on the continent. Can outrun anything on four legs."

"They're beautiful," Lydia said, watching as the herd disappeared over a rise.

"And smart. They've learned to stay clear of humans. Time was, they'd graze alongside buffalo herds without much concern."

As the day wore on, the trail began to ascend more noticeably, winding through pine-covered hills. The air grew cooler, fragrant with the scent of evergreens and rich earth. Lydia breathed deeply, the clean mountain air a stark contrast to the sooty atmosphere of New York.

"Nearly there," Joseph said, nodding toward a wide valley that had come into view as they crested a rise. "Ranch is on the other side of that stand of pines."

Lydia leaned forward, eager for her first glimpse of Joseph's home. The valley stretched before them, a patchwork of meadows and woodlands, with a creek winding through its center like a silver ribbon. Cattle grazed in scattered groups across the grasslands, dark dots against the verdant green. And there, nestled at the base of a gentle slope, stood a collection of buildings that must be the ranch headquarters.

As they approached, details emerged. The main house was a log structure with a covered porch across the front. A large barn stood nearby, along with corrals, a bunkhouse, and various outbuildings. It was not grand or pretentious, but solid and well-maintained, speaking of careful stewardship.

"It's lovely," Lydia said sincerely, taking in the setting. The house sat with its back to a pine-covered slope, looking out across the valley toward distant mountains. The positioning offered both shelter from storms and a commanding view of the ranch lands.

Joseph made a noncommittal sound, but she thought she detected a hint of pride in his posture as he guided the team down the long approach to the ranch yard. "It serves its purpose."

A dog, a large black and tan animal with the look of a shepherd, came bounding from the direction of the barn, barking a greeting. Joseph called out, "Bear! Down now," and the dog immediately ceased barking, though his tail continued to wag vigorously as he paced alongside the wagon.

They pulled into the yard, and Joseph brought the team to a halt near the house. The dog circled excitedly, clearly delighted by his master's return.

"Bear, sit," Joseph commanded, and the dog immediately dropped to his haunches, though his entire body quivered with barely contained enthusiasm.

Joseph set the brake and wrapped the reins around the handle before stepping down from the wagon. He moved around to Lydia's side, offering his hands to help her descend. She placed her hands on his shoulders as his grip encircled her waist, the brief contact oddly intimate despite its practicality.

The moment her feet touched the ground, the dog abandoned his sitting position and approached, sniffing curiously at her skirts. Joseph made a sharp sound, and Bear backed up a pace, though his tail continued to wave like a flag.

"He won't hurt you," Joseph said. "Just curious about strangers."

Lydia smiled, extending her hand for the dog to sniff. "Hello, Bear. Aren't you a handsome fellow?" Bear's tail wagged harder, and he pushed his nose into her palm, apparently accepting her presence.

Joseph watched the interaction with an unreadable expression before turning to unhitch the team. "I'll take care of the horses and your luggage. You can wait on the porch if you'd like."

Grateful for the chance to stretch her legs properly, Lydia made her way to the covered porch that ran along the front of the house. The boards were worn smooth by years of use, the whole structure solid and well-built. She paused at the top of the steps, taking in the view that spread before her, the valley, the distant mountains, and the vast Montana sky arching overhead.

It was, quite simply, the most beautiful place she had ever seen. Not manicured or cultivated like the Connecticut countryside, nor dramatic and picturesque like the Hudson Valley. This was raw, elemental beauty, a landscape of immense scale and profound silence, broken only by the occasional lowing of cattle or cry of a hawk high overhead.

"Thank You, Lord, for bringing me to this magnificent place," she whispered, overcome by the majesty before her. "Help me to see it clearly and capture some small portion of its wonder."

Joseph led the team and wagon toward the barn, his movements efficient and purposeful. Bear trotted at his heels, occasionally glancing back at Lydia as if to ensure she remained where she should be.

She watched them go, struck by how naturally Joseph fit into this setting. This was his domain, and he moved through it with the sure confidence of a man who knew exactly where he belonged in the world.

The journey had been long and tiring, but standing here, drinking in the vista before her, Lydia felt a surge of renewed purpose. This was why she had come, to witness and document this way of life, this magnificent country that was changing even as she observed it. She might not yet understand Joseph Calloway or the demons that clearly haunted him, but she understood with perfect clarity that this place was worthy of her artistic efforts.

Chapter 5

Joseph returned from the barn, carrying her trunk and valises with apparent ease. Bear pranced ahead of him, casting occasional glances back as if to ensure his master followed. When they reached the porch, Joseph paused.

"I need to explain the sleeping arrangements," he said, not quite meeting her eyes.

"Of course," Lydia replied, following him into the house.

The interior was surprisingly spacious, with a large central room that served as both living and dining area. A stone fireplace dominated one wall, its hearth swept clean though laid with kindling ready for lighting. The furniture was simple but well-crafted—a sturdy table with four chairs, a pair of wooden armchairs near the fireplace, shelves holding books and various necessities of ranch life. The wooden floors were partially covered with woven rugs that added warmth to the space.

Joseph set her things down and stood awkwardly, hat in hand, looking distinctly uncomfortable. "The bedroom's through there," he said, nodding toward a door off the main room. "It's clean. Fresh sheets and blankets."

Lydia glanced toward the indicated door, then back at Joseph. "And where will you sleep, Mr. Calloway?" she asked directly, sensing his discomfort with the topic.

He cleared his throat. "In the bunkhouse with my ranch hand."

"I wouldn't want to displace you from your home," Lydia began, but Joseph shook his head firmly.

"It's not proper for us to be under the same roof at night," he said stiffly. "I'll be fine. Bear usually sleeps there or in the barn, anyway."

Lydia nodded, acknowledging the propriety of the arrangement. While frontier life might be less formal than Eastern society, certain basic conventions of respectability still applied, particularly given that they were virtual strangers.

"Very well, Mr. Calloway. Thank you for your consideration."

He seemed relieved by her easy acceptance. "Kitchen's over there," he continued, gesturing to an adjoining room. "Stove's simple enough to operate if you're familiar with wood burning. There's a pump for water by the sink, and a pantry with basic provisions." He paused, seeming to search for what else might be important to tell her. "The Outhouse is out back, about thirty yards from the kitchen door. There's a washroom off the bedroom with a basin and such."

"I'm sure I'll manage just fine," Lydia assured him, touched by his evident concern for her comfort despite his general reticence.

Joseph nodded, still looking somewhat ill at ease in his home with her present. "I've got work to see to—cattle to check, fence line to ride. Might be gone for a few hours. Help yourself to whatever you need. If you get hungry, there's bread and preserves in the pantry, cold ham in the springhouse."

"Thank you. I'll settle in and perhaps explore a bit around the immediate area."

"Bear will stay close," Joseph said, whistling for the dog, who had been investigating Lydia's trunk with interest. "He's good company and will let you know if there's anything to be concerned about... not that there should be. The ranch is pretty peaceful."

He moved to the door, clearly eager to escape the unfamiliar situation of having a woman in his home. At the threshold, he paused, turning back with a look of uncertainty that seemed oddly vulnerable on his stern features.

"Miss Hayes... I know this isn't what you're used to. It's plain living out here."

"It's far more comfortable than I anticipated for a frontier ranch, Mr. Calloway," she replied honestly. "You have a lovely home."

A flicker of surprise crossed his face, followed by something that might have been pleasure. "It's nothing fancy," he said gruffly. "But it keeps out the weather."

With that, he settled his hat back on his head and departed, leaving Lydia alone in the silent house. Through the window, she watched him stride toward the barn, Bear trotting at his heels. A few minutes later, he emerged mounted on a tall black gelding, riding out across the meadow with the easy seat of a man who had spent most of his life on horseback.

Lydia turned back to the room, taking in the details she had missed initially. Despite its rustic nature, there was a subtle beauty to the space—the way light slanted through the windows to warm the wooden floors, the careful craftsmanship of the furniture, the practical organization that spoke of a methodical mind. It was a man's home, without feminine touches, yet not without a certain austere charm.

Moving to explore further, she pushed open the door to the bedroom. Like the main room, it was simple but well-appointed. A large bed with a carved headboard dominated the space, covered with a patchwork quilt in shades of blue and gray. A chest of drawers stood against one wall, a washstand in the corner held a basin and pitcher, and a small braided rug softened the wooden floor. The window looked out toward the mountains, offering a view that any grand hotel would envy.

On the bedside table lay a Bible, its leather binding worn smooth from handling. Lydia touched it gently. This evidence of Joseph's faith was a reminder that beneath his gruff exterior and evident pain lay a spiritual foundation they shared, however differently expressed.

"You're a complex man, Joseph Calloway," she murmured to the empty room. "Far more than you want anyone to see."

She returned to the main room and retrieved her valises from beside the trunk, carrying them to the bedroom to unpack the essentials. Her riding clothes, including the split skirt, would be needed when they began their proper excursions. For now, though, she was grateful for the chance to wash away the dust of travel and rest briefly before exploring her new surroundings.

The small washroom yielded another basin and pitcher of fresh water, a cake of simple soap, and clean towels. Lydia poured water into the basin and removed her jacket and collar, washing her face and hands with relief. The cool water revived her, washing away not just the physical dust of the journey, but some of the tension that had built during the long hours of travel.

Refreshed, she changed into a simpler skirt and shirtwaist, suitable for walking around the ranch. She left her hair in its practical braid but removed the pins that had secured it tightly to the back of her head for travel, relieving the pressure on her scalp.

Bear was waiting on the porch when she emerged from the house, his tail wagging in greeting. "Hello again," Lydia said, patting his broad head. "Are you to be my guardian while your master is away?"

The dog gave what sounded remarkably like a confirmatory "woof" and fell into step beside her as she descended the porch steps. With Bear as her guide and protector, Lydia set out to explore the immediate surroundings of the ranch house.

The yard was neat and well-organized, with clear paths between the various buildings. Behind the house, a kitchen garden showed signs of recent planting, with neat rows marked by string lines. A chicken coop stood nearby, several hens scratching contentedly in a fenced run. Beyond that, a small orchard of what looked like apple trees was just beginning to blossom, their pale flowers catching the afternoon light.

"He's quite the farmer as well as a rancher," Lydia observed to Bear, who watched her with intelligent eyes. The level of care and attention evident in these plantings spoke of a man who was committed to this place.

She continued her exploration, keeping the house in sight as she wandered. The barn was a substantial structure, with a hayloft above and stalls below. Through the open door, she could see the orderly arrangement of tack and tools, everything in its place. Even the scent was pleasant—fresh hay, leather, the clean smell of healthy animals.

Beyond the immediate buildings, the land opened up into pastures and meadows. Cattle grazed in the distance, dark shapes against the green grass. The creek she had seen from above wound through the property, its banks lined with willows and cottonwoods. In every direction, the views were spectacular: mountains, forest, open range, all under that immense sky that seemed somehow larger and more vivid than the Eastern heavens she knew.

Lydia found herself drawn to a small rise near the house, where a single pine tree stood sentinel. From this vantage point, she could see much of the valley, including Joseph's distant figure, riding along a fence line far to the west. The afternoon light bathed everything in a clear, pure illumination that revealed every detail with startling clarity.

She sat beneath the tree, Bear settling comfortably beside her, and took out her sketchbook again. This time, she worked more deliberately, creating a more detailed panorama of the valley from this elevated perspective. As she drew, she found herself adding Joseph's distant figure on horseback, a small but essential element that somehow anchored the vast landscape.

"He belongs here," she murmured to herself as she sketched. "It's in every movement, every gesture."

Yet, there was something in Joseph that suggested wounded history, a past that still shadowed his present. The way he spoke of the buffalo, the changing West, the reference to "taking what isn't yours to take"—all hinted at experiences that had left their mark on him.

Lydia closed her sketchbook, leaning back against the trunk of the pine. Bear had fallen asleep beside her, his large body radiating warmth in the cooling afternoon. She closed her eyes, listening to the sounds of this new place, the whisper of wind through pine needles, the distant lowing of cattle, the chatter of birds.

"Lord," she prayed softly, "thank You for bringing me safely to this beautiful place. Help me to see it truly, not just through my preconceptions or romantic notions. And help me to understand my guide, this complicated man whose pain seems as vast as the land he loves. Give me patience with his gruffness, and wisdom in my words and actions."

She opened her eyes, gazing out at the expansive view. For all its beauty, there was an undercurrent of melancholy to this place, or perhaps that was simply the projection of Joseph's evident sorrow onto the landscape. Either way, she felt it keenly, this sense of something precious passing away even as she arrived to document it.

Bear stirred beside her, lifting his head alertly. A moment later, Lydia heard the rhythm of approaching hoofbeats. She turned to see Joseph riding toward the house, his black gelding moving at an easy lope across the meadow. Man and horse made a striking silhouette against the late afternoon light, a vision straight from the frontier paintings she had studied back East, yet this was real, vital, and alive in a way no painting could fully capture.

She rose, dusting off her skirt. Bear was already racing down the slope to greet his master, barking joyfully. Joseph dismounted in the yard below, pausing to ruffle the dog's fur before leading the horse toward the barn. He glanced up, spotting Lydia on the rise, and lifted a hand in acknowledgment.

Taking that as an invitation, or at least permission, Lydia made her way down to the yard. By the time she reached the barn, Joseph had unsaddled the gelding and was brushing him down in the aisle between stalls.

"Did Bear show you around?" he asked, not looking up from his task.

"He was an excellent guide," Lydia replied, maintaining a respectful distance from the large horse. "You have a beautiful property, Mr. Calloway."

Joseph's hands stilled briefly on the brush before resuming their rhythmic strokes. "It does well enough," he said, but there was a hint of pride in his voice. "Land's good when you treat it right."

"The views are spectacular," Lydia continued. "I was doing some sketching from that pine-covered rise."

"Old Sentinel," Joseph supplied. "That's what I call that spot. Good place to watch the valley."

"It must be gratifying to look out over your land and see the results of your hard work."

Joseph led the gelding into a stall, securing the door before turning to face her. In the barn's dimmer light, his features were softer somehow, less guarded.

"It is," he admitted. "There's satisfaction in building something, making something work when others couldn't." He hung the brush on a nearby hook, his movements precise. "Thunder here knows every inch of this place as well as I do, don't you, boy?"

The black gelding nickered softly, pushing his nose against Joseph's shoulder in what looked like genuine affection. Joseph stroked the horse's neck, a rare smile softening his stern features. The tenderness of the gesture caught Lydia by surprise, revealing a gentleness she hadn't yet seen in her taciturn guide.

"He's beautiful," she said. "How long have you had him?"

"Eight years. Bought him as a half-broke three-year-old when I first got the ranch. We learned together." There was real fondness in Joseph's voice as he spoke of the horse. "He's steady. Doesn't spook at much anymore."

Lydia ventured closer, tentatively extending a hand toward Thunder. The gelding stretched his neck, nostrils flaring as he sniffed her palm.

"He's decided you're not too objectionable," Joseph commented, that ghost of a smile lingering. "High praise from Thunder. He doesn't suffer fools gladly."

"Like his master, perhaps?" The words slipped out before Lydia could reconsider them.

To her surprise, Joseph didn't take offense. "Fair observation," he acknowledged, turning to gather his saddle. "We get along because we understand each other."

"I should like to understand Montana that well someday," Lydia said wistfully, watching as Joseph efficiently stored his tack.

Joseph glanced at her, his expression thoughtful. "Takes time. And willingness to learn, not just see what you expect to see." He hesitated, as if weighing his next words. "Most Easterners don't stay long enough for that."

"I have two months," Lydia reminded him. "And while I realize that's not long in the grand scheme of things, I intend to make the most of every day."

Joseph considered her for a moment, those gray eyes assessing. "We'll head out early tomorrow. First light. There's a valley to the north that might interest you, a good variety of terrain, some interesting rock formations."

"That sounds perfect. I'll be ready at first light."

He nodded, seeming satisfied with her assurance. "I need to check on a few things before dark. Make yourself at home in the house. There's a fireplace if it gets cool tonight. Wood's stacked by the hearth."

"Thank you. I'll manage fine." Lydia paused, then added, "Would you like me to prepare some supper? It seems only fair since you're providing lodging."

Joseph looked genuinely surprised by the offer. "You don't need to do that."

"I'd like to. I may not be an expert in frontier living, Mr. Calloway, but I do know my way around a kitchen."

He studied her for a moment, as if trying to determine whether this was some kind of test or trick. Finally, he gave a slight nod. "If you're offering, I won't refuse. Nothing fancy needed."

"I'll see what I can put together," Lydia said, pleased to have a practical way to contribute. "What time should I expect you?"

"About an hour."

"Supper will be ready," she promised, turning toward the house. Behind her, she heard Joseph murmur something to Thunder before the sound of his boots on the barn floor indicated he was moving to another task.

Chapter 6

Lydia surveyed the kitchen with a practical eye. It was, like the rest of the home, simple but well-organized. The wood stove looked to be in good condition, its surface clean and ready for use. A quick check of the pantry revealed basic staples: flour, sugar, coffee, salt, and various preserves in glass jars. In the springhouse, she found ham, eggs, and butter, kept cool in the stone structure built over a natural spring.

Working efficiently, she soon had a fire going in the stove and a skillet heating for ham and eggs. She found potatoes in a bin and sliced them thinly, frying them in the rendered fat from the ham. Bread from the pantry would complete the simple meal.

As she worked, Lydia hummed softly, oddly content in this unfamiliar kitchen. There was something satisfying about the practical tasks, about creating a meal from these basic ingredients in this place so far from the elaborate cuisine of New York society.

"I could get used to this simplicity," she murmured to herself as she turned the potatoes in the skillet, enjoying their savory aroma.

By the time she heard boots on the porch steps, the table was set with plates and two of the mismatched mugs she'd found on a shelf. The coffee was brewing, its rich scent filling the kitchen, and the food was nearly ready.

Joseph paused in the doorway, hat in hand, looking momentarily disoriented at the sight of a woman in his kitchen. His eyes traveled from Lydia to the set table, then to the stove where supper sizzled.

"Smells good," he said, his voice holding a note of surprise.

"I hope you like ham and eggs," Lydia replied. "And fried potatoes. I found some preserves in the pantry that might go nicely with the bread."

Joseph nodded, moving to hang his hat on a peg by the door. She noticed he'd washed up, his face clean of the dust from the day's riding, his dark hair damp at the temples.

"Sit down, Mr. Calloway," Lydia said, gesturing to the table. "The coffee's hot."

He hesitated only briefly before taking a seat at the table. Lydia served generous portions of ham, eggs, and potatoes onto both plates. She added a plate of sliced bread and a jar of what appeared to be apple preserves to the table before sitting down across from him.

"Would you mind saying grace?" she asked.

Joseph looked up, an expression of surprise flashing across his features, before he composed himself and nodded. He bowed his head, and Lydia followed suit.

"Lord," he began, his deep voice steady, "thank You for this food and the hands that prepared it. Bless this meal to our bodies and us to Your service. Amen."

It was simple and direct, like the man himself, but Lydia was touched by the sincerity in his tone. She raised her head to find his eyes on her, an unreadable expression on his face.

"Thank you," she said. "Please, eat while it's hot."

They ate in silence for several minutes, the only sounds the clink of utensils against plates and the occasional appreciative murmur from Joseph. Lydia studied him covertly as she ate, noting the strength in his hands as he cut his ham, the slight furrow between his brows that seemed permanent. The way the light from the window caught the streaks of copper in his dark hair.

"This is good," Joseph said finally, breaking the silence. "Thank you."

Lydia smiled, pleased by the simple compliment. "You're welcome. It's the least I could do, given your hospitality."

Joseph shifted in his chair, a hint of discomfort crossing his features. "Not much of a host," he muttered. "Leaving you to fend for yourself on your first day here."

"You had work to do," Lydia said reasonably. "I understand that. Besides, I enjoy cooking. It's satisfying to create something useful with your hands."

He looked at her with that assessing gaze again, as if she'd said something unexpected. "Most ladies I've come across from out east consider kitchen work beneath them."

"Then you've come across a limited selection of ladies, Mr. Calloway," Lydia replied with a slight smile. "Many women of my acquaintance cook, though perhaps with more servants around to handle the messy parts."

"Fair enough."

Encouraged by this small breakthrough, Lydia decided to press her advantage. "May I ask you something, Mr. Calloway?"

"Depends on what you're asking," he replied.

"Where did you grow up?" Lydia kept her tone casual, reaching for her coffee mug. "You seem to know this country very well, but I was wondering if you're from Montana originally."

Joseph took a bite of potatoes, chewing thoughtfully before answering. "No. Grew up in Missouri, near the Kansas border. Farming country, mainly. Father had a small spread."

"And what brought you west?" Lydia asked, genuinely curious.

Something flickered across his face, a shadow of memory, perhaps regret. "Same thing that brought most men. Opportunity. Space. Chance to make something of myself."

"You were young when you came west?"

Joseph nodded, cutting another slice of ham. "Sixteen. Left home after my father died. Mother had already passed years before. Nothing keeping me there."

Lydia tried to imagine it, a sixteen-year-old boy setting out alone into the vast unknown territories. "That must have been frightening," she said softly.

Joseph's eyes met hers, a hint of surprise in them. "Never thought of it that way. Was just what needed doing." He paused, taking a sip of coffee. "Wasn't alone for long. Fell in with other travelers, learned from them. The West teaches you quick or breaks you."

"And you learned," Lydia observed.

"Had to." He set down his fork, his expression growing more distant. "Did a lot of different jobs. Worked cattle drives in Texas. Trapped in the mountains of Wyoming and Colorado. Scouted for the army for a spell." He stopped, as if the list contained entries he preferred not to mention.

"How did you end up in Montana?" Lydia prompted gently.

Joseph's jaw tightened almost imperceptibly. "Montana seemed right. Less crowded than some places. Good grazing land, plenty of water. When I had enough saved, I bought this place."

Lydia sensed there was much more to the story, but his clipped responses made it clear he was uncomfortable with the topic. She changed tack.

"Your house is lovely," she said.

"Originally, it was just a smaller cabin. I expanded it over the years, added the bedroom."

"You're quite skilled with your hands."

Joseph shrugged, but she could see he was pleased by the observation. "Necessity. Out here, you learn to do for yourself or go without."

"A philosophy I've always admired," Lydia said sincerely. "Self-reliance is a virtue too often overlooked in society circles."

Joseph studied her, his gray eyes intent. "You're not what I expected," he said.

"Oh? And what did you expect, Mr. Calloway?"

"Joseph," he said abruptly. "Since we'll be traveling together, might as well use my given name."

The concession surprised her. "Thank you... Joseph. And you may call me Lydia, if you wish."

He nodded, looking slightly uncomfortable with the sudden informality. "To answer your question... I expected someone more..." He hesitated, seeming to search for a diplomatic word.

"Helpless?" Lydia supplied. "Pampered? Demanding?"

A faint color touched his cheekbones. "Something like that."

"I may be from New York, Joseph, but I'm not incapable of adapting." Lydia spread a bit of the apple preserves on a piece of bread. "Though I will admit, everything here is new to me. I'm grateful for your guidance."

Joseph seemed to relax slightly at her acknowledgment. "It's a hard country, but fair in its way. Doesn't lie to you about what it is."

"Unlike people?" Lydia asked perceptively.

His eyes flickered to hers, a hint of respect in them. "Sometimes."

They ate in silence for a moment, but it felt less strained now, more companionable. Lydia decided to shift the conversation away from him for a while.

"Aren't you curious about me, Joseph? You've barely asked me anything since we met."

He looked up from his plate, a wry expression crossing his features. "Figured you'd tell me what you wanted me to know. City folks usually do."

Lydia laughed softly. "A fair observation. But perhaps there's something specific you'd like to know?"

Joseph considered the question, taking a sip of his coffee. "How'd you end up drawing for National Geographic? Doesn't seem a common occupation for a lady."

"It's not," Lydia admitted. "But I've been drawing since childhood. My grandfather encouraged me. He was something of an amateur naturalist and appreciated my detailed renderings of plants and animals on his estate." She smiled at the memory. "When I grew older, I continued studying art, though more discreetly than I would have liked. My father doesn't entirely approve of my artistic pursuits."

"Why not?" Joseph asked, seeming genuinely curious.

"He believes a woman's role is to make a suitable marriage and manage a household, not pursue a career of any sort." Lydia tried to keep the bitterness from her voice. "Drawing is acceptable as a genteel accomplishment, but not as a serious endeavor."

"Yet here you are, in Montana Territory, on assignment."

"Yes. It took some doing. I submitted my work under my initials only at first, L.C. Hayes. The editor was impressed enough to request a meeting, and by then, it was too late for him to rescind the offer simply because I was a woman." Lydia smiled at the memory of the editor's shocked face. "To his credit, he recognized quality work regardless of the artist's gender."

"That's how you convinced your father to let you come?"

Lydia's smile faded slightly. "Not exactly. He... he didn't give his blessing. I came anyway."

Joseph's eyebrows rose. "That took courage."

"Or foolishness," Lydia replied softly. "Sometimes I'm not sure which."

"Bit of both, maybe," Joseph said, surprising her with his insight. "Most worthwhile things are."

Their eyes met across the table, and for a moment, Lydia felt a connection, as if they understood each other in some fundamental way despite their different backgrounds.

The moment stretched between them until Joseph cleared his throat and reached for his coffee again. "Your father will come around when he sees your work," he said gruffly. "If it's as good as the editor thought."

Lydia wasn't certain whether that was a compliment or a challenge. "I hope my work will be worthy of the subject," she replied diplomatically.

Joseph's expression softened almost imperceptibly. "Montana will give you plenty to work with."

"Speaking of which," Lydia said, gathering her courage, "what should I expect at first on our journey? How much should I pack?"

Joseph seemed relieved to be back on practical ground. "We'll head north first, through Shields Valley. Good views of the Bridger Range, some interesting creek landscapes. Then east toward the Crazies. Different terrain there, more dramatic. Good place to see wildlife, too. Many more places I'm still considering as well."

"It sounds wonderful," Lydia said sincerely. "What should I bring?"

"Pack light, but warm," Joseph advised. "Nights get cold in the mountains, even this time of year. I've got camping gear ready—two tents, two bedrolls, cooking equipment, the essentials."

"Two tents?" Lydia whispered, a slight flush touching her cheeks.

Joseph's expression remained impassive, though she thought she detected a hint of color in his face as well. "Of course. Propriety demands it."

"Of course," Lydia agreed quickly. "I just... I wasn't sure what the arrangements would be. Thank you for your consideration."

Joseph nodded, a bit stiffly. "We'll travel on horseback. I've got a gentle mare you can ride."

"That sounds perfect," Lydia said, relieved. While she could ride, she wasn't an expert horsewoman and had been concerned about managing a spirited western mount.

They fell silent as they finished their meal. When Joseph set down his fork, Lydia gathered her courage for the question that had been on her mind since their first meeting.

"May I ask you something, Joseph? Something rather direct?"

His expression grew guarded, but he nodded once.

"Why did you agree to be my guide?" She met his eyes steadily. "You're obviously a successful rancher with responsibilities here. This is... well, it's a rather odd arrangement, isn't it? A single woman from the East and a single man of the West, traveling alone together. I can't help but wonder why you would take on such a task."

Joseph was silent for a long moment, his eyes studying her with that penetrating gaze. When he finally spoke, his voice was measured.

"Money's part of it," he said frankly. "Spring's a quieter time on the ranch. Sam, my ranch hand, can manage the day-to-day while I'm away." He paused, seemingly weighing his next words. "But that's not the whole of it."

"What is the rest, then?" Lydia prompted gently when he didn't continue.

Joseph's jaw worked slightly, as if he were chewing over his response. "The Geographic editor, Mr. Mitchell... he's an old acquaintance. Asked me as a personal favor."

This surprised Lydia. "You know Mr. Mitchell? How?"

A shadow crossed Joseph's features. "From before. When I first came to Montana." Again, that sense of something left unsaid, a history deliberately obscured.

"I see," Lydia said, though she didn't, not really. "And out of friendship, you agreed."

Joseph's mouth quirked in what might have been a smile or a grimace. "Wouldn't call us friends exactly. But we have... an understanding." He met her eyes directly. "He said you were determined to come. He figured if someone was going to show you Montana, better it be someone who respects the land."

"Instead of someone who might exploit it?" Lydia guessed.

Joseph nodded. "Too many men would see a city woman alone as an opportunity for profit or worse. Out here, two months is a long time to be at someone's mercy."

The stark truth of this assessment sent a chill through Lydia. She had been so focused on winning her independence that she perhaps hadn't fully considered the vulnerability of her position.

"Thank you for your honesty," she said. "And for accepting the responsibility."

"Don't thank me yet," Joseph replied, his tone lightening slightly. "Four or five days in the saddle might change your mind about this whole venture."

Lydia smiled, grateful for the shift in mood. "I'm more resilient than I appear, Mr. Calloway."

"Joseph," he reminded her.

"Joseph," she amended. "And I hope to prove that to you in the days ahead."

He studied her for a moment longer, then nodded. "We'll see." He pushed back from the table and stood. "Thank you for supper. It was good."

"You're welcome. I'll clear up."

"I can help," he offered, surprising her again.

"There's no need—"

"My house, my dishes," he interrupted mildly. "I'll wash you dry."

Lydia found herself smiling at his unexpected insistence. "Very well."

They worked together, Joseph washing each item thoroughly in a basin of hot water he'd poured from the kettle, Lydia drying them with a clean cloth and returning them to their proper places. The domesticity of the scene struck her as both odd and oddly comfortable.

"Where did you learn to cook?" Joseph asked suddenly as he handed her the last plate.

"My grandmother taught me the basics when I was young. Later, I used to slip into the kitchen when our cook was in a good mood. She'd show me how to make simple dishes." Lydia smiled at the memory. "My mother was horrified when she found out, but by then I'd developed a taste for it. There's something satisfying about creating a meal from raw ingredients."

Joseph nodded. "My mother taught me. Said a man ought to know how to feed himself. After she passed, it was just my father and me. We took turns."

This glimpse into his childhood touched Lydia. "She sounds like a wise woman."

"She was."

As Lydia put away the last dish, Joseph moved to the door. "I'll be heading to the bunkhouse now. We leave at first light. Be ready to ride by sunrise. Pack what you need tonight, so there's no rush in the morning."

"I will. Thank you, Joseph."

He paused at the door, hat in hand. "There's a bar for the door there," he said, nodding toward a heavy wooden beam leaning against the wall. "Slot it into those brackets after I leave. Bears are waking up, other critters about. Just a precaution."

"All right." Lydia was touched by his concern for her safety.

"Good night, then." He settled his hat on his head and stepped onto the porch.

"Good night, Joseph." Lydia watched as he crossed the yard toward the bunkhouse, his tall figure outlined against the darkening sky. Only when he had disappeared inside did she close the door, securing it with the heavy wooden bar as instructed.

Alone in the quiet house, she moved through the rooms, lighting a lamp against the gathering dusk. The fire in the stove had died down to embers, casting a gentle glow through its iron grate. Outside the windows, the mountains were turning purple with the approach of night, the valley below already in deep shadow.

Lydia stood for a moment at the window, gazing out at this wild, beautiful land that was to be her home for the next two months. Tomorrow would bring new adventures, new landscapes to capture, and perhaps new insights into the enigmatic man who was to be her guide.

With a small smile, she turned from the window and headed to the bedroom to begin packing. She would be ready at dawn, just as she'd promised.

Chapter 7

"How are your legs?" he asked as they walked back to the horses.

"Better," Lydia said truthfully. The rest had helped, and the stunning scenery had distracted her from her discomfort. "I'll be fine."

Joseph raised a skeptical eyebrow but didn't argue. He helped her mount, then checked Penny's saddle once more before swinging up onto Thunder's back.

"We'll follow the creek for another few hours," he explained as they set off again. "There's a good camping spot at the base of that far ridge where the creek widens into a small pool."

The afternoon passed in relative quiet, broken occasionally when Joseph would point out some feature of the landscape or identify an animal or bird for her benefit. They saw deer drinking in the creek, a red-tailed hawk circling overhead, and once, a fox darting through the underbrush.

Each time, Lydia would make quick notes or crude sketches in her sketchbook as best she could. Joseph seemed to approve of her attentiveness, sometimes slowing or stopping entirely to allow her a better view.

As the afternoon wore on, Lydia found herself growing more comfortable in the saddle, her body adapting to the rhythm of Penny's steady gait. The country they passed through grew incrementally more rugged, the gentle valley giving way to steeper slopes and rockier terrain. The creek they followed cut deeper into the land, forming small waterfalls and pools as it descended through the changing landscape.

The shadows were lengthening when Joseph finally guided them off the main trail toward a sheltered clearing near the creek. A semicircle of large rocks created a natural windbreak, and flat ground offered an ideal spot for their camp.

"We'll stop here for the night," he announced, dismounting and moving to help Lydia down. This time when her feet touched the ground, she managed not to wince, though her muscles protested the movement.

"It's beautiful," she said, looking around at their campsite. The clearing was bordered on one side by a stand of aspens, their slender trunks white against the darker pines beyond. The creek widened here into a small, clear pool before continuing its journey downward. Above them, the ridge rose steeply, its upper reaches still touched by the late afternoon sunlight, while the clearing lay in deepening shadow.

Joseph nodded, already beginning to unload the horses. "Been using this spot for years. Good water, shelter from the wind, plenty of dead wood for a fire."

Lydia moved to help, reaching for her saddlebags and portfolio. "What can I do?" she asked, determined to pull her weight.

Joseph glanced at her with a slightly raised eyebrow. "You can gather some of that smaller deadwood for the fire while I see to the horses and set up the tents."

Grateful for a concrete task, Lydia nodded and moved toward the stand of aspens where fallen branches lay scattered among last autumn's leaves. Her body ached from the day's ride, but the simple physical task of gathering wood felt good, stretching different muscles and giving her a sense of contributing to their camp.

She worked methodically, collecting an armful of dry branches and twigs. As she bent to retrieve a particularly promising piece, she noticed a cluster of delicate white flowers pushing up through the carpet of old leaves. Their star-shaped blooms seemed to glow in the fading light, a touch of pure beauty in the wilderness.

"Spring beauties," came Joseph's voice from behind her.

Lydia turned to find him standing a few paces away, watching her with those observant gray eyes.

"They're lovely," she said. "I'd like to sketch them before we leave tomorrow."

He nodded. "They don't last long. First flowers after the snow melts." He gestured to her armload of wood. "That's enough for now. I'll show you where to put it."

She followed him back to the clearing, where he had already unloaded their supplies and unsaddled the horses. Thunder and Penny were tethered on long leads that allowed them to graze comfortably near the creek.

Joseph had selected a spot for the fire within the semicircle of rocks and quickly arranged stones to contain it. Lydia placed her gathered wood nearby as instructed, watching as he built a fire, starting with a small nest of dry pine needles and bark, then gradually adding larger pieces as the flames took hold.

"Where did you learn to do that?" she asked, fascinated by the efficiency of his movements.

"Necessity," he replied simply. "Fire means survival out here." He looked up at her, the growing flames casting flickering shadows across his face. "You know how to cook over an open fire?"

"Theoretically," Lydia admitted. "Though I've never actually done it."

The corner of his mouth quirked up slightly. "First time for everything. I'll show you tonight. You can try tomorrow."

As the fire strengthened, Joseph turned his attention to setting up their sleeping arrangements. He had brought two small canvas tents. He positioned them several yards apart, with the fire between them, close enough for safety but far enough for propriety.

Lydia watched as he drove stakes into the ground with efficiency, securing the canvas with quick, sure movements. When he finished, he nodded toward the smaller tent.

"That one's yours. Ground cloth inside should keep the damp out. There's extra blankets if you need them."

"Thank you," Lydia said sincerely. "I appreciate your thoroughness."

Joseph simply nodded and turned his attention to preparing their evening meal. From one of the packs, he produced a small iron pot and skillet, beans, coffee, and some dried meat. He worked quietly, measuring coffee into the pot and setting it near the fire to boil.

"Is there anything I can do to help?" Lydia asked, feeling somewhat useless.

Joseph considered her for a moment. "If you intend to draw, now's a good time. Light's what artists call 'interesting,' isn't it?"

Lydia smiled, surprised and touched by his consideration. "Yes, it is. The golden hour, we call it."

While Joseph tended to the food, Lydia retrieved her sketchbook and settled on one of the larger rocks where she could capture the scene. The light was indeed perfect, warm, golden, and directional, casting long shadows and illuminating the edges of trees and rocks with an almost ethereal glow.

Her pencil moved swiftly across the paper, capturing the essential elements of their campsite, the aspens with light filtering through their leaves, the clear pool of the creek reflecting the sky, the rugged line of the ridge above them. She worked quickly, knowing the light would soon fade, adding notes about colors to guide her later work.

Joseph moved about the camp, occasionally glancing her way but never interrupting. As the aroma of coffee and cooking beans filled the air, he spoke.

"Food's nearly ready."

Lydia finished the last few strokes of her sketch and closed her book. "It smells wonderful," she said, rising to join him by the fire.

They ate seated on logs Joseph had positioned near the fire, plates balanced on their knees. The meal was simple, beans cooked with dried meat, hard biscuits from the day before, and strong black coffee, but to Lydia, it tasted better than any formal dinner she had attended in New York.

"This is delicious," she said between mouthfuls.

Joseph looked up, surprise clear on his face. "It's just trail food."

"Perhaps it's the setting that makes it special," Lydia mused, gazing around at their campsite now bathed in the deepening blue of twilight. "Or the satisfaction of a day well spent."

Joseph nodded slowly, thoughtful. "There is something to that. Food tastes better when you've earned it."

The sounds of the crackling fire, the soft nickering of the horses, and the gentle bubbling of the creek surrounded them as they ate.

Above them, stars began to appear, first one by one, then in brilliant clusters against the darkening sky.

"I've never seen so many stars," Lydia whispered, gazing upward as more appeared with each passing minute. "In New York, the gaslights and coal smoke obscure all but the brightest."

"Reminds us how small we really are."

Lydia looked at him across the fire, struck by the unexpected philosophical tone. "That's a comfort to you? Feeling small?"

He considered her question seriously. "In a way. Problems seem less overwhelming when you remember how vast creation is." He gestured upward. "Hard to stay too caught up in yourself under a sky like this."

"It puts things in perspective," Lydia agreed softly. "Makes you wonder what really matters."

Joseph's eyes met hers across the flames, and for a moment, she glimpsed something vulnerable in his usually guarded expression.

"What matters," he said quietly, "is living right with the land and with others. Doing more good than harm. The rest is just... details."

The simplicity and wisdom of his statement touched her deeply. "I believe you're right," she said. "Though it can be difficult to remember in the midst of society's expectations."

He nodded, understanding in his eyes. "Society has different expectations out here. Simpler ones, maybe. Can you ride? Can you work? Will you keep your word? That's what counts."

"It sounds refreshingly straightforward," Lydia said, a smile tugging at her lips.

"Most times," Joseph agreed. He drained the last of his coffee and set the cup aside. "We should turn in soon. Dawn comes early, and tomorrow's trail is more challenging."

Lydia nodded, though part of her was reluctant to end this moment of connection. "What should I do with my plate?"

"Just rinse it at the creek's edge. I'll wash them properly in the morning."

After cleaning her dishes, Lydia retrieved her saddlebags and headed toward her tent. Joseph remained by the fire, adding a few more small logs to sustain it through part of the night.

"Good night, Joseph," she said, pausing at the entrance to her tent. "Thank you for today. It was... extraordinary."

He looked up, his face half in shadow, half illuminated by the firelight. "Sleep well, Lydia. Call out if you need anything."

Chapter 8

A sharp crack jolted Lydia from sleep. She bolted upright, momentarily disoriented by the unfamiliar canvas walls surrounding her. Another loud pop followed, and her racing heart slowed as understanding dawned, the campfire. Just the sound of wood settling in the flames.

She rubbed her eyes, surprised to find that despite sleeping on the ground, she felt remarkably well-rested. Pale gray light filtered through the canvas, suggesting dawn was not far off. Moving carefully on limbs stiff from yesterday's ride, Lydia reached for her mother's Bible, drawing comfort from its familiar weight in her hands. She read a few verses from Psalms, then closed her eyes in silent prayer, thanking God for safety through the night and asking for strength for the day ahead.

Outside, she heard movement, the soft thud of Joseph's boots on the earth, the quiet nickering of horses, the metallic clink of the coffee pot being positioned over the rekindled fire. Taking a deep breath, Lydia quickly dressed. She braided her hair, pinning it securely, before tucking her hat under her arm and ducking through the tent opening.

The crisp morning air carried the scent of pine, damp earth, and brewing coffee. Joseph crouched by the fire, stirring something in a skillet. He glanced up as she emerged, his expression unreadable in the half-light.

"Morning," he said, his voice low and rough from disuse. "Coffee's almost ready."

"Good morning," Lydia replied, taking in the scene around her. The landscape looked different in the dawn light, softer, shrouded in a fine mist that clung to the creek's surface and wound between the trees like pale ribbons. "It's beautiful."

Joseph nodded, returning his attention to the skillet. "Slept alright?"

"Better than I expected," Lydia admitted, stretching to ease the lingering stiffness in her muscles. "Though I imagine I'll feel yesterday's ride when I get back on Penny."

A ghost of a smile touched Joseph's lips. "That's the way of it. Second day's always worse than the first." He gestured toward the creek with a tilt of his head. "Water's cold but clean if you want to wash up properly. I won't look."

"Thank you." Lydia appreciated his consideration for her privacy. She retrieved her small bag of toiletries from her tent and made her way to the creek's edge, selecting a spot partially screened by a cluster of aspens.

The water was indeed shockingly cold, sending a gasp through her as she splashed it over her face and neck. Yet it was invigorating, washing away the last vestiges of sleep and leaving her feeling refreshed and alert. She quickly cleaned her teeth with tooth powder and a small brush, then smoothed her hair where wisps had escaped her braid.

By the time she returned to the fire, Joseph had filled two tin plates with a mixture of cornmeal mush and what appeared to be dried apples reconstituted in the cooking. He handed her a plate and a steaming cup of coffee.

"Thank you," she said, settling on the same log she'd used the night before. "This looks good."

"Simple trail breakfast," Joseph replied with a shrug. "But it'll keep you going."

They ate in companionable silence for a few minutes, watching as the day brightened around them. The mist began to burn away, revealing the deeper blue of the creek and the vivid green of new spring growth on the surrounding trees.

"What will we see today?" Lydia asked, breaking the silence.

Joseph swallowed a mouthful of coffee before answering. "Heading into more rugged country. Some interesting rock formations by midday. Good views of the Crazy Mountains by late afternoon, if the weather holds." He glanced upward at the clearing sky. "Should be fine. The barometer's steady."

"I've been meaning to ask," Lydia ventured, "how did the Crazy Mountains get their name?"

Joseph set his empty plate aside. "Story goes, a woman got lost there in winter, years back. Survived somehow, but when they found her in spring, her mind was gone." He reached for the coffeepot, refilling his cup. "Crow Indians called them 'Mad Mountains' long before that, though. Some places just have that feel about them."

"Sounds ominous," Lydia said.

Joseph shook his head slightly. "Just wild. Powerful. The kind of place that reminds you humans aren't in charge." He offered her more coffee, which she accepted with a grateful nod. "We won't be going deep into them. Just skirt the western edge. Good drawing spots there."

"I look forward to seeing them," Lydia said sincerely. Despite the hint of foreboding in Joseph's description, she was genuinely excited.

After breakfast, they broke camp efficiently. Joseph taught Lydia how to properly extinguish the fire, demonstrating how to douse it thoroughly with water from the creek and stir the ashes to ensure no embers remained hidden.

"Never leave a fire unless you're certain it's completely out," he said seriously. "One spark can destroy thousands of acres in dry conditions."

Lydia nodded, taking his lesson to heart. "My grandfather taught me something similar when I was young. 'Respect fire as you would a wild animal,' he used to say. 'Useful when controlled, devastating when it escapes.'"

"Your grandfather sounds like a sensible man."

"He was," Lydia agreed, a touch of sadness coloring her voice. "He taught me to appreciate the natural world when most girls my age were learning only about fashionable bonnets and proper tea service."

While Joseph dismantled the tents and repacked their supplies, Lydia made a quick sketch of the spring beauties she'd noticed the previous evening. The delicate white flowers with their distinctive pink stripes were even lovelier in the morning light.

Joseph approached as she was finishing, peering over her shoulder at the drawing. "You've got a good eye," he commented. "Most people wouldn't notice something so small."

Lydia smiled up at him, pleased by the compliment. "Beauty exists at every scale. Sometimes, the smallest things are the most perfect."

He nodded, then gestured toward the horses, now saddled and ready. "Time to move out if we want to make a good distance before the heat of the day."

Mounting was easier this morning than she expected, though Lydia couldn't completely suppress a wince as her muscles protested. Joseph pretended not to notice, a courtesy she appreciated. Once she was settled, he swung up onto Thunder's back with grace, and they set off, following the creek upstream toward higher ground.

The trail narrowed as they ascended, sometimes disappearing altogether where it crossed exposed bedrock. Joseph led the way with confident ease, occasionally pointing out landmarks or identifying birds and plants for Lydia's benefit. She was struck by his extensive knowledge of the landscape, not just the geography, but the intricate relationships between the land and its inhabitants.

"How long have you lived in Montana?" she asked as they paused to let the horses drink from a clear rivulet crossing the trail.

Joseph considered the question, his eyes on the distant horizon. "Going on twelve years now. Came when I was twenty-four."

Lydia did the quick calculation. "So you're thirty-six?"

He nodded, a slight furrow appearing between his brows. "Does it matter?"

"Not at all," Lydia replied honestly. "I was just trying to place you in time. To understand your perspective on the changes you've witnessed here."

The furrow eased somewhat. "A lot can change in twelve years. When I first came, there were still vast buffalo herds. Indian tribes followed traditional ways. Now..." He trailed off, his expression darkening.

"You miss it," Lydia observed softly. "The way it was before."

Joseph was quiet for a long moment, gathering Thunder's reins in his hands. "Parts of it," he admitted. "Not all. There was much hardship too. But there was a balance that's been lost." He clicked his tongue, urging Thunder forward. "Let's keep moving. Daylight's wasting."

They rode in silence for a time, climbing steadily through terrain that grew increasingly dramatic. Stands of pine gave way to scattered, wind-twisted trees that clung tenaciously to rocky slopes. The creek they followed became more turbulent, forming small waterfalls and cascades as it tumbled over the uneven ground.

By mid-morning, they emerged onto a high plateau dotted with remarkable rock formations. Weathered pillars of stone stood like sentinels across the landscape, their surfaces sculpted by centuries of wind and water into fantastical shapes.

"Oh my," Lydia breathed, drawing Penny to a halt beside Joseph. "It's like a garden of stone giants."

Joseph nodded, satisfaction evident in his expression. "Thought you might appreciate this spot. Good place to rest the horses and for you to sketch, if you want."

"I'd love to," Lydia said eagerly, already reaching for her portfolio.

They dismounted near a particularly impressive formation, a balanced rock perched atop a slender pedestal of stone that seemed to defy gravity. Joseph helped Lydia from her saddle, his strong hands steadying her as her feet touched the ground. This time, she couldn't hide a grimace as her sore muscles protested.

"Saddle-sore?" he asked, his tone matter-of-fact rather than mocking.

"Yes," Lydia admitted, seeing no point in pretense. "But I'll manage."

Joseph nodded, releasing her once he was certain she had her balance. "Walking helps. Stretch your legs while I tend to the horses."

Lydia did as suggested, moving carefully at first, then with increasing confidence as her muscles warmed. She wandered among the stone formations, marveling at their shapes and the play of light and shadow across their weathered surfaces. Selecting a spot with a good view of several formations, she settled on a flat rock and opened her sketchbook.

Time slipped away as she worked, her pencil capturing the essential lines and textures of the scene before her. She was so absorbed that she startled slightly when Joseph's shadow fell across her page.

"Sorry," he said, stepping back. "Didn't mean to startle you."

"It's fine," Lydia assured him, glancing up with a smile. "I tend to lose myself when I'm drawing."

Joseph stood a respectful distance away, his eyes on her sketch. "May I?" he asked, gesturing toward her work.

"Of course," Lydia replied, turning the sketchbook so he could see it better.

Joseph studied the drawing with serious attention, his expression thoughtful. "You've captured it," he said finally. "The feeling of the place, not just how it looks."

The simple observation pleased Lydia more than a thousand flowery compliments.

Joseph glanced at the sky. "We should move on soon. Still have a good distance to cover before nightfall."

Chapter 9

The song started softly, almost under his breath, but gradually strengthened. His voice was a rich baritone, clear and unexpectedly melodious. The tune was unfamiliar to Lydia, something with a gentle rhythm that matched their horses' steady pace. The words spoke of wide-open spaces, of freedom found under vast skies, of a wanderer's heart finally coming home.

Lydia remained silent, afraid to interrupt this unexpected revelation. She watched Joseph's back as he rode ahead of her, noting how the tension seemed to flow out of his shoulders as the song continued. His voice carried across the empty landscape, echoing slightly from distant rocky slopes, filling the vast space with human emotion.

When he finally fell silent, Lydia held her breath, uncertain whether to acknowledge what she'd heard or pretend it hadn't happened. After a moment's hesitation, she decided on honesty.

"That was beautiful," she said. "You have a remarkable voice."

Joseph glanced back at her, a hint of color touching his cheeks. "My apologies, old habit when riding alone."

"Please don't apologize," Lydia said quickly. "It was truly lovely."

Joseph turned forward again, but not before she caught a fleeting smile. "Trail song. Learned it from an old cattle driver years back. Has a rhythm that keeps the horses moving steady."

"Would you... would you mind singing more?" Lydia asked hesitantly. "Unless I'm interrupting your thoughts."

There was a pause, long enough that Lydia feared she'd overstepped, but then Joseph's voice rose again, this time in a different melody. This song was more narrative, telling of a cowboy's life on the open range, the joys, and hardships, the bonds formed with horses and the land itself.

They continued this way for some time, Joseph singing and Lydia listening as they traveled across the rolling terrain. Occasionally, he would explain the origin of a particular song or teach her a simple chorus that she could join in on. It transformed their journey, creating a sense of shared experience that hadn't existed before.

During a lull between songs, Lydia gathered her courage. "May I ask where you learned to sing like that? Did someone teach you?"

Joseph was quiet for a moment before answering. "My mother. She sang all the time, working in the garden, cooking, mending. Said music made the work go faster." His voice softened with memory. "She had the voice of an angel, at least to my ears. Mine's rougher, but she taught me to carry a tune."

"She taught you well," Lydia said. "Music was important in my home too, though in a different way. Formal lessons, appropriate songs for young ladies to perform in drawing rooms." She smiled at the memory. "I used to sneak down to listen when the kitchen staff would sing their work songs. They had such life to them, so much more interesting than the polite pieces my instructor assigned."

Joseph glanced back at her, a new understanding in his eyes. "You've got wandering in your blood too, don't you? Not just in miles, but in how you see the world."

The observation struck Lydia as profoundly insightful. "I suppose I do," she agreed. "I've always been drawn to what lies beyond the expected path."

"That's why you're here," Joseph said, not a question but a realization. "Not just for the magazine assignment."

"Yes," Lydia admitted. "The commission was the opportunity, but the desire to see and understand this place was already there." She hesitated, then added, "My father calls it my 'unfortunate restlessness.' He believes it's unbecoming in a woman."

"Seems to me restlessness has its purpose. Drives people to discover, to create." He turned in his saddle slightly, meeting her eyes. "Without it, none of us would be here. This country was built by the restless."

His words settled in Lydia's heart like a balm, easing a hurt she hadn't fully acknowledged. All her life, she'd felt somewhat wrong for wanting more than the confined existence prescribed for women of her station. To hear her yearning described not as a flaw but as a strength was profoundly affirming.

"Thank you," she said simply.

Joseph nodded once, then turned forward again, seeming to understand the depth of her gratitude without requiring elaboration.

They rode on through the rolling grassland, the landscape gradually changing as they approached the foothills of a new mountain range. By early afternoon, the distant peaks Joseph had called the Crazy Mountains came fully into view—a dramatic, jagged line cutting across the horizon. Even from a distance, they had a formidable presence, their higher reaches still capped with snow despite the spring warmth in the valleys.

"Oh my," Lydia breathed, unconsciously drawing Penny to a halt. "They're magnificent."

Joseph reined Thunder in beside her. "They are," he agreed, his eyes on the distant peaks. "Different from other ranges. More isolated, standing apart from the main Rockies. Creates their own weather, their own rules."

Lydia studied the mountains, trying to commit their distinctive silhouette to memory for later sketching. "You said the Crow called them the Mad Mountains?"

Joseph shifted in his saddle. "Story I heard was that the spirits in those mountains were especially powerful, sometimes driving people to visions or madness. Some of their medicine men would go there deliberately, seeking dreams to guide the tribe." He shrugged slightly. "Don't know how much is truth, how much is tale. But there is something about them that feels... different."

Lydia nodded, understanding what he meant. Even from here, the mountains had a presence that seemed to demand respect. "Will we get closer?"

"Close enough," Joseph replied. "There's a good campsite in those foothills," he pointed to where the grassland began to rise toward the mountains. "We'll aim for that tonight. Tomorrow, I'll take you to a viewpoint with a good perspective on the range."

They continued their journey; the mountains growing more imposing with each mile. The grassland gradually gave way to more varied terrain, patches of forest, rocky outcroppings, small streams cutting across their path. Joseph led them confidently through this changing landscape, occasionally pointing out wildlife or interesting features.

By late afternoon, clouds had gathered around the mountain peaks, obscuring their summits and casting deep shadows across the land-scape. Joseph glanced at the sky with a practiced eye.

"Mountain weather," he commented. "Changes quick. We should make camp soon."

They rode another hour before Joseph led them off the main trail toward a grove of pines sheltering a small meadow. A clear stream ran along one edge, and the trees provided good protection from the wind that had begun to pick up.

"This is where we'll stop for the night," Joseph announced, dis-mounting and moving to help Lydia from her saddle.

This time, when her feet touched the ground, Lydia was prepared for the stiffness and managed to stand without grimacing. Joseph raised an eyebrow, a hint of approval in his expression.

"Getting your trail legs," he observed.

"I suspect I'll still be sore tomorrow."

"Takes time," Joseph said simply, his hand lingering briefly on her arm before he turned to unsaddle the horses.

While Joseph tended to the animals, Lydia gathered firewood, as she had the previous evening. By the time she had collected a good supply, Joseph had cleared a spot for their fire and was unpacking their supplies.

"Can I help with the tents?" Lydia asked, setting down her armload of wood.

"Yes. I'll show you how to set up yours. Useful skill to have."

For the next several minutes, Joseph patiently demonstrated how to properly pitch the small canvas tent, how to position it for drainage if rain came, and how to secure the guy ropes to withstand wind. Lydia listened attentively, asking questions when needed and following his instructions.

When they had finished, she stood back to survey their work. The tent looked sturdy and inviting.

"Not bad," Joseph commented, the closest thing to praise she'd heard from him about her practical abilities. "Gets easier with practice."

"I appreciate you taking the time to teach me," Lydia said sincerely. "I'd rather learn to do things myself than always depend on others."

Joseph nodded. "Good attitude to have out here."

They worked together to set up the second tent. The task going more quickly now that Lydia understood the process.

"Need to get a fire going before the rain comes," Joseph said, glancing at the darkening sky visible between the pine branches overhead.

With the fire crackling steadily, Joseph turned his attention to their meal and Lydia wrote in her journal, recording observations about the day's journey and making preliminary notes and sketches for future reference.

"May I ask you something?" Lydia said, closing her journal as Joseph stirred the pot hanging over the fire.

He glanced up, wariness flickering briefly in his eyes, but nodded. "You can ask. Might not answer."

Lydia smiled at his candor. "Fair enough. Tell me more about your ranch. What was it like when you first bought it?"

The question seemed to relax him somewhat. "It was just a small cabin and some cleared land."

"You've built it up considerably," Lydia said. "It must have taken a great deal of work."

Joseph nodded. "Piece by piece. Built the barn first, then expanded the house. Added fencing as I could afford it. Took in strays—horses no one wanted, cattle from ranchers who couldn't winter them. Started breeding my own stock about five years ago."

"You did all this alone?" Lydia asked, impressed by the scope of his achievement.

"Mostly. Hired hands when I needed them for specific jobs—barn raising, spring roundup. Sam came on permanent about three years back." He paused, then added, "Neighbors help too. That's the way out here. Everyone pitches in when there's a big job to do."

"It sounds like a true community," Lydia said, thinking of the stark contrast to the often superficial social connections in New York society.

"It is, in its way," Joseph agreed. "Not always smooth, plenty of disagreements and feuds. But when it matters, people stand together." He stirred the beans in the pot once more. "This is ready. Get your plate."

They ate under the shelter of the pines, rain steadily heading their way.

"The Crazy Mountains—do people live there? Or is it too remote?" She asked.

"Some. Trappers, a few prospectors still hoping to strike it rich. One or two small ranches in the lower valleys. Not easy country to tame."

"And the Blackfoot? Do they still use these areas?"

Joseph's expression grew more serious. "Some. Their traditional hunting grounds were further north, but as they've been pushed onto smaller territories, some bands move through this region seasonally. Relations with settlers have been... strained."

"I can imagine," Lydia said soberly. "Losing their lands, their way of life... it must be devastating."

Joseph studied her face, perhaps searching for sincerity in her concern. Whatever he saw seemed to satisfy him.

"It has been," he confirmed. "Old Thomas, the elder I mentioned before, he's seen it all. Lost family in the smallpox epidemics, witnessed the decimation of the buffalo herds, and survived the army campaigns. Now he's trying to help his people adapt without losing who they are." He paused, adding quietly, "Not an easy path."

"I would very much like to meet him," Lydia said. "Not just for my assignment, but to personally understand. Do you think he would be willing?"

"I'll ask when we get closer to their settlement. Can't promise anything. They've had their fill of curious people treating them like exhibits."

"I understand," Lydia said. "And I respect that. I don't want to intrude where I'm not welcome."

Joseph nodded.

They finished their meal and cleaned up after dinner, the rain still steadily moving their way.

"Hopefully, this rain will be gone by morning," Joseph observed, glancing upward.

Lydia followed his gaze and noticed the stars beginning to emerge above them. "It's almost overwhelming how vast and beautiful it is out here," she said softly. "In the city, it's easy to forget what the sky truly looks like."

Joseph nodded, understanding in his expression. "The city has its own beauty, I suppose. But this," he gestured toward the heavens, "this reminds us of our place in creation."

"'When I consider thy heavens, the work of thy fingers, the moon, and the stars, which thou hast ordained; what is man, that thou art mindful of him?'" Lydia quoted softly.

Joseph looked at her with surprise. "Psalms," he identified the passage.

"Yes," Lydia confirmed. "It comes to my mind often out here."

A moment of connection passed between them, a shared understanding of the spiritual dimension of the natural world surrounding them. Joseph's expression softened, revealing a glimpse of the man beneath the rugged exterior.

"My mother used to say that God speaks clearest through His creation. That if you listen properly, you can hear His voice in the wind and the trees and the running water."

"I believe she was right," Lydia replied, touched by this personal revelation.

Joseph nodded, then seemed to catch himself opening up and retreated slightly behind his usual reserve. "Getting late," he said, his tone more practical. "Should turn in. Tomorrow's trail is more challenging."

Lydia accepted the shift, recognizing it wasn't a rejection, but rather Joseph's habitual guardedness reasserting itself. "Of course," she agreed, rising from her seat by the fire. "Thank you for everything you're teaching and showing me."

He looked up at her, firelight casting his features in warm light and deep shadow. "You're a good student," he said simply. "Quick to learn, willing to try."

Coming from Joseph, Lydia knew this was high praise indeed. "Good night, then," she said with a small smile. "Until morning."

"Good night, Lydia." Joseph remained by the fire. "Sleep well."

In her tent, Lydia changed quickly in the chill air, wrapping herself in the blankets. Despite the hard ground beneath her bedroll, she felt a deep contentment that had nothing to do with physical comfort. Today had brought new understanding between her and her taciturn guide, small glimpses behind his careful façade, hints of the man shaped by both joy and sorrow.

She said her prayers, giving thanks for safety and for new perspectives, then settled into her blankets. Outside, she could hear Joseph moving around the camp, checking on the horses, and ensuring all was secure for the night as the rain softly started hitting her tent. There was something deeply reassuring about his presence, a sense of capability and care that allowed her to relax completely.

As sleep began to overtake her, Lydia found herself recalling Joseph's voice as he sang across the open grassland, rich and unexpectedly beautiful, like a hidden stream suddenly revealed. It was, she realized, a perfect metaphor for the man himself, depths concealed beneath a surface that most never troubled to look beyond.

Her last conscious thought before drifting off was a prayer of gratitude for the chance to discover those depths, and a hope that Joseph might one day trust her enough to reveal more of himself willingly.

Chapter 10

Morning came with brilliant clarity, the air washed clean by the previous night's rain and the sky a flawless dome of blue stretching across the horizon. Lydia woke to birdsong and the gentle sounds of Joseph already moving about the camp. She dressed quickly, eager to begin the day.

When she emerged from her tent, she found breakfast already well underway—coffee brewing and something that smelled deliciously like flapjacks cooking in a skillet over the fire.

"Good morning," she called, approaching the fire where Joseph crouched, flipping a golden-brown cake with ease.

He glanced up, a hint of morning stubble darkening his jaw and his hair still slightly damp, suggesting he'd already washed in the stream. "Morning," he replied. "Coffee's ready if you want some."

"Thank you," Lydia said, pouring herself a cup from the pot, keeping warm at the edge of the fire. "Those smell wonderful."

"Sourdough starter," Joseph explained, sliding the finished flapjack onto a plate where several others were stacked. "Brought it along in a jar. Makes better bread than baking powder."

"I've heard of sourdough, but never tried it," Lydia admitted, intrigued.

"Common out here. Some miners and trappers keep starters going for decades." He poured more batter into the skillet. "There's honey in that small jar if you want it for these."

Lydia found the jar and soon was enjoying what might have been the best breakfast she'd had since leaving New York. The flapjacks were light and tangy, perfect with the dark honey and strong coffee.

"These are delicious," she said sincerely. "You're quite the camp cook."

Joseph shrugged off the compliment, but she caught the small smile of satisfaction as he turned to bank the fire. "Practical skill," he said. "Like any other."

As they ate, Joseph outlined the day's plan. "There's a ridge about three hours' ride from here," he explained, pointing toward the foothills of the Crazy Mountains. "Good viewpoint that gives perspective on the whole range. Thought we'd head there first, give you time to sketch, then make our way toward the settlement where Elder Thomas lives. Won't reach it today, but can set up a good halfway camp."

"That sounds wonderful," Lydia agreed, excitement building at the prospect of both the mountain views and the possibility of meeting the Blackfoot elder.

They broke camp efficiently, Lydia taking more responsibility this time, folding her tent correctly after Joseph showed her how, helping to pack the cooking equipment, ensuring the fire was completely extinguished. By the time the sun had fully cleared the eastern horizon, they were mounted and ready to depart.

The morning's ride took them through terrain that grew increasingly dramatic as they approached the mountains. They followed game trails through stands of pine and aspen, crossed meadows brilliant with wildflowers, and forded shallow streams still running high with snowmelt from the peaks above.

Joseph was more talkative than he had been previously, pointing out tracks of elk and deer, identifying birds by their calls, explaining how the landscape had been shaped by ancient glaciers and ongoing erosion. Lydia absorbed it all eagerly, asking questions that revealed her genuine interest and intelligence.

As they climbed higher into the foothills, the vegetation changed subtly. The trees becoming smaller and more gnarled, and the wildflowers had different varieties than those before. The air grew thinner and cooler, carrying the crisp scent of snow from the higher elevations.

"Almost there," Joseph announced as they rounded a bend in the trail. "Ridge is just ahead."

They emerged from a stand of twisted pines onto a rocky promontory that thrust out from the mountainside like the prow of a great stone ship. The view that opened before them was breathtaking. The entire range of the Crazy Mountains spread out in a jagged panorama, their peaks sharp against the sky, valleys, and canyons cutting deep into their flanks.

Lydia gasped, instinctively drawing Penny to a halt. "Oh my," she breathed, her artist's eye already cataloging the play of light and shadow across the dramatic landscape. The textures of rock, the subtle variations in color from the forested lower slopes to the bare rock and ice of the summits.

Joseph dismounted and moved to help her down, his strong hands steadying her as she slid from the saddle. This time, her legs felt stronger, the soreness from previous days' riding beginning to fade.

"Worth the ride?" Joseph asked, a note of pride in his voice as he gestured toward the view.

"Beyond worth it," Lydia replied fervently. "It's magnificent."

They secured the horses to a pine at the edge of the clearing, giving them room to graze on the sparse mountain grass. Joseph helped Lydia find a comfortable spot to sit where she could work, then settled nearby, content to watch the landscape while she sketched.

For nearly two hours, Lydia worked steadily, first capturing the overall composition of the mountain range, then focusing on details that caught her artist's eye, a dramatic cliff face, a waterfall visible as a silver thread in a distant canyon. The interplay of light and shadow as clouds occasionally drifted across the peaks.

Joseph watched her work with undisguised interest, sometimes asking quiet questions about her techniques or observing details she was including. His genuine respect for her craft touched Lydia deeply, so different from the patronizing attitude she often encountered in New York society, where her art was viewed as a genteel accomplishment rather than serious work.

"You see things differently," Joseph commented as she worked on a particularly detailed section of the drawing. "Notice what most people miss."

Lydia glanced up, her pencil pausing mid-stroke. "Is that a good thing?"

"Yes," he replied, his eyes on the mountains. "Seeing clearly keeps you alive. Noticing details others miss, which berries are safe, how clouds form before a storm, the subtle shift in an animal's posture before it bolts or charges." He gestured toward her sketch. "You're capturing what these mountains actually are, not just what you expected to see."

"That's the highest compliment you could give my work," she said, returning to her drawing. "To truly see something requires pushing aside preconceptions. It's harder than most realize."

Joseph nodded. "Most folks just see what fits their ideas. Indians are savages, mountains are obstacles, land is something to be conquered." His voice held a trace of bitterness. "Few take the time to understand what's actually before them."

Lydia continued sketching, occasionally glancing up to find Joseph's eyes on her work, thoughtful and assessing. Where once his scrutiny might have made her uncomfortable, now she found it oddly reassuring.

When she finally set her sketchbook aside, flexing her cramped fingers, Joseph handed her a canteen of fresh water.

"Thank you," she said, taking a long drink. The cool mountain water tasted sweeter than any beverage she'd been served in New York's finest establishments.

"Ready to move on?" Joseph asked, standing and stretching his long frame. "Still have a good distance to cover before nightfall."

Lydia nodded, carefully storing her sketches in her portfolio. "These mountains... I can understand why the Crow considered them powerful places for visions. There's something about them that feels...ancient and knowing."

Joseph helped her gather her supplies, his movements efficient but unhurried. "Some places have that effect. Like they were here long before us and will remain long after, watching our brief lives with indifference."

"Yet not with cruelty," Lydia added, glancing back at the majestic peaks. "There's a strange comfort in that permanence, don't you think? In knowing that some things endure beyond our troubles."

Joseph studied her face for a moment. "Yes," he said finally. "There is."

They mounted their horses and began the descent from the ridge, following a different trail than the one they had ascended. This path wound along the shoulder of the mountain before dropping into a narrow valley thick with pine and aspen. Water trickled everywhere—small springs emerging from rocky crevices, tiny streams crisscrossing the trail, the earth still saturated from the previous night's rain.

As they descended, the air warmed and softened, filled with the scent of pine resin and wildflowers. Birds called from the surrounding forest, and once, a flash of movement through the trees revealed a deer bounding away, startled by their approach.

"This valley leads toward Blackfoot country," Joseph explained as they rode. "We'll be traveling along the boundary between settler ranches and lands they still use seasonally. It's...complicated territory."

"In what way?" Lydia asked, sensing the tension in his voice.

Joseph guided Thunder around a fallen log before answering. "Treaties get made and broken. Boundaries shift. Some ranchers respect the Blackfoot claims to certain hunting grounds and water sources. Others don't." He glanced back at her. "Creates conflict. Hard feelings on both sides."

"Where do you stand in this?" Lydia asked carefully.

"I try to live respectfully. My ranch isn't on contested ground. I have agreements with Elder Thomas about water rights and hunting passage." His jaw tightened slightly. "Not all my neighbors appreciate my position."

"It must be difficult being caught between worlds," Lydia observed.

"Difficult for everyone," Joseph replied. "But hardest for the Blackfoot. They're the ones losing ground with each passing year."

They emerged from the forest into a meadow alive with wildflowers, purple lupine, scarlet paintbrush, and golden balsam root, creating a tapestry of color against the green grass. The sight was so beautiful it made Lydia's breath catch.

"Oh!" she exclaimed softly. "Could we stop, just for a moment? I'd like to make a small color study."

Joseph nodded, reining Thunder to a halt. "Good place for the horses to rest anyway," he said, dismounting fluidly. "Not much further to where we'll camp tonight."

Lydia worked quickly, using her watercolors to capture the vibrant palette of the meadow flowers. Joseph watched for a few minutes, then moved off to check on something he'd noticed at the edge of the clearing. When he returned, his expression was somber.

"What is it?" Lydia asked, sensing the shift in his mood.

"Tracks," he said simply. "Riders came through here recently. Four, maybe five horses."

"Is that unusual?"

"This isn't a main trail," Joseph explained, glancing toward the forest beyond the meadow. "And the tracks are heading into Blackfoot territory."

"Perhaps traders?" Lydia suggested.

Joseph shook his head. "Not likely. No trading post that way, and legitimate traders would use the established routes." He frowned slightly. "Could be nothing. But I don't like it."

The carefree mood of the day evaporated, replaced by a subtle tension that Lydia could feel radiating from him. He helped her pack away her art supplies, his movements reflecting a new alertness.

"We should move on," he said, his voice low and serious. "Be in camp before dusk."

They rode at a brisker pace now, Joseph frequently scanning the surrounding landscape, occasionally pausing to examine something only he could detect, broken twigs, disturbed earth, and marks Lydia couldn't begin to interpret. His vigilance both impressed and unnerved her.

"Are we in danger?" she asked finally, keeping her voice steady.

Joseph glanced back at her. "No immediate danger," he assured her. "Just being cautious. Montana's still wild country. Best to know who's moving through it and why."

"Who do you think left those tracks?"

Joseph's jaw tightened. "Could be hunters. Could be men looking for trouble." He guided Thunder around a rocky outcropping. "There are those who resent the Blackfoot's remaining claims to this land. Some act on that resentment."

The implications settled heavily in Lydia's mind. "You're worried about the settlement Elder Thomas lives in."

It wasn't a question, but Joseph nodded anyway. "Worrying doesn't help, but being aware does."

They continued through the afternoon, the landscape gradually changing as they moved from the mountain foothills into more open country. By late afternoon, they had reached a small plateau overlooking a broad valley. A river wound through the center, flanked by cottonwoods and willows still bright with spring green.

"That's where we'll camp," Joseph said, pointing to a stand of trees near a bend in the river. "Good water, sheltered from the wind, not far from the trail we'll take tomorrow."

They made their way down to the river, where Joseph selected a campsite with the same careful attention he'd shown at previous stops.

As they unpacked the horses, he remained vigilant, his eyes frequently scanning the surrounding landscape.

Lydia set up her tent with minimal assistance, proud of her improving skills. While Joseph gathered firewood, she arranged their cooking supplies and prepared the fire pit, as she'd seen him do. Working together without much need for conversation, they established their camp efficiently.

As twilight settled over the land, they sat by the fire eating a simple meal of beans, jerky, and hardtack softened in the bean broth. Joseph had been quieter than usual, his attention seemingly divided between their immediate surroundings and distant concerns.

"May I ask you something?" Lydia ventured, setting aside her empty plate.

Joseph nodded, his eyes reflecting the dancing flames.

"How did you come to know Elder Thomas? You speak of him with respect, but also a familiarity that suggests more than passing acquaintance."

Joseph was silent for so long that Lydia thought he might not answer. When he finally spoke, his voice was low, almost contemplative.

"Found myself near Blackfoot territory during a hard winter. Got caught in a blizzard, horse died, ended up half-frozen in a ravine."

He paused, memories clearly playing across his features.

"Thomas's son found me. He could have left me there, many would have, given what white men had done to their people. Instead, he brought me to their winter camp." Joseph's eyes remained on the fire. "Thomas's family nursed me back to health. Fed me when they had little enough for themselves. Taught me things about surviving in this country that I'd never known."

Lydia listened, touched by both the story and the fact that he was sharing it with her.

"When spring came, I helped them hunt, shared what skills I had. Didn't balance the scales, not even close, but it was what I could offer." He glanced up at her. "Later, when I bought my ranch, I made sure to seek Thomas out, to establish more respect between us. We've maintained that over the years."

"That's a remarkable story."

Joseph nodded once. "We should turn in. Tomorrow will bring us closer to their settlement, and I want to arrive with daylight to spare."

Despite his suggestion, Joseph remained by the fire after Lydia retired to her tent. Through the canvas, she could see his silhouette, still and watchful, a sentinel between her and whatever concerns had shadowed his thoughts throughout the afternoon.

As she drifted toward sleep, Lydia found herself praying—for Joseph, for Elder Thomas and his people, and for whatever lay ahead on their journey. There had been a shift today, a sense that they were riding toward something more complicated than mountain views and artistic studies. The tracks in the meadow had unsettled Joseph deeply, and his concern had transmitted itself to her.

Yet alongside this new uneasiness, Lydia realized there was also a deepening trust between them. Joseph had shared a significant piece of his past with her, revealing vulnerability and depth she hadn't glimpsed before. Something was changing in their relationship, evolving from the wary formality of guide and client into something more nuanced and genuine.

Chapter 11

The crack of a rifle shot shattered the morning stillness.

Lydia's heart lurched as Joseph's arm shot out, halting her horse beside his. His body tensed, head cocked to one side, listening intently.

"Was that—" she began.

"Quiet," Joseph whispered, his voice barely audible above the rustling leaves. His hand moved to the Winchester rifle in his saddle holster, though he didn't draw it yet.

They sat motionless for several long moments, Penny shifting nervously beneath Lydia, while Thunder remained statue-still under Joseph's steady hand. The surrounding forest seemed to hold its breath. Birds had ceased their calls.

Then came distant voices, floating up from somewhere ahead on the trail.

Joseph's jaw tightened. "Stay here," he murmured, swinging down from his saddle in one fluid motion. "Don't move unless I call for you."

"But Joseph—"

"Please, Lydia." His eyes met hers, and something in their grave intensity stopped her protest. "I need to know you're safe while I scout ahead."

She nodded reluctantly, watching as he handed her Thunder's reins. He moved with surprising stealth for such a large man, his footfalls nearly silent on the pine-needle covered ground as he disappeared into the trees.

Lydia sat rigid in her saddle, straining to hear anything beyond the nervous shifting of the horses and her own quickened breathing. She murmured the Twenty-third Psalm under her breath, drawing comfort from the familiar words as minutes stretched endlessly.

When Joseph finally reappeared, emerging from the shadows of the pines so suddenly that she startled, the tight lines around his mouth told her something was wrong before he spoke.

"Hunters," he said, his voice low and controlled, but Lydia detected an undercurrent of anger. "Four men camped by the stream ahead."

"Are they hunting deer?" Lydia asked.

He looked away, his profile hard as granite against the dappled forest light. "They've shot a buck out of season. But that's not what concerns me." He took Thunder's reins back from her. "They're camped directly on a Blackfoot trail, one used regularly to reach fishing grounds. And from their talk, that's no accident."

"You think they're deliberately provocative?"

Joseph swung back into his saddle. "I know they are. Recognized two of them, brothers named Garrett who've had run-ins with the Blackfoot before. Bad blood there." He guided Thunder off the main trail. "We'll go around. I know another way to reach Elder Thomas's settlement."

They picked their way carefully through the thicker forest, Joseph leading them on what seemed to Lydia an invisible path. Branches occasionally brushed her shoulders, and twice she had to duck low over Penny's neck to avoid low-hanging limbs. The detour would surely add length to their journey, but Joseph's tension was palpable enough that she didn't question the necessity.

It was approaching midday when they finally emerged from the dense woodland onto a gentle slope overlooking a wide, grassy valley. The land below spread out in a verdant patchwork of meadows and scattered copses, bisected by a shimmering river that wound like a silver ribbon through the center. Near a bend in the river, Lydia could make out what appeared to be a small settlement—a gathering of structures quite different from the log cabins and frame houses she'd seen in frontier towns.

"Is that...?" she began.

Joseph nodded. "Elder Thomas's people. One of the smaller Blackfoot settlements, but they've held this ground for generations." His expression softened slightly. "Good bottom land for growing things. River full of fish. Sheltered from the worst winter storms by those hills to the north."

Lydia studied the distant collection of dwellings with keen interest. Even from this distance, she could see they weren't the teepees depicted in the popular illustrations she'd studied before her journey, but more substantial structures that spoke of a settled community.

"I thought the Blackfoot were primarily nomadic," she said, careful to keep curiosity rather than presumption in her tone.

"They were when buffalo were plentiful. Following the great herds was their way for countless generations. But those days..." He trailed off, and Lydia didn't need him to finish the thought.

"The buffalo hunts," she said softly.

He nodded once, a sharp motion. "Some bands adapted. Became more settled, growing crops, raising some livestock, fishing more. Thomas's people are among them." He hesitated before adding, "It wasn't a choice freely made."

They guided their horses down the gentle slope, following a well-worn trail that zigzagged toward the valley floor. As they descended, Joseph began to share more about what to expect.

"Thomas is respected not just for his age but for his wisdom. He speaks English well. He was educated for a time at a mission school, though he returned to his people's ways afterward." Joseph glanced at her. "His wife, Sarah Dove, is a healer with knowledge of plants that would put most doctors to shame. Their son, Michael, is now a leader among the younger men."

"The son who found you in the blizzard?" Lydia asked.

"Yes. He had every reason to leave me there, considering..." Joseph's voice tightened. "I'd been a buffalo hunter. He knew it could tell from my gear. He still brought me in."

They rode in silence for several minutes before Lydia ventured another question. "Will they welcome me? A stranger with a sketchbook might not be a welcome sight, given their experiences."

Joseph considered this. "Thomas understands the power of images to tell the truth, if that's truly your intention." He looked at her directly. "It's trust in me that will open the door for you. Don't make me regret that."

"I won't," Lydia promised earnestly.

"Follow my lead. There are courtesies to observe. And Lydia—" he hesitated, "—listen more than you speak, at least at first. Silence is respected."

As they neared the settlement, Lydia noticed subtle signs of human presence intensifying. A carefully managed stand of berry bushes, a stack of firewood arranged with precision, a corral containing several horses. Evidence of lives deeply connected to this particular piece of earth.

Their approach had not gone unnoticed. As they came within a hundred yards of the first dwellings, three men appeared on horseback, moving to intercept them. Joseph raised his hand in what Lydia recognized as a gesture of peace.

"Michael," he called, recognizing the man in the center.

The man returned the gesture, his face impassive as they drew closer. He appeared to be in his early thirties, broad-shouldered and straight-backed, with intelligent eyes that assessed them carefully. His dark hair was cut shorter than Lydia had expected, and he wore a mixture of traditional clothing and items clearly acquired through trade. Buckskin leggings paired with a cotton shirt, moccasins adorned with intricate beadwork, and a wide-brimmed hat similar to Joseph.'s.

"Joseph Calloway," Michael said, his voice carrying a slight accent. "It has been many moons."

"Too many," Joseph agreed, reining Thunder to a halt at a respectful distance. "I bring news, and a visitor." He gestured toward Lydia. "This is Miss Lydia Hayes, from New York. An artist commissioned to document the Montana Territory."

Michael's dark eyes shifted to study her, his expression revealing nothing of his thoughts. Lydia inclined her head respectfully, remaining silent as Joseph had advised.

After a long moment, Michael looked back at Joseph. "My father expected you might come. There is much happening that concerns us all." He glanced at the two men flanking him, then back at Joseph. "You know of the hunters?"

"We encountered their camp this morning," Joseph confirmed, his tone grim. "The Garrett brothers among them."

Michael's jaw tightened almost imperceptibly. "Yes. They have been watching our movements, shooting game that crosses paths used by our children." His eyes held Joseph's. "They want conflict."

"That won't happen," Joseph said firmly. "Not if we can prevent it."

"May we speak with Elder Thomas?" Lydia asked, unable to remain silent any longer. "I would very much appreciate learning from his wisdom, if he's willing."

All eyes turned to her, and Lydia feared she had spoken out of turn. But after a moment, Michael's expression softened slightly.

"My father would not forgive me if I turned away a genuine seeker of understanding," he said. "You may come." His gaze returned to Joseph. "Both of you."

He wheeled his horse around and led the way into the settlement, the other two men falling in behind Joseph and Lydia. As they rode, Lydia took in the community with keen interest, noting details that contradicted many of the depictions she had seen in Eastern publications.

The dwellings were a mixture of traditional structures. Some conical lodges covered with hides and canvas that she recognized as teepees, though more permanent than the transportable versions she had imagined, and more recent rectangular buildings constructed of logs or sod with sturdy roofs. Around them, the life of the community continued: women working at tanning hides or tending gardens, children playing a game involving hoops and sticks, elderly men sitting in the shade engaged in what appeared to be a serious discussion.

Many paused to observe the newcomers, their expressions ranging from curiosity to wariness. Lydia felt a sudden self-consciousness under their scrutiny, aware of how foreign she must appear with her Eastern clothing and pale skin.

They dismounted near a larger dwelling set slightly apart from the others. An older man sat on a bench outside, watching their approach with alert eyes that belied his advanced years. Even seated, Lydia could tell he had once been tall and imposing; age had bent but not broken his frame. Deep lines etched his copper-hued face, each one seeming to hold a story of its own.

"Father," Michael said, stepping forward. "Joseph Calloway has come, and brings a visitor."

Elder Thomas rose slowly, his movements deliberate but not frail. He regarded Joseph for a long moment before extending his hand in the white man's manner of greeting.

"Many moons have passed since you sat at my fire, Joseph Calloway," he said, his voice rich and resonant despite his age.

Joseph clasped the offered hand firmly. "Too many, Elder Thomas. I should have come sooner."

"A man rides when the path calls him, not before." Thomas's gaze shifted to Lydia, studying her with the same quiet intensity. "And who is this who travels in your company?"

Joseph performed the introduction more formally than he had with Michael, explaining Lydia's purpose in Montana Territory with careful attention to her genuine interest in understanding the land and its people truthfully.

When he finished, Thomas regarded Lydia thoughtfully. "So you make pictures that will travel far to the East, to show those who have never seen this land what it truly is?"

"Yes, sir," Lydia replied, meeting his gaze respectfully. "I hope to create honest images that reflect the beauty and complexity of Montana, including its people."

"And what of our struggles? Will your pictures show those as well?" The question was direct but not hostile, a test of her intentions.

Lydia considered her answer carefully. "If you're willing to share them with me, yes. I believe understanding comes only through truth, however difficult it may be to face."

Thomas nodded slowly. "Good words. We will see if the heart behind them is equally good." He gestured toward the dwelling behind him. "Come. Sarah Dove will have food prepared, and we have much to discuss."

The interior of Elder Thomas's home was cool and dim after the bright sunlight outside. Lydia blinked after entering, allowing her eyes to adjust as the scent of cooking food and aromatic herbs enveloped her. The single room was spacious and meticulously organized, with sleeping platforms along one wall, and a central hearth where an older woman was tending a pot suspended over glowing coals.

She turned as they entered, wiping her hands on a cloth tied around her waist. Though clearly of similar age to Thomas, Sarah Dove moved with grace and purpose, her silver-streaked hair plaited in two braids that framed a face etched with the same deep lines as her husband's. Her dark eyes were sharp and assessing, but not unkind, as they came to rest on Lydia.

"Welcome, travelers," she said, her English accented but clear. "You have journeyed far."

"Thank you for your hospitality," Lydia replied, touched by the greeting. She had read enough to know that offering food to visitors was a sacred obligation in many indigenous cultures, and one not extended lightly to strangers.

Sarah gestured for them to sit on woven mats arranged around the hearth. As they settled themselves, she ladled a rich-smelling stew into wooden bowls, passing them first to the guests, then to Thomas and finally to Michael, who had joined them inside.

"Eat," Thomas said, reaching for his own bowl. "We will speak of serious matters afterward."

The meal was delicious. A hearty mixture of game meat, wild roots, and berries that Lydia couldn't identify but found flavorful and satisfying. They ate in silence, as Joseph had advised was customary, though the quiet felt comfortable rather than strained.

When they had finished, Sarah collected the bowls and offered a tea brewed from herbs that tasted of mint and something deeper, earthier that Lydia couldn't name. Only then did Thomas lean forward, signaling the beginning of a more serious conversation.

"The hunters your path crossed—they are not the first," he began, addressing Joseph. "Since the snow melted, we have seen strangers watching our movements, testing boundaries."

Joseph nodded grimly. "The Garrett brothers have a reputation for pushing where they're not wanted."

"It goes beyond them," Michael said, his voice tight with controlled anger. "Two weeks past, our hunters found surveyor's stakes on land clearly defined as ours by the last treaty. When our people removed them, they were threatened at gunpoint by men claiming to represent the territorial government."

"The stakes returned the next day," Thomas added. "The message was clear."

Lydia felt a chill despite the warmth of the dwelling. The subtle erosion of treaty lands was not an unfamiliar story, but witnessing its reality in the concerned faces around her made it immediate in a way no newspaper account could convey.

"There is more," Sarah Dove spoke up unexpectedly. "Three days ago, two of our children were gathering berries near the northern creek and reported seeing men with measuring instruments walking the ridgeline. When asked their purpose, these men spoke of 'progress' and 'development' coming soon."

· "Railroad interests, most likely," Joseph said, his expression darkening. "They've been pushing for a spur line through this valley for years. The timber and water access would be valuable to them."

Thomas nodded slowly. "So we believe. The path of iron brings many changes quickly."

"But surely, they can't simply ignore established treaty boundaries?" Lydia asked, unable to contain her indignation.

Elder Thomas regarded her with eyes that had witnessed decades of such "progress." "Treaties are paper promises, easily forgotten when valuable things lie beneath them. We have seen this pattern before." There was no bitterness in his voice, only a weary acceptance that stirred something painful in Lydia's chest.

Joseph leaned forward, his forearms resting on his knees. "What can I do to help?"

"Be our witness," Thomas replied simply. "You walk in both worlds, Joseph Calloway. Your voice may be heard where ours would be dismissed." He glanced at Lydia. "And perhaps the artist's pictures can show truths that word alone cannot convey."

"I would be honored to document whatever you believe would help," Lydia said sincerely. "If seeing the reality might influence hearts and minds back East..."

Michael made a soft sound of skepticism, but Thomas silenced him with a subtle gesture.

"Hearts and minds are like rivers," the elder said. "They find new courses slowly, over much time. But yes... we would show you our life here, if your intention is truth."

"It is," Lydia assured him. "I want to understand, not merely observe."

Thomas nodded, seemingly satisfied. "Then you will stay as our guests for two nights. You will see how we live now, not as wanderers following the buffalo, but as people adapting to a changing world without abandoning who we are."

The conversation turned to practicalities, where Joseph and Lydia would stay, the schedule for the following days, and the current conditions in the wider territory. As they spoke, Lydia noticed young children peering curiously through the doorway, only to be shooed away by older siblings. One small face lingered longer than the others, a boy of perhaps nine or ten with bright, intelligent eyes.

Sarah Dove noticed Lydia's gaze and smiled. "My grandson, Little Crow. He is very curious about your arrival." She called something in their native language, and the boy stepped hesitantly into the dwelling.

"Hello," he said in carefully pronounced English, glancing between Lydia and Joseph.

"Hello, Little Crow," Lydia replied warmly. "I'm very pleased to meet you."

The boy's eyes lingered on her sketchbook, which protruded from her satchel. "You make pictures?" he asked.

"I do," Lydia confirmed. "Would you like to see some?"

At his eager nod, Lydia drew out her sketchbook and opened it to some of the landscape studies she had made during their journey. Little Crow moved closer, his curiosity overcoming his shyness as he examined the drawings with serious attention.

"You caught the mountains' spirit," he said finally, pointing to her sketch of the Crazy Mountains. "Grandfather says they speak to those who listen properly."

"Your grandfather is very wise," Lydia replied, touched by the boy's perception. "I tried to listen with my eyes and my heart while drawing them."

Little Crow nodded as if this made perfect sense to him. He pointed to a blank page. "Will you draw our home too?"

"If your elders permit it, I would be honored to," Lydia said, glancing toward Thomas for approval.

The old man nodded. "Little Crow can show you our settlement tomorrow. His eyes are good, and he knows what is important."

"I would like that very much," Lydia said, smiling at the boy, who straightened with pride at being given this responsibility.

As the day progressed, more members of the community stopped by Thomas's dwelling, some out of curiosity about the visitors, others to discuss community matters. Lydia observed the interactions carefully, noting the deep respect accorded to the elder, and the structured yet relaxed way decisions seemed to be made. There was a sense of connection and mutual responsibility that felt profoundly different from the competitive individualism she knew from Eastern society.

Eventually, Sarah Dove led Lydia and Joseph to a small but clean dwelling where they would stay during their visit. Two sleeping platforms had been prepared on opposite sides of the space, with sufficient privacy for propriety.

"Rest now," Sarah told them.

After she left, Joseph and Lydia found themselves alone for the first time since arriving. The small dwelling felt suddenly intimate in the late afternoon light filtering through the smoke hole above.

"I appreciate you bringing me here, more than I can express in words," Lydia said quietly, arranging her belongings on the platform assigned to her.

Joseph stood near the doorway. "You've earned their trust," he said, his voice low. "The way you spoke with Thomas, with Little Crow—you weren't condescending or romanticizing. You listened."

"I meant what I said. I want to understand the truth, not just what fits comfortable narratives." She hesitated, then added, "But I'm nervous. I want to do this justice, to create images that truly honor these people and their reality."

Joseph moved closer, his expression softening. "You will. Your art has integrity because you do." There was a warmth in his voice that sent a flutter through Lydia's chest. "Just keep seeing with that honest heart of yours."

Their eyes met, and something shifted in the air between them—a recognition, perhaps, of how far they had come from their tense first meeting. The moment stretched, filled with unspoken thoughts and feelings too new to name.

Joseph broke it first, clearing his throat and stepping back. "I should check on the horses, make sure they're settled properly." He paused at the doorway. "Elder Thomas has called a council fire tonight. All are welcome to attend. It would be a good opportunity for you to observe."

"I'd like that," Lydia said, still feeling the lingering warmth of the moment they'd shared.

After Joseph left, Lydia sat on her sleeping platform, allowing the events of the day to settle in her mind. From the tension of their encounter with the hunters to the solemnity of their discussion with Elder Thomas, it had been a day of profound contrasts and realizations. She felt humbled by the trust being placed in her and determined to prove worthy of it.

Taking out her sketchbook, she began to record her impressions while they were still fresh—not just visual details for later artwork, but the emotional truths she had witnessed: the dignity with which Thomas's people faced encroachment on their world, the complex bond between Joseph and this community born of past redemption, the weight of history pressing against the present moment.

When Joseph returned, he found her still writing and drawing, deep in concentration. He moved quietly, settling on his platform and occupying himself with checking his gear, offering her the space to complete her thoughts.

"I keep thinking about what Elder Thomas said regarding treaties," Lydia said finally, closing her sketchbook. "About them being 'paper promises easily forgotten.'" She looked up at Joseph, troubled. "Is there truly no recourse when agreements are violated so blatantly?"

Joseph's expression was grim. "The law is written by those with power and enforced selectively. Thomas's people have witnessed promises broken since the first white traders arrived."

"It's wrong," Lydia said simply, the inadequacy of the words burning in her throat.

"Yes," Joseph agreed, no attempt to soften the harsh truth. "It's one of the shadows I carry, being part of the wave that changed everything for them." He met her eyes directly. "You asked once about my past as a buffalo hunter. That's part of it, participating in the destruction of their way of life, however unintentionally."

Lydia considered this, seeing more clearly now the complex layers of Joseph's relationship with the Blackfoot community. "Yet they've welcomed you, accepted you as a friend."

"Thomas sees beyond surface judgments," Joseph said. "He recognized my regret was genuine, my desire to live differently was real. Their generosity in allowing me to make amends..." He trailed off, emotion tightening his voice.

Lydia moved across the small space to sit beside him, their shoulders nearly touching. "That kind of forgiveness is rare," she said softly. "A reflection of true faith."

Joseph nodded, his profile strong against the fading light. "Thomas follows different traditions than we do, but his understanding of grace would put many church-going Christians to shame."

They sat close enough that Lydia could feel the warmth radiating from him.

"The council fire will begin soon," Joseph said eventually, though he made no move to rise. "We should prepare."

"What should I expect?" Lydia asked, reluctant to break the quiet intimacy of the moment.

"Stories shared, concerns raised, decisions considered," Joseph explained. "It's how the community addresses important matters together. As guests, we'll mostly listen."

"Will they discuss the hunters? The survey stakes?"

"Likely. And how to respond." Joseph's voice held concern. "Thomas favors peaceful solutions, but younger men like Michael have seen too many peaceful approaches fail. There's growing tension within the community about the best path forward."

Lydia thought of the warning shot they'd heard that morning, the Garrett brothers deliberately pushing boundaries. "And what do you think is the right approach?"

Joseph turned to face her fully, their proximity suddenly acute in the dimming light. "I think confrontation plays into the hands of those who want to portray the Blackfoot as aggressive, dangerous. It gives them the excuse they're looking for." His eyes held hers with unwavering intensity. "But I also understand the frustration of always being the one to step back, to compromise, to lose ground inch by inch."

The weight of his words settled between them, along with an awareness of how their conversation had transcended the formal relationship of guide and client. They were sharing thoughts, concerns, and convictions.

A call from outside, a summoning to the council fire, broke the moment. Joseph rose to his feet, offering Lydia his hand. She took it, feeling the strength and calluses of his fingers as they closed around hers, steady and secure as he helped her up.

He didn't immediately release her hand, and Lydia found herself unwilling to be the first to let go. They stood for a heartbeat longer than necessary, connected by this simple touch, by the understanding that had grown between them.

"We should go," Joseph said, his voice lower than usual. He released her hand.

"Yes," Lydia agreed, though part of her wished they could remain in this quiet moment of connection. She reached for her shawl, wrapping it around her shoulders against the evening chill. "I'm ready."

Chapter 12

Flames leapt skyward, sending sparks spiraling into the darkening Montana sky like fireflies seeking stars. The council fire burned at the center of a wide circle where members of the Blackfoot community gathered, their faces illuminated by the dancing light. Lydia sat beside Joseph on a woven mat, their shoulders nearly touching as Elder Thomas raised his hand for silence.

The murmur of voices faded. In the newfound quiet, Lydia could hear the soft crackling of the fire, the distant call of a night bird, and the gentle rustle of cottonwood leaves stirred by the evening breeze. She was acutely aware of being welcomed into something ancient and sacred. A gathering not meant for outsider eyes, yet opened to her through Joseph's trust and her own sincere desire to understand.

"We come together as we have since the time of our ancestors," Thomas began, his deep voice carrying easily across the circle. "To speak with honest tongues, to listen with open ears, to seek the path that serves not just one but all."

Lydia watched, captivated, as the firelight played across the elder's weathered face. His words were translated by Michael for those who preferred their native tongue, though many nodded their understanding of the English. She felt a gentle nudge and turned to find Joseph offering a small wooden cup filled with what appeared to be tea.

"Mint and sage," he whispered close to her ear. "A traditional offering at council gatherings."

She accepted it with a grateful nod, her fingers brushing his in the exchange. The warm liquid carried a complex flavor—earthy and aromatic—that seemed to settle her mind even as it warmed her body against the growing chill of the evening.

Thomas gestured toward a middle-aged man sitting across the circle. "Running Elk has news from the north. We will hear him."

The man rose, his bearing dignified as he addressed the gathering. "Three days past, I traveled to the trading post at White Water. There I heard talk of new settlers coming, twenty families or more, before the snow falls again." He paused, his gaze sweeping the attentive faces. "They speak of building a town where Beaver Creek meets the river."

A murmur rolled through the assembly. Lydia didn't need a translation to understand the implications. The location described was perilously close to the settlement's northern boundary, if not encroaching upon it.

"The white trader, Parker, he showed me papers. Maps with marks and lines, names written by men who have never walked this land." Running Elk's voice remained measured, but Lydia detected the strain beneath his control. "Our hunting grounds by the eastern ridge are marked as 'available parcels.'"

Michael stood abruptly, his restraint visibly fraying. "Available? Those lands have belonged to our people since before their grandfathers were born! The treaty of '55 confirmed them as ours!"

"Treaties change," an older man said quietly from his place near Thomas. "The ink is barely dry before new papers appear."

"And each time, our lands shrink," a younger man added bitterly. "Each time, we are told to be grateful for what remains."

The discussion intensified, voices overlapping as various members of the community expressed concerns, anger, and uncertainty. Lydia watched, mesmerized by this democratic process, so different from the political machinations she'd witnessed in New York, where power and influence determined whose voice carried weight.

Here, each speaker was given respectful attention, regardless of age or station. Young men spoke with passion of resistance, elders counseled caution and strategic thinking, women voiced practical concerns about crops already planted and children's security.

Joseph leaned close to Lydia, his breath warm against her cheek as he provided a context in a low murmur. "The settlement has already been moved twice in the last decade. Each relocation means rebuilding homes, establishing new gardens, learning the patterns of a different piece of land."

"But surely the territorial government must honor established boundaries?" Lydia whispered back, her indignation rising.

Joseph's expression was grim in the firelight. "Should and do are different matters entirely."

Their attention returned to the circle as Sarah Dove rose to speak, her silver-streaked braids gleaming in the firelight. The community fell silent immediately, respect for the elder woman evident in their attentive faces.

"I have lived long enough to see many changes," she began, her accented English clear and deliberate. "I have seen great herds vanish like morning mist. I have seen our people move from the wide plains to smaller and smaller pieces of land." She looked around the circle, meeting eyes both young and old. "Each time, we are told, 'This is progress. This is necessary.'"

She paused, drawing herself up with quiet dignity. "But I have also seen our strength. We have planted where before we only hunted. We have built permanent homes where once we followed the buffalo. We have kept our stories, our beliefs, our ways, even as the world around us transforms." Her gaze settled briefly on Lydia. "Now we must decide: How do we face this new challenge while remaining who we are?"

A moment of profound silence followed her words. Lydia felt the weight of them, understanding suddenly that she was witnessing not just a discussion about land boundaries, but an entire people's struggle to maintain their identity amid relentless pressure to disappear.

Elder Thomas nodded to Sarah with deep respect before addressing the gathering once more. "We must consider our options carefully. Running Elk, what more did you learn at the trading post?"

"The surveyor's stakes are but the first step. There is talk of the railroad bringing men to assess the valley within the month." Running Elk's expression darkened. "And I heard whispers that those who seek our removal have friends in the territorial government. They say papers are already being prepared that will redraw the boundaries established in the last treaty."

"Always the same pattern," Michael said, anger evident in his taut posture. "First come the surveyors, then the papers declaring our land 'unused' or 'needed for progress,' then the soldiers, if we refuse to move."

"What of the agent assigned to our people?" asked a woman Lydia hadn't yet been introduced to. "Would he not speak for our rights?"

A bitter laugh came from somewhere in the circle. "Agent Willis hasn't been seen in four months. He collects his government salary while spending his days in Helena, far from our concerns."

Thomas held up his hand again, calming the rising tension. "We have a guest who walks in both worlds," he said, turning toward Joseph. "Joseph Calloway, what counsel would you offer?"

All eyes shifted to Joseph, and Lydia felt him straighten beside her, the responsibility of the moment evident in his bearing.

"I cannot claim to have easy answers," he began, his deep voice steady. "But I know that when paperwork is already being prepared, direct opposition often plays into the hands of those who wish to portray you as obstacles to progress." He paused, choosing his words with evident care. "However, there are still those in positions of authority who believe in honoring commitments made. The challenge is reaching them before decisions are finalized."

"And how would we do this?" Michael asked, skepticism clear in his tone. "Our words disappear like smoke when we speak them in government offices."

Joseph nodded, acknowledging the bitter truth in this observation. "Which is why witnesses matter. People whose voices are heard in those same offices." His hand gestured slightly toward Lydia. "People who can carry the truth to places where it might make a difference."

Lydia felt the weight of many gazes turning toward her, assessing and hopeful. Her heart pounded with the sudden responsibility placed upon her shoulders.

"I—" she began, then steadied herself. "I was commissioned to document the Montana Territory through my art. That commission includes showing the truth of the lives being lived here, and the challenges being faced." She met Thomas's steady gaze across the fire. "If my sketches and written accounts could help make your situation visible to those who might influence these decisions, I would consider it an honor to create them."

Her words seemed to hover in the air, met with expressions ranging from hope to skepticism across the fire lit faces.

Thomas studied her for a long moment before speaking. "Pictures have power. They can show what words alone cannot convey." He turned to the assembly. "We will show Miss Hayes our life here, not as curiosities to be examined, but as people with deep roots in this land, roots that should not be severed lightly."

A murmur of agreement spread through the circle, and Lydia felt both relief and a deepening sense of responsibility. She had come to Montana seeking beautiful landscapes and frontier characters to render into art. Now she found herself potentially advocating for a community's right to exist as they chose, on land that was rightfully theirs.

The council continued as various practical matters were discussed. The need to send messengers to other Blackfoot settlements with news of the potential threat, contingency plans for the crops should relocation be forced upon them, strategies for documenting their continuous presence on the disputed lands.

Lydia listened intently, making mental notes of details that might strengthen her eventual writings and illustrations. Beside her, Joseph remained a steady presence, occasionally leaning close to provide context for matters she might not fully understand.

"They're discussing whether to proceed with the summer gathering," he explained during one such moment. "It's an important cultural event that brings scattered bands together, but some fear it would leave the settlements more vulnerable if many able-bodied men are away."

The proximity of his voice sent a shiver through Lydia that had nothing to do with the cooling night air. She was becoming increasingly aware of his presence. The subtle cedar scent that clung to his clothing, the quiet strength in his profile as firelight played across his features, the respectful attention he gave to each speaker regardless of age or status.

As the council progressed, Little Crow slipped silently through the gathered adults to settle beside Lydia, his bright eyes reflecting the dancing flames. He carried a small wooden flute, which he showed to her with evident pride.

"My grandfather made this for me," he whispered. "Later, I will play for the stories."

"Stories?" Lydia whispered back, careful not to disrupt the ongoing discussion.

The boy nodded solemnly. "After the serious talk ends, there are always stories. It's how we remember who we are."

His simple explanation touched Lydia deeply. In her world of galleries and drawing rooms, stories were entertainment, diversions. Here, they were vessels of identity and continuity, carrying the community's essence through generations of change.

As the practical discussions concluded with plans for the coming days, the atmosphere around the fire subtly shifted. Two elderly men brought out drums, and several younger people produced flutes similar to Little Crow's. Sarah Dove moved to sit near Thomas, and the community arranged themselves more comfortably, expectation evident in their postures.

"Now," Thomas announced, his voice warmer than it had been during the council's more serious deliberations, "we remind ourselves of who we have always been, and who we will continue to be."

At his nod, the drummers began a gentle, hypnotic rhythm. Little Crow raised his flute and, after a moment's hesitation, began to play a haunting melody that seemed to rise and fall like the very landscape around them. Other flutists joined gradually, creating a layered harmony that raised goosebumps along Lydia's arms.

Thomas began to speak, his words flowing into a story about the creation of the mountains and rivers, how they came to be shaped as they were, and why certain animals and plants lived among them. It was not translated into English, but Joseph leaned close to provide brief explanations at key moments, allowing Lydia to follow the narrative's essence, if not its every detail.

"He's explaining why the river bends sharply near their fishing grounds," Joseph murmured at one point. "How it was formed when a great spirit being dragged by his tail across the land while pursuing a trickster who had stolen fire."

The stories continued, some told by Thomas, others by different community members. Some were clearly ancient legends, while others recounted more recent history, the coming of horses that transformed their ancestors' way of life, early encounters with white trappers and traders. The gradual loss of the buffalo herds that had sustained them for countless generations.

Lydia was transported by the combination of music, firelight, and narrative. Her artist's mind captured mental images that she knew would find their way onto paper, the dignified profile of Thomas as he gesticulated toward the stars while describing a celestial battle. The curve of Sarah Dove's hands as she mimicked a falcon's flight. The rapt expressions of children hearing their people's stories preserved through yet another telling.

"They're sharing their creation story now," Joseph explained softly as an elderly woman took up the narrative. "How the world was formed from mud brought up from the depths by a water creature." He hesitated, then added, "Not so different from some interpretations of Genesis when you consider it."

"The medium differs, but the meaning feels familiar," Lydia agreed, thinking of the Bible stories she'd grown up with. "Explaining our place in creation, our relationship to the land and its creatures."

Joseph nodded, a look of appreciation crossing his features at her understanding. "Most folks I've met can't see past the surface differences to recognize the common threads."

Their eyes met in the flickering light, and Lydia felt a deepening connection that transcended their disparate backgrounds. Here was a man who had learned to see beyond his own cultural assumptions, to recognize value in traditions different from those he'd been raised with.

The storytelling continued, and eventually, Little Crow was invited to play his flute alone while Thomas recited what Joseph explained was a prayer of gratitude for the land's bounty and beauty. The boy's playing was hesitant at first but grew more confident as he progressed, his small fingers moving deftly over the instrument's holes.

When the music faded, a comfortable silence settled over the gathering. Stars blazed overhead in the vast Montana sky, more numerous and brilliant than Lydia had ever seen in New York. The fire had burned down to glowing embers that cast just enough light to illuminate the circle of faces, each lost in thought or memory.

Thomas spoke one final time, his words carrying the weight of formal closure. "We have shared our concerns, made our plans, and remembered our stories. Now we rest. Knowing tomorrow brings new challenges and new opportunities to live honorably upon this land that sustains us."

The council dispersed quietly, families moving toward their dwellings, some stopping to exchange a few words with friends or relatives. The rhythms of community life continued even as the formal gathering ended.

Joseph rose and offered Lydia his hand. She took it, grateful for the support, as her legs had stiffened from sitting cross-legged for so long. His hand remained around hers a moment longer than necessary, warm and steadying in the cool night air.

"Thank you," she said, "for translating, for explaining. I would have missed so much without your guidance."

His expression softened in the fading firelight. "You saw more clearly than many who've spent years in these territories. You have a gift for looking beneath the surface."

Little Crow appeared at her side, his flute carefully tucked away in a beaded leather case.

"Did you like the stories?" he asked eagerly. "Did Mr. Joseph explain the one about how Raven brought light to the world?"

Lydia smiled at the boy's enthusiasm. "He did, and I found it beautiful. You played wonderfully as well. How long have you been learning the flute?"

"Since last winter," Little Crow replied, pride evident in his voice. "Grandfather says I have good breath control for my age." He glanced toward Joseph. "Mr. Joseph plays the mouth harp sometimes when he visits. Will you play tomorrow?"

"Perhaps, if there's time, after all the important things your grandfather wants to show Miss Hayes."

"My flute and your mouth harp could make music together," Little Crow suggested, his eyes bright with the possibility.

"That they could," Joseph agreed. "Now, shouldn't you be heading to your family's lodge? It's growing late."

The boy nodded reluctantly, then turned to Lydia. "Tomorrow, I will show you the best places to make pictures. Places that show why this land matters to us."

"I look forward to that very much," Lydia replied sincerely.

Little Crow beamed, then darted off toward a dwelling where a woman his mother, Lydia presumed, waited patiently.

Chapter 13

"What did you make of the council meeting?" Joseph asked as they walked back to their assigned shelter.

Lydia considered the question carefully, wanting to offer more than superficial observations. "I was struck by how democratic it was, each voice respected, and even when opinions differed sharply. And how the practical concerns were balanced with the need for continuity of their traditions and identity." She paused. "It makes the threats to their land all the more heartbreaking, knowing how deeply rooted their connection to this specific place has become."

Joseph nodded, satisfaction evident in his expression. "Many who visit tribal councils see only the exotic elements, such as the drums or the unfamiliar language. They miss the sophisticated governance happening before their eyes."

"The stories afterward," Lydia continued, "they reminded me of evenings from my childhood when my grandfather would read Bible stories by the fire. The same sense of passing down not just tales but values, a way of understanding the world."

"Thomas would appreciate that comparison," Joseph said. "He sees parallels between different faith traditions more readily than most, whether from his people or from Christian teachings."

They reached their shelter, and Joseph held the hide covering aside for Lydia to enter. A small oil lamp had been left burning inside, casting soft illumination across the simple interior. The space seemed even more intimate after the communal experience of the council fire.

"I should write down some impressions and make a few drawings while they're fresh," Lydia said, moving toward her sleeping platform where her sketchbook waited. "There were images tonight I don't want to lose."

Joseph nodded, settling on his platform, and busying himself with removing his boots. "I've noticed you writing each evening. Detailed observations, I imagine?"

"Yes," she confirmed, sitting cross-legged on her bedding. "Visual notes primarily, but also thoughts and feelings that might inform the final works." She opened her sketchbook, the familiar weight of it comforting in her hands. "This project has become something more meaningful than I initially envisioned."

"The best work often does," Joseph observed quietly. "Starts as one thing, becomes another through honest engagement with what's actually there, not just what you thought you'd find."

Lydia looked up, struck by the insight. "Is that what happened with you and Montana? You came for one purpose but found another meaning altogether?"

A shadow crossed his features. "In a manner of speaking. Though my transformation was born more from regret than inspiration." He met her gaze directly. "I came to hunt buffalo for hides and profit. I stayed to try to make amends for the damage done, to find a better way to live with this land."

The frank admission hung in the air between them. Lydia had suspected as much from hints he'd dropped, but hearing it stated openly carried a different meaning.

"That takes courage," she said after a moment. "To acknowledge a wrong path and change direction completely."

Joseph's laugh held little humor. "Courage had little to do with it. After my last buffalo hunt, I couldn't continue. Simple as that." His eyes grew distant with memory. "Stood surrounded by carcasses stripped of their hides, meat left to rot, knowing there were fewer each season, knowing what that meant for people like Thomas and his family."

Lydia set her sketchbook aside and moved to sit closer to him, drawn by the raw honesty in his voice. "But many others continued. They didn't change their ways as you did."

"Some still haven't," he said grimly. "Men like the Garrett brothers were late to the buffalo trade, angry they missed the peak years of easy profit. Now they turn that resentment toward the Blackfoot, as if they're to blame for the herds' decline."

"Is that what motivates them? These provocations on the hunting grounds and fishing areas?"

Joseph sighed, running a hand through his hair. "Partly. It's also about the land itself. The Blackfoot holds some of the best water access in the region. With the railroad potentially coming through, that land rises in value." His jaw tightened. "Creating tension serves those who'd prefer to see Thomas's people removed entirely."

"That's unconscionable," Lydia said, indignation coloring her voice.

"It's Montana," Joseph replied simply. "Beautiful and brutal in equal measure. The same mountain stream that nurtures life can flood and destroy without warning. The same open plains that offer freedom can turn deadly in winter storms." He looked at her directly. "The same people capable of extraordinary kindness can commit unthinkable cruelty when fear or greed drives them."

His words painted a complex portrait of the territory she'd come to document, far more nuanced than the romantic wilderness she'd initially imagined. Not for the first time, Lydia found herself grateful for Joseph's unflinching honesty, even when it challenged her preconceptions.

"Tomorrow," he continued, his tone softening slightly, "you'll see the reality of their lives here—neither the noble savages of dime novels nor the obstacle to progress that railroad men would paint them as. Just people with a different way of seeing and being, trying to adapt without surrendering who they are."

"I want to capture that," Lydia said earnestly. "Not just the external trappings, but the essence—their connection to this specific place, their resourcefulness in the face of change."

Joseph studied her face in the lamp's soft glow, something like admiration warming his gray eyes. "If anyone can, I believe you will." He hesitated, then added more quietly, "Your vision goes deeper than most."

The simple compliment affected Lydia more profoundly than the most effusive praise she'd received in New York salons. Coming from Joseph, who measured his words so carefully and valued authenticity above all, it felt like a precious gift.

For a moment, neither spoke. The silence between them charged with unspoken thoughts and growing awareness. Lydia found herself noticing details she'd overlooked before. The way the lamplight caught the silver threads beginning to appear at his temples, the fan of fine lines around his eyes that spoke of years scanning distant horizons. The surprising gentleness in hands strong enough to break a wild horse or build a cabin from raw timber.

Joseph cleared his throat softly, breaking the moment. "We should rest. Tomorrow will bring many new impressions for your journaling and sketchbook."

"Yes, of course," Lydia agreed, returning to her sleeping platform. She took a moment to make a few quick notes about the council fire before preparing for bed.

As she settled beneath the warm blankets, listening to Joseph's quiet movements as he extinguished the lamp, Lydia found her mind still swirling with images from the evening—firelight on solemn faces, the haunting melody of Little Crow's flute, Thomas's hands gesturing toward the star-filled sky as he recounted ancient stories. Woven through these impressions was a growing awareness of Joseph himself, no longer just her guide to Montana's physical landscape, but a man whose own journey of redemption and transformation touched something profound within her.

"Joseph?" she said softly into the darkness.

"Yes?" His voice came from across the shelter, low and attentive.

"I'm glad I didn't get a different guide. I'm glad it was you." The words emerged before she could reconsider them, honest in their simplicity.

A moment's silence followed, long enough that Lydia wondered if she'd overstepped some boundary.

"As am I," he finally replied, his deep voice carrying a warmth that eased any uncertainty. "More than I expected to be."

With that gentle acknowledgment hovering in the darkness between them, Lydia closed her eyes, allowing exhaustion to finally claim her. Her last conscious thought was a prayer of gratitude, for the trust shown to her by Thomas's community, for the chance to create a work that might truly matter, and for the unexpected gift of Joseph Calloway's companionship on this journey. It was transforming her in ways she had never anticipated.

Chapter 14

Orning came with the soft murmur of voices and the scent of wood smoke drifting through the settlement. Lydia woke to find Joseph already gone from their shelter, his bedding neatly arranged. Sunlight filtered through the smoke hole above, illuminating dust motes dancing in the golden beam.

She dressed quickly in her most practical attire, the split riding skirt and sturdy shirt waist that had proven so useful on their journey. After splashing her face with cool water and pinning her hair into a simple coil at the nape of her neck, she gathered her essential art supplies in the leather satchel Joseph had helped her fashion for easier carrying.

Outside, the settlement was alive with morning activity. Women worked at cooking fires, children carried water from the nearby river, men mended tools or prepared for hunting expeditions. The orderly purposefulness struck Lydia immediately. This was no haphazard camp but a functioning community with established routines and clear cooperation.

She spotted Joseph across the central area, deep in conversation with Michael and two other men. They bent over what appeared to be a map spread across a flat stone, pointing and discussing something with serious expressions. Joseph looked up, catching sight of her, and raised a hand in greeting before returning to the discussion.

"Miss Hayes." The voice came from behind her, and Lydia turned to find Sarah Dove approaching with a small ceramic cup. "Morning tea. Good for strength before a day of much walking."

"Thank you," Lydia said, accepting the offering gratefully. The warm liquid tasted of herbs she couldn't identify but found refreshing. "Your hospitality is very kind."

Sarah studied her with keen eyes that missed nothing. "You watched well at the council fire. Many visitors look but do not see."

Before Lydia could respond to this perceptive comment, Little Crow appeared at his grandmother's side, practically vibrating with excitement.

"I am ready to show you our special places," he announced, importantly adjusting the small bag slung across his shoulder. "Grandfather says I should start with the river bend where the healing plants grow."

Sarah smiled fondly at her grandson. "Little Crow knows every path and hidden corner of our lands. He will be a good guide." She turned back to Lydia. "Joseph Calloway will join you soon. He and my son are discussing the hunters' movements."

As if summoned by her words, Joseph approached, followed by Michael. Both men's expressions were serious, though they softened when they reached the women and the eager boy.

"The Garrett brothers and their companions were spotted this morning," Joseph explained to Lydia in a low voice. "Still camped where we avoided them yesterday, but they've been scouting nearby ravines."

"Looking for what?" Lydia asked.

"Trouble, most likely," Michael answered grimly. "Or opportunity. Sometimes, they're the same thing." He nodded toward Little Crow. "Keep to the settlement and the nearby grounds today. No venturing to the northern boundaries."

The boy's face fell slightly, but he nodded with the solemnity of one accepting an important instruction.

"Michael will ride out with two others to keep watch on their movements," Joseph continued. "Meanwhile, we'll proceed with showing you the settlement as planned."

"We'll begin at the river," Little Crow announced, recovering his enthusiasm. "Where the medicine plants grow, and the fish traps are set."

"A good starting point," Thomas agreed, joining their small gathering. The elder seemed to move through his community like its living center, aware of all activities while maintaining a calm presence that clearly provided stability. "The river is the lifeblood of our settlement. Understanding our connection to it helps explain why this specific place matters to us."

They set out soon after, a small procession consisting of Lydia, Joseph, Little Crow, Thomas, and two young women who were introduced as skilled gatherers of the medicinal plants they would be showing Lydia. The morning air was cool and sweet with the scent of wildflowers as they walked the well-worn path toward the river's edge.

"Before the buffalo grew scarce, we followed seasonal patterns," Thomas explained as they walked. "Summer camps near good hunting grounds, winter camps in sheltered valleys. We traveled light, taking only what was needed." He gestured toward the permanent structures of the settlement visible behind them. "Now we build differently, plant foods that must be tended, stay in one place through all seasons."

"Was that transition difficult?" Lydia asked, genuinely curious about how the community had adapted.

Thomas's weathered face revealed a lifetime of witnessing change. "For the old ones, yes. Very difficult. Some never accepted it, preferred to die following the old ways." His eyes held a distant sadness before refocusing on her. "For the young, like Little Crow, this is the only life they know. They learn our stories, our values, but in new forms."

They reached the river, which flowed clear and swift with late spring runoff from distant mountains. Along its banks grew a lush variety of plants, some Lydia recognized and many she did not. Little Crow ran ahead eagerly, pointing out features he clearly felt were important for her to notice.

"Look! Fish traps there, where the water narrows," he called, indicating ingeniously designed basket-like structures positioned to catch fish while allowing smaller ones to escape. "And here, the special mud for pottery. And over there, the best willow branches for basket making!"

The two young women, Morning Sky and Willow Woman, began showing Lydia the various plants they gathered for medicine and food. They worked with practiced efficiency, explaining each plant's properties and uses while harvesting only what was immediately needed.

"This one stops bleeding," Morning Sky explained, carefully digging around a plant with delicate white flowers to expose its root. "We dry the root, grind it to powder, apply it to wounds that won't close."

"And this," Willow Woman added, indicating a different plant with broad leaves, "reduces fever. Very important during winter sickness."

As they moved along the riverbank, Joseph occasionally added context that helped Lydia understand the significance of what she was being shown. Thomas observed quietly, sometimes offering deeper historical perspective that connected present practices to their ancestors' knowledge.

Lydia sketched continuously, filling page after page with detailed renderings of the plants, the fish traps, the gathering techniques, and the river itself. She was careful to include the people in these drawings, not as exotic curiosities but as knowledgeable practitioners of a sophisticated relationship with their environment.

"You capture both the plant and how it is used," Thomas remarked, watching over her shoulder as she completed a sketch of Morning Sky demonstrating how to harvest a particular root without damaging the parent plant. "Most who come to look at our ways see only things, not understanding."

"Understanding is what I'm seeking," Lydia replied earnestly. "The relationship between your people and this specific place. How you've adapted while maintaining core traditions."

Thomas nodded, satisfaction evident in his expression. "This is what we hoped to show you. Not just what we do, but why it matters."

They continued along the river to where it bent sharply around a rocky outcropping. Here, Little Crow insisted on showing Lydia a small cave in the rock face where, he explained importantly, special clay for ceremonial pottery could be found.

"Only once each year do we gather it," he said, his voice taking on the cadence of a story he'd clearly heard many times. "When the river is at its lowest, after the hot moons, but before the cold returns."

As the morning progressed into afternoon, they moved from the river back toward the settlement, stopping at garden plots where women tended carefully organized plantings of corn, beans, and squash. These were not the neat rows of Eastern farms, Lydia noted, but a more integrated approach where different plants supported each other's growth.

"The tall corn provides climbing support for the beans," one of the gardeners explained, seeing Lydia's interest. "The beans give back to the soil what the corn takes away. The squash leaves shade the ground, keeping moisture in and weeds out." She smiled. "They help one another, as all things should."

Lydia sketched these gardens, fascinated by their practical wisdom and the way they reflected a worldview that emphasized interconnection rather than domination of nature. Joseph remained near her throughout, sometimes engaging in conversation with community members in their native tongue, sometimes translating nuances that might be lost in simpler English explanations.

By mid-afternoon, they had toured the settlement thoroughly. Lydia's sketchbook was filled with detailed drawings—women scraping hides using traditional tools, men crafting arrow points with techniques passed down through generations, children learning these skills through careful observation and guided practice. She had documented the adaptations as well: metal pots hanging alongside traditional clay vessels, trade cloth incorporated into otherwise traditional clothing, a carefully maintained rifle for hunting now that buffalo were scarce.

Throughout it all, Thomas ensured she understood the context. How each activity connected to the community's deeper values, how they had adjusted without abandoning the core of who they were. Little Crow remained an enthusiastic assistant, clearly proud to be showing his people's ways to an interested outsider.

They ended at the center of the settlement, where several community members had gathered in preparation for the evening meal. Cooking fires were being built, food preparations were underway. Sarah Dove supervised the activity with quiet authority, occasionally offering direction or assistance.

"Rest now," Thomas suggested to Lydia, noting her fatigue after hours of intense observation and sketching. "Tonight there will be a special meal to honor guests. Afterward, if you wish, you may share what you have drawn with any who are interested."

As Thomas moved away to speak with the other elders, Joseph guided Lydia to a shaded spot where they could sit and rest. Little Crow had reluctantly departed for his own chores, though he extracted a promise from Lydia that she would show him her completed sketches later.

"You've impressed them," Joseph said quietly, handing Lydia his canteen. "Particularly, Thomas and Sarah."

She took a grateful drink before replying. "They've been remarkably generous in sharing their knowledge and traditions. I only hope my work can do justice to what they've shown me."

"It will," Joseph said with simple confidence. "You see with honest eyes." He glanced toward where Michael and his companions were returning from their scouting mission, their expressions grim. "Excuse me for a moment. I should hear their report."

While Joseph conferred with the returning scouts, Lydia reviewed her day's work, adding notes and details to her sketches while the observations were still fresh. She was so absorbed in this task that she didn't immediately notice Sarah Dove's approach.

"Your pictures speak truth," the older woman said, startling Lydia slightly. "May I see more?"

"Of course," Lydia replied. She carefully turned the pages of her sketchbook, showing Sarah the various drawings she'd made throughout the day.

Sarah studied each one with careful attention, occasionally nodding or tracing a particular detail with her weathered finger. When she came to a portrait Lydia had quickly sketched of Thomas as he explained the significance of a particular ceremony, Sarah's expression softened noticeably.

"You have caught his spirit," she said quietly. "Not just his face, but the wisdom in his eyes, the strength that has carried him through many hard seasons."

"He's a remarkable man," Lydia replied sincerely. "Both of you are remarkable people. To have witnessed so much change, to have guided your community through it while preserving what matters most, it's truly inspiring."

Sarah's dark eyes held Lydia's for a long moment, assessing something beyond words. "You understand more than most who come from the outside world." She glanced toward where Joseph stood in serious conversation with Michael and Thomas. "He has chosen well in bringing you here."

Before Lydia could respond to this cryptic statement, Sarah rose. "Rest now. The evening meal will begin when the sun touches the western ridge."

Chapter 15

The sharp clang of metal against metal silenced the evening chatter. All eyes turned toward Elder Thomas, who stood beside the communal fire, a ladle in one hand. The impromptu bell had served its purpose—bringing immediate attention from everyone gathered for the special meal.

"We share food together," Thomas announced, his deep voice carrying across the settlement's central gathering area. "As we have since the time of our ancestors. Tonight, we welcome friends who seek to understand, not judge."

Lydia sat cross-legged on a woven mat between Joseph and Little Crow. The afternoon's rest had refreshed her, and now the tantalizing aromas of the feast being laid out made her realize how hungry she'd become after a day spent walking the settlement.

Women moved with efficiency, setting wooden bowls and platters on blankets spread in the center of the gathering. Men carried spits of roasted venison from cooking fires, the meat sizzling and releasing fragrant steam into the evening air. Children darted between adults, carrying smaller dishes of berries, roots, and bread made from ground corn and wild grains.

"First, we offer thanks," Thomas continued, raising his hands toward the darkening sky. He spoke in his native language, the words mysterious to Lydia but their reverent tone unmistakable.

Joseph leaned closer, his breath warm against her ear. "He's thanking the Creator for the animals who give their lives to sustain the people, for the plants that offer healing and nourishment, for the water that brings life to all things."

The prayer continued, Thomas's weathered hands gesturing toward the mountains, the river, and finally the gathered community. When he finished, a soft murmur of agreement rippled through the assembly.

"Now, we eat together," he announced, turning to Lydia and Joseph with a gracious nod. "Our guests will be served first, as is our way."

Sarah Dove approached with two beautifully crafted wooden bowls. She presented them with dignity, first to Lydia and then to Joseph. "The best portions for those who come in peace," she said, her English deliberate and clear.

Lydia received her bowl with both hands, recognizing the gesture's significance. Inside was a portion of venison, rich with dark meat still steaming from the fire, surrounded by unfamiliar vegetables and berries that formed a colorful mosaic. A flat bread lay beside the meat, its golden-brown surface marked with grill patterns.

"Thank you," she said, meeting Sarah's eyes with genuine appreciation. "For this meal and for all you've shared today."

Little Crow nudged her gently. "The meat is from a deer I helped track," he said proudly. "My first successful hunt. Grandfather says it brings honor to share it with guests."

Lydia's heart warmed at the boy's earnest pride. "Then I'm especially honored," she told him seriously. "This is a very important moment for you."

The boy beamed before accepting his portion from an older woman Lydia recognized as his mother.

As the food was distributed throughout the gathering, conversation resumed. Unlike formal dinners in New York society, where rigid etiquette dictated every interaction, the meal had a comfortable familial quality. People spoke freely across groups, children were included rather than segregated, and laughter punctuated serious discussions without seeming out of place.

The venison was more tender than Lydia expected, seasoned with herbs she couldn't identify but found delicious. She followed Joseph's example in how to eat the unfamiliar items, using the flat bread to scoop up a mixture of meat and vegetables.

"The bread is made from corn and wild rice," Joseph explained between bites. "The purple berries are serviceberries harvested last fall and preserved. The roots are similar to turnips but sweeter."

"Everything is delicious," Lydia replied sincerely. "And so beautifully presented."

Michael, who sat nearby with his wife and young daughter, overheard her comment. "Food nourishes more than the body," he said. "How it looks and how it's shared feeds the spirit as well."

This simple observation struck Lydia as profound. In her experience, elaborate meals in New York were often more about displaying wealth and social position than genuine nourishment or connection. Here, despite having far fewer material resources, the community created a more meaningful experience through intention and presence.

As the meal progressed, she noticed how seamlessly younger members anticipated the needs of elders, offering water or additional portions before being asked. Children were gently corrected when necessary, but otherwise trusted to participate appropriately. There was reverence without stiffness, respect without fear.

When most had finished eating, Thomas signaled for attention once again.

"As is our custom when welcoming visitors who come with good hearts, we will share stories and music." He gestured toward a group of men who had assembled with drums and flutes. "But first, we invite our guests to speak, if they wish."

Joseph nodded at Thomas's expectant look. He rose, standing tall in the firelight, his face serious but open.

"I am grateful for your hospitality and trust," he began, his deep voice carrying easily across the gathering. "Many here remember when I first came to your camp, half-frozen and near death. You had every reason to turn away a buffalo hunter whose kind had destroyed so much of your way of life."

A murmur passed through the older members of the group, acknowledging this shared history.

"Instead, you taught me a better way to live with this land," Joseph continued. "To take only what's needed, to respect all living things, to understand that true wealth isn't counted in pelts or gold but in the right relationship with the world around us."

He paused, his eyes moving to Thomas and Sarah. "That lesson changed my path forever. Though I can never fully repay that debt, I stand ready to help however I can with the challenges you now face."

Thomas nodded, satisfaction and approval evident in his expression.

Joseph turned slightly, gesturing toward Lydia. "Miss Hayes came to Montana seeking to document the territory through her art. What she's finding, I believe, is much more valuable. The truth that lies beneath surface appearances, and the wisdom your people have preserved through generations of change."

All eyes shifted to Lydia, and she realized Joseph had created an opening for her to speak. She rose slowly, grateful for his lead, but suddenly nervous before so many attentive faces illuminated by firelight.

"I'm deeply grateful for your willingness to share your lives and traditions with me," she began, her voice steadier than she expected. "Where I come from, in New York, many have strong opinions about the West and its people, despite having never ventured beyond their comfortable parlors."

This brought a ripple of knowing smiles.

"My commission was to create images showing Montana's landscapes and frontier life," she continued. "But what I've discovered is how incomplete such pictures would be without understanding the deep relationship between the people and the land. A relationship your community embodies so beautifully."

She glanced down at Little Crow, who was watching her with rapt attention. "Today, I learned more than how to identify medicinal plants or how fish traps are constructed. I learned about a way of seeing the world where everything is connected. Where wisdom is passed through generations not just in words but in actions. Where adapting to change doesn't mean abandoning who you are."

Lydia reached for her satchel, drawing out her sketchbook. "With your permission, I'd like to share some of the drawings I made today, and perhaps explain how I hope they might help others see beyond their preconceptions."

At Thomas's encouraging nod, she opened to the first page of the day's work, a detailed rendering of the river bend where the women had gathered medicinal plants, their movements purposeful and knowledgeable in the landscape.

"May I?" Little Crow asked eagerly, reaching for the sketchbook.

With Lydia's permission, he stood and carried it carefully around the circle, holding it up, so all could see while she explained each image and why she had composed it as she had.

"Here, I wanted to show not just the plants themselves, but how carefully they're harvested to ensure they'll return in future seasons," she explained as Little Crow displayed a detailed sketch of Morning Sky demonstrating proper harvesting technique. "This knowledge, passed down through generations, shows a relationship with the land based on respect and sustainability."

The images moved through the circle, gardens with companion planting, craftspeople at work, children learning traditional skills alongside adaptations to changing circumstances. With each drawing, Lydia explained how she hoped to convey the sophistication and resilience of the community's way of life.

When they reached the portrait of Thomas that had moved Sarah earlier, a reverent murmur passed through the gathering. The drawing captured not just the elder's physical features but something of his essential character, the dignity of his bearing, the intelligence in his eyes, the weight of experience carried with grace.

"This," Lydia said, her voice softening, "I hope might help those far from here understand that the decisions affecting your lands and lives impact real people, not abstract concepts or obstacles to progress, but individuals with profound wisdom and legitimate connections to specific places."

Thomas studied the portrait for a long moment. When he looked up, his eyes held both approval and a trace of sadness.

"You have captured what many cannot see," he said. "But will those with power to make decisions look with your eyes?"

The question hung in the air, its weight felt by all present. Lydia couldn't offer false reassurances—she knew too well how entrenched views could be, especially when economic interests aligned with prejudice.

"I don't know," she answered honestly. "But I believe truth has its own power. These images, along with the written accounts I'll provide, may reach some whose minds remain open, whose hearts can still be moved by human connection."

Thomas nodded, accepting her sincerity if not fully convinced of its potential impact. He turned to the assembled musicians. "Now, let us share the songs and stories of our people, that our guests may carry them in memory when they return to their own world."

What followed was a feast for the senses, as rich as the meal had been. Drums established hypnotic rhythms while flutes wove melodic patterns above them. Singers chanted in harmonies that raised goosebumps along Lydia's arms, their voices seeming to call to something ancient and half-remembered in the human soul.

Between musical performances, storytellers shared tales, some humorous, drawing peals of laughter from the audience and others deeply spiritual, explaining how features of the landscape came to be or how certain animals acquired their distinctive traits.

Joseph occasionally leaned close to translate nuances or provide context, his presence beside her a steady comfort. Lydia was acutely aware of him. The clean scent of his soap mingling with leather and wood smoke, the controlled strength in his posture, and the genuine respect with which he listened to each performance.

When one elderly man finished a particularly moving story about a great flood that had shaped the nearby mountains, Joseph whispered, "Now Thomas will ask me to play, as he always does when I visit."

True to his prediction, Thomas turned toward them with a warm smile. "Joseph Calloway, will you honor us with your mouth harp, as in days past?"

Joseph inclined his head in acknowledgment. He reached into his pocket and withdrew a harmonica that gleamed softly in the firelight. "Only if Little Crow will join me with his flute, as he suggested earlier."

The boy's eyes widened, a mixture of excitement and nervousness crossing his expressive face. He looked to his grandfather, who nodded encouragement.

"What shall we play?" Joseph asked as Little Crow retrieved his flute from the leather case on his belt.

"Do you know the Meadowlark Song?" the boy asked hopefully.

Joseph smiled. "I do. Your grandfather taught it to me during that long winter when I stayed with your people." He turned to Lydia. "It imitates the call of the meadowlark, but also tells of how spring returns after hardship, how life persists even when the path is difficult."

He raised the harmonica to his lips and began to play. The melody that emerged was hauntingly beautiful, starting with a phrase that indeed echoed the meadowlark's distinctive call before developing into something more complex yet strangely familiar, like a half-remembered dream.

Little Crow waited through the introduction, listening intently, then joined with his flute. The boy's playing carried a pure, clear quality that perfectly complemented Joseph's lower tones.

Lydia found herself unexpectedly moved as the two instruments conversed, separated by octaves but finding harmony in the ancient melody. It seemed to perfectly symbolize what she'd observed throughout the day, different traditions finding common ground, past wisdom informing present challenges, disparate elements creating something greater than either could alone.

The duet concluded to appreciative murmurs from the gathering. Little Crow beamed with pride as his grandfather nodded approval.

Eventually, as younger children began to drowse against their parents' shoulders and the fire burned lower, Thomas signaled that the gathering was concluding.

"We have shared food, music, and stories," he announced, rising slowly to his feet. "Tomorrow brings new work, new challenges. Rest well, knowing we face them together."

People began dispersing to their dwellings, exchanging quiet good nights. Sarah approached Lydia and Joseph, her silver-streaked braids gleaming in the dying firelight.

"Walk with me," she said to Lydia. "There is something I wish to show you before you sleep."

Joseph raised an eyebrow in question, but Sarah reassured him. "She will be safe with me, Joseph Calloway. We won't go far."

Chapter 16

Lydia followed Sarah Dove along a path that led slightly away from the main settlement, curious about this unexpected invitation. They stopped beside a small, dome-shaped structure unlike the other dwellings she had seen during the day.

"This is our medicine lodge," Sarah explained, her voice low with respect. "A place of healing for body and spirit."

In the dim light, Lydia could make out bundles of dried plants hanging from the framework, stones arranged in a circle at the center, and various implements whose purpose she couldn't immediately determine.

"Few outsiders are brought here," Sarah continued. "But I believe you should see it, to understand another part of our way."

"I'm honored by your trust," Lydia replied sincerely.

Sarah studied her face for a long moment. "You have a healer's eyes, observant, compassionate, seeking to understand before acting. In my people's way, such gifts carry responsibility."

"I'm not sure that I understand," Lydia admitted.

"Your pictures. They are not just marks on paper. They have power to heal misunderstanding, to bridge what divides. Or they can wound further, if created without care."

The responsibility inherent in this observation struck Lydia forcefully. Her art wasn't merely documentation, it was interpretation that would shape how others perceived this community and its way of life.

"I will try to be worthy of that trust," she promised.

Sarah nodded, seemingly satisfied. "One more thing I would show you." She reached into a small pouch at her waist and withdrew what appeared to be a square of tanned leather, about the size of Lydia's hand.

Unfolding it carefully, she revealed an image painted on the surface. A scene showing riders on horseback, stylized yet recognizable figures, pursuing buffalo across a grassy plain.

"My grandmother made this," Sarah explained. "Before I was born, when the buffalo were still many and our people followed them across the open lands." Her weathered fingers traced the painted figures with reverence. "This is how we kept our stories when there was no paper, no books. Images that carried meaning."

Lydia studied the painting with appreciation. The figures were simplified but communicated essential information through posture, relationship, and symbolic elements. Despite the different aesthetic approach, she recognized a shared purpose with her own work, capturing truth through visual means.

"Your grandmother was an artist," she said softly. "As you are in your healing work, knowing which plants to use, how to prepare them, how to apply them where needed."

Sarah's eyes crinkled at the corners, pleased by this understanding. "Different tools, same purpose, to preserve what matters, to help others see clearly." She carefully refolded the leather square. "Remember this when you return to your world of paper and ink. The power of true seeing is a gift not everyone possesses."

They walked back toward the settlement in silence, Lydia turning this unexpected wisdom over in her mind. When they reached the dwelling she shared with Joseph, Sarah touched her arm lightly.

"He too has healer's eyes," she said, with a slight nod toward the shelter where Joseph presumably waited. "Though his wounds run deep, and some still bleed." Before Lydia could respond to this cryptic observation, Sarah had melted into the darkness, her footsteps whisper-quiet on the packed earth.

Inside the shelter, a small oil lamp burned low, casting soft shadows across the simple space. Joseph sat on his sleeping platform, a book open in his hands—Lydia recognized it as the Bible he carried in his pack.

He looked up as she entered, his expression unreadable in the dim light. "Everything all right?"

"Yes," Lydia replied, moved by Sarah's insights but uncertain how much to share. "She wanted to show me their medicine lodge and talk about... the responsibility that comes with creating images of their way of life."

"Sarah sees deeply. She recognized something in you from the start."

"What do you mean?" Lydia asked, settling onto her platform and removing her boots.

He considered his words carefully. "The Blackfoot believe certain people are born with special abilities to bridge worlds, physical and spiritual, past and present, and different ways of knowing. They recognize such traits early, nurture them differently." His eyes met hers across the small space. "Sarah saw something similar in your ability to truly see her people, not just look at them."

"She showed me a painting her grandmother made," Lydia said, still processing the exchange. "It helped me understand how art serves a similar purpose across different traditions, preserving what matters, and communicating across boundaries."

"That's a rare honor. Those family items aren't often shared with outsiders."

Lydia prepared for sleep, removing her shawl and loosening her hair from its pins. The day's experiences swirled in her mind. The community's generous sharing of their traditions, Little Crow's eager guidance, the portrait of Thomas that had moved the gathering, Joseph's harmonica playing with the boy's flute. Each image contained layers of meaning beyond what might be immediately apparent to outsiders.

"Joseph?" she asked, an idea forming as she brushed out her hair. "Would it be possible to stay one more day beyond what was planned? There are additional sketches I'd like to make, perspectives I didn't capture today."

He looked up from his Bible, studying her face in the lamplight. "I suppose so if Thomas agrees. Any particular reason?"

"Sarah helped me realize something important about the work I'm creating," Lydia explained, setting her brush aside. "These images need to show not just activities or physical features, but relationships. How the community connects to this specific place, how traditions adapt without being abandoned, and how wisdom passes between generations." She gestured toward her sketchbook. "I've made a good start, but I need more time to do it justice."

"I suspect Thomas would welcome that request, especially given how you've approached your work so far." He closed his Bible, marking his place with a slender ribbon. "I can ask him in the morning."

"What were you reading?"

His hand paused, and in the lingering light, she caught a glimpse of something vulnerable cross his features. "Psalms," he admitted. "Particularly the ones about finding grace after failure. They've...spoken to me since my buffalo hunting days."

The simple admission revealed more about his inner journey than any lengthy explanation could have.

Chapter 17

A sharp, urgent cry pierced the dawn stillness, yanking Lydia from sleep. She bolted upright on her sleeping platform, momentarily disoriented in the gray half-light filtering through the smoke hole above.

"Joseph?" she called, turning toward his sleeping area.

His bed was empty. The sound came again, not human distress as she'd initially feared, but the high, keening call of an eagle soaring above the settlement. Lydia pressed a hand to her racing heart, willing it to slow as she gathered her bearings.

Outside, the settlement was already stirring to life. Voices murmured in quiet conversation, and the scent of wood smoke drifted through the air.

She was pinning her hair into a simple twist when Joseph appeared at the entrance of their shelter.

"Good morning," he said, ducking his head beneath the low doorway. "Sleep well?"

"Until an eagle decided to announce sunrise," she replied with a smile, securing the last pin.

"Ah. Their hunting cry carries for miles." Joseph's expression softened slightly. "Elder Thomas gave his permission for us to stay another day. Sarah Dove's already asked after you. She and Thomas have planned a journey to a place they rarely show outsiders."

Interest immediately kindled in Lydia's chest. "What kind of place?"

"Sacred ground. Where generations of their people have gone to seek visions and mark important transitions. Thomas will explain better than I can." He hesitated, then added, "It's a considerable honor, Lydia. I've known Thomas for years and have never been invited there."

"I'll need my sketch materials."

"And sturdy boots. It's not a difficult journey, but parts will be rocky." He gestured to a small bundle in his hands. "Sarah Dove sent food. We'll leave when you're ready."

Lydia quickly ate flatbread wrapped around dried berries and nuts, while gathering her essential art supplies. Joseph waited patiently.

"Did you sleep at all?" she asked, noticing the shadows beneath his eyes.

He shrugged. "Enough. Morning Sky's youngest was feverish in the night. I helped fetch water while Sarah Dove tended to him."

This glimpse of Joseph's integration into the community's life touched Lydia. Not merely a visitor or former patient, but someone who stepped in when needed.

Outside, the morning air carried a crisp sweetness that promised warmth later. Little Crow was already waiting, and Elder Thomas and Sarah Dove approached, dressed for travel with small packs slung across their shoulders. Both moved with purpose and energy that belied their age.

"You slept well?" Thomas asked by way of greeting.

"Very well, thank you," Lydia assured him. "And I'm deeply grateful for this additional day to learn from your community."

Thomas nodded, satisfaction in the small gesture. "Today we take you to Whispering Ridge, where our ancestors have sought wisdom for many generations." He gazed at the distant hills, visible as purple shadows against the brightening sky. "It is a three-hour journey if we walk steadily."

"I'm ready whenever you are," Lydia assured him, adjusting her satchel of art supplies.

Sarah stepped forward, handing Lydia a walking stick of polished wood. "The path grows steep in places," she explained. "This will help steady your steps." Her dark eyes, clear and penetrating, studied Lydia's face. "You rested, but your mind worked through the night. Dreams spoke to you?"

The observation was startlingly accurate. Lydia had indeed experienced vivid dreams—fragments of images and conversations from the previous day reshaping themselves in her sleeping mind.

"Yes," she admitted. "How did you know?"

Sarah smiled. "Your eyes carry the look of one who has traveled in sleep. Sometimes, the spirit understands before the mind does."

"Dreams are messages," Little Crow said. "We must listen to them like voices carried on wind."

Joseph, who had been quietly checking Lydia's equipment, rejoined them. "All ready here. Michael has asked to join us if that's acceptable. He'll catch up along the trail."

Thomas nodded. "My son honors the old ways, though sometimes he struggles to balance them with the new path we must walk. This journey will be good for his spirit."

Their small group set out as the sun cleared the eastern ridge, bathing the settlement in soft morning light. They followed a narrow trail that wound through stands of cottonwood before beginning a gradual ascent into the surrounding hills. Little Crow ranged ahead, then doubled back repeatedly, pointing out features he deemed important. A patch of ripening berries, a hawk's nest high in a lightning-struck pine, and the tracks of deer that had crossed the path before dawn.

Lydia walked beside Sarah, with Joseph and Thomas following close behind, their deeper voices a reassuring rumble of occasional conversation. The elder woman moved with remarkable grace, her moccasined feet finding secure placement on even the rockiest portions of the trail.

"The place we go to," Sarah explained as they climbed, "has been sacred to my people since before the memory of the oldest stories. A place where the veil is thin between worlds."

"Worlds?" Lydia asked, intrigued.

Sarah gestured to the physical landscape around them. "This world we touch and see, and the spirit world that flows beneath and through it. Most people notice only the surface of things, but some places allow deeper seeing." Her weathered hand traced a shape in the air. "Like ripples on water, revealing what moves beneath."

Lydia considered this perspective thoughtfully. Growing up, she'd been taught that God was everywhere, yet she'd also experienced moments, usually when drawing, when the separation between herself and what she observed seemed to dissolve, allowing a deeper perception of truth.

"I think I understand, at least a little," she offered. "Sometimes when I'm drawing something with complete focus, it feels as though I'm not separate from what I'm seeing, but connected to its essence in a way that's difficult to explain."

Sarah's expression warmed with approval. "Yes. The artist's way of seeing. This is why Thomas believes your pictures might speak a truth others would miss."

The trail steepened, requiring more breath for climbing and less for conversation. Joseph moved forward to walk beside Lydia, matching his longer stride to her pace.

"Need a rest?" he asked after a particularly challenging section.

Lydia shook her head, though she gratefully used the walking stick Sarah had provided. "I'm fine. Good, actually."

"Montana's changing you," he observed, a hint of approval in his tone. "You've grown stronger since we left Bozeman."

The simple observation warmed her unexpectedly. "In more ways than one, I think."

Their eyes met briefly, a current of understanding passing between them. Joseph's gaze lingered on her face before he turned his attention back to the trail, but not before Lydia caught a softening around his eyes that sent a flutter through her chest.

After about two hours of steady walking, with brief rests when the terrain demanded it, they reached a small plateau where a clear spring bubbled from between rocks. The view from this vantage point was breathtaking. The valley spread below them like a living map, with the settlement visible as a small cluster of structures beside the silver ribbon of the river.

"We rest here," Thomas announced, lowering himself to a flat rock beside the spring. "When Michael joins us, we will proceed to the sacred ground."

Little Crow immediately dropped his small pack and darted to the spring, cupping his hands to drink the crystal water. "Best water anywhere," he declared, water dripping from his chin. "Grandfather says it comes from the heart of the mountain."

Joseph helped Sarah Dove arrange herself comfortably on a smooth boulder, then took out his canteen to refill it from the spring.

"May I?" Lydia asked, extending her water container.

He took it with a nod, their fingers brushing briefly in the exchange. Such small, incidental touches had begun to register more prominently in Lydia's awareness, each one leaving a lingering warmth like the echo of a gentle word.

As Joseph filled their canteens, Little Crow approached Lydia, his expression suddenly serious.

"Will you draw this place too?" he asked. "So people far away will know it matters to us?"

Lydia studied the boy's earnest face. "I'd like to if your grandfather approves. Though some places are perhaps too sacred to capture in drawings."

Thomas, overhearing, nodded thoughtfully. "A wise observation. There are indeed some aspects of our sacred grounds that should not be shown to outside eyes. But the beauty of the place, the feeling it creates in the heart—these can be shared without revealing what should remain private."

"I understand," Lydia assured him. "I would never want to depict anything that might violate your community's trust."

A movement on the trail below caught their attention. Michael appeared, climbing with powerful strides that ate up the distance. Despite the steep ascent, he showed little sign of exertion when he reached them, merely a light sheen of perspiration on his forehead.

"Father," he greeted Thomas respectfully. "I had to help resolve a boundary question with Two Bears' family before I could leave."

Thomas nodded in acknowledgment. "All is settled?"

"For now." Something in Michael's tone suggested the issue was more complex than his simple answer indicated, but he didn't elaborate. Instead, he accepted the water from Joseph with a grateful nod before turning to Lydia.

"You wish to understand our connection to this land more deeply."

"I do," she confirmed.

Michael studied her face, his expression guarded but not hostile. "Many white people see land as something to be owned, divided with fences and papers. For us, the relationship is different. More like being part of a family. You belong to each other. Perhaps your pictures will help some understand what words alone have failed to convey."

After their brief rest, they continued upward, the trail narrowing as it wound between massive boulders and stands of twisted pine that clung tenaciously to the rocky soil.

Joseph walked immediately behind Lydia, close enough that she could occasionally feel his presence, particularly when the path grew treacherous. Once, when loose stones shifted beneath her feet, his hand materialized instantly at her elbow, steadying her with gentle strength before withdrawing once she regained her footing.

The small gesture of protection, offered and then retracted without comment, touched her deeply. Joseph's care was neither possessive nor patronizing, but a natural extension of his awareness, like his vigilance regarding weather patterns or animal tracks.

Finally, Thomas led them through a narrow passage between towering rocks, and they emerged onto a sunlit shelf of stone that extended like a natural balcony from the mountainside. The view was breathtaking. Miles of Montana territory spread before them, from the distant smudges of mountain ranges to the emerald ribbon of river valley below.

"Whispering Ridge," Thomas announced simply, but with reverence that made the name sound like a prayer.

Lydia stood transfixed by the panorama, her artist's eye trying to absorb the vastness of sky and land unfolding before her. The sensation was almost overwhelming, not just visual beauty, but something deeper that seemed to reverberate in her chest like distant thunder.

"It's magnificent," she whispered, inadequate words for what she was experiencing.

"Listen," Sarah instructed quietly, moving to stand beside her.

Lydia closed her eyes and focused on her hearing. At first, she was aware only of the wind and distant bird calls. Then, gradually, she perceived a subtle sound—a continuous whisper, like many voices speaking just below the threshold of comprehension.

Her eyes opened in wonder. "What is that?"

"The ridge speaks," Thomas said simply. "Wind through the stone passages below us creates voices. Our ancestors believed these were the spirits of those who came before, offering guidance to those who listen properly."

"In the vision seeking time," Little Crow added importantly, "young men would sit alone here for days with no food or water, waiting for the spirits to speak clearly to them."

Lydia listened again, mesmerized by the ethereal quality of the sound. It did indeed resemble distant conversation, rising and falling like the murmur of a crowd just out of earshot.

"There's more," Sarah said, gesturing for Lydia to follow her toward the far end of the stone shelf.

There, partially sheltered by an overhanging ledge, was a smooth section of rock face covered with ancient paintings. Ochre and carbon figures depicted human forms, animals, celestial bodies, and symbols whose meanings weren't immediately apparent. The images had faded with time but remained visible, some appearing recent, others so ancient they seemed part of the stone itself.

"The story of our people's journey," Thomas explained, coming to stand beside them. "Each generation has added to this record, beginning with our earliest ancestors." His weathered hand hovered reverently near but didn't touch a series of figures that appeared to be following a trail of animal tracks. "Here is the story of how we came to this land, following the buffalo. Here," he indicated another section, "the great sickness that came after the first white traders visited."

Lydia studied the paintings with deep respect, recognizing them as historical documentation as significant as any written archive.

"May I move closer to see better?" she asked, not wanting to presume.

Thomas nodded. "Yes. But draw only what I indicate is appropriate for outside eyes to see."

For the next hour, Thomas guided Lydia through the visual history depicted on the stone canvas. He identified which elements represented community knowledge meant for all to see, and which depicted sacred ceremonies or spiritual teachings that should remain private.

Lydia sketched carefully, focusing on the stylized animals, migration patterns, and historical events Thomas approved for documentation. She was drawn to the elegant economy of the ancient artists' technique. How a few simple lines could convey movement, relationship, and meaning with remarkable clarity.

"These paintings tell of seasons of plenty and times of hardship," Thomas explained, indicating a sequence showing tall grasses and abundant game, followed by stark figures and bare landscapes. "Our people have always understood that life moves in cycles, like the moon above us."

"The colors have lasted remarkably well," Lydia observed, examining the rich pigments.

Sarah nodded. "Made from earth and mixed with fat from animals. The stone itself protects them from rain and too much sun."

As Lydia worked, she found herself adopting elements of the rock paintings' straightforward visual language in her sketches, simplifying forms to their essential characteristics, emphasizing relationship rather than detail. The ancient artists had understood storytelling in visual terms, communicating complex ideas through deceptively simple means.

Joseph had remained somewhat apart, sitting near the ridge's edge with Michael, their conversation too low to overhear. Occasionally, Lydia glanced their way, noting the intensity of their discussion, Joseph's face grave as he listened to the younger man.

Little Crow alternated between watching Lydia sketch and exploring the perimeter of the ridge, though never straying far from his grandfather's sight. The boy moved with the natural confidence.

"Here," Thomas said finally, indicating the most recent section of paintings, "is our current struggle." The images showed square shapes representing settlers' buildings encroaching on traditional lands, straight lines cutting across what had been open territory.

"The most recent addition," he explained, pointing to markings that appeared fresher than the others. "Made last autumn, when the surveyors first came."

Lydia studied the stark visual testimony, understanding more clearly now why Thomas had wanted her to see this place. It wasn't merely a historical record but a continuing narrative, one in which his community faced perhaps its greatest challenge.

"I see why this place matters so deeply," she said. "It holds your people's memory, your connection to the past, and your understanding of the present."

Thomas nodded, satisfaction in his eyes. "You understand better than most who come from outside. This ridge has witnessed every important moment in our history. From here, our ancestors could see enemies approaching or buffalo herds moving. Here, they made decisions that ensured survival through difficult times." He gestured toward the valley below. "To lose our connection to this place would be to lose part of ourselves."

As the sun climbed higher, Sarah approached with a small bundle of food, dried meat, berries, and corn cakes, which they shared sitting in a semicircle facing the immense landscape. The whisper of the stone continued beneath their conversation, an ancient counterpoint to their words.

"The paintings you've made," Sarah said to Lydia, "what will become of them when you return to the East?"

Lydia considered the question thoughtfully. "They'll accompany my written observations as part of the commission for National Geographic. Selected images will be published alongside the article, reproduced for readers across the country."

"And those who see them, will they understand?" The elder woman's question carried genuine concern.

"Not completely," Lydia admitted honestly. "No picture can convey the full reality of being here, of hearing the whispering stone or feeling the connection that spans generations. But if my work can help even a few people recognize the importance of your relationship to this land, perhaps it will make some difference."

Thomas's weathered face remained impassive, but something in his eyes suggested he appreciated her lack of false promises.

"The world is changing rapidly," Joseph said, speaking for the first time since they'd reached the ridge. "Not all changes can be prevented. But how they happen, and whether they occur with respect for what came before—that's what's at stake."

Michael stirred restlessly. "Words and pictures haven't protected our hunting grounds or kept settlers from encroaching on our land before. Why should these be different?"

"Because they'll show truth rather than imagination," Lydia responded quietly. "Most Eastern publications show either hostile warriors or romanticized noble savages—rarely real people with complex histories and legitimate connections to specific places."

Michael held her gaze, measuring her sincerity. "Perhaps," he finally conceded. "Though I remain skeptical."

"Skepticism is warranted," Thomas acknowledged. "But we must try all paths available to us. Miss Hayes's pictures may reach people we cannot."

The conversation fell into natural silence as they finished their simple meal. Lydia used the time to add final details to her sketches, trying to capture not just the visual elements but something of the feeling of this sacred place. The sense of time's passage marked in charcoal, the whispered voices of the stone, and the view that connected earth and sky in panoramic splendor.

When Thomas finally signaled it was time to depart, Lydia felt a reluctance to leave, as though the ridge had temporarily claimed her as part of its ongoing story.

As they gathered their belongings, Little Crow approached her with something clutched carefully in his hand.

"For your pictures," he said solemnly, opening his palm to reveal a piece of ochre stone. "The color of our paintings." His serious eyes met hers. "So you remember the true color when you make your final drawings."

The simple gift, offered with such genuine purpose, touched Lydia deeply. "Thank you," she said, carefully wrapping the ochre in a clean handkerchief. "I'll use it with respect."

Their descent followed a different path, steeper but more direct. Joseph stayed close behind Lydia, while Thomas led with Sarah beside him. Michael brought up the rear, his watchful gaze frequently scanning the surrounding terrain.

The journey downward was largely silent, each person absorbed in their thoughts. For Lydia, the experience at Whispering Ridge had shifted something fundamental in her perspective. What had begun as artistic documentation now felt like a deeper responsibility, carrying forward the trust placed in her by Thomas's community.

As the settlement came back into view below them, Joseph drew alongside her. "You've been quiet," he observed.

"I'm still processing everything," she admitted. "The responsibility feels much greater now."

Joseph nodded understanding. "That's how it should be. True seeing always carries obligation with it." His gray eyes met hers. "But I believe you're equal to it."

The simple vote of confidence warmed her. "Today has been... transformative."

"I could see it happening," he said quietly. "Watching you on the ridge, the way you absorbed not just the images but their meaning." A hint of admiration softened his expression. "Few people ever achieve that level of understanding."

They continued in companionable silence until they reached the settlement's edge. The afternoon was waning, golden light slanting across the valley and burnishing the simple structures with warm radiance.

"There's still daylight left," Lydia observed. "I'd like to make a few more sketches before we depart tomorrow."

"Of course," Joseph agreed. "I have some matters to discuss with Michael regarding the Garrett brothers. We'll reconnect for the evening meal."

As they parted ways, Lydia felt a curious mixture of emotions—gratitude for the experiences of the day, satisfaction in the work she'd accomplished, and an unexpected pang at the thought of leaving this place and its people the following morning. The settlement had ceased to feel foreign, becoming instead a place of genuine connection and profound learning.

She settled on a flat rock overlooking the river, where several women worked at various tasks while keeping watchful eyes on children playing nearby. Opening her sketchbook to a fresh page, Lydia began to draw, not individual portraits but the interconnected activities that formed the community's daily rhythm. Women conversing as they worked, children observing and sometimes imitating their elders, the easy flow of knowledge passing between generations.

As her pencil moved across the paper, Lydia found herself integrating what she'd learned at Whispering Ridge—the economy of the line, the emphasis on relationship rather than detail, the ability to suggest deeper meaning through simple visual elements. The resulting sketches captured something essential about the community that her earlier, more technically precise drawings had sometimes missed.

By the time shadows lengthened across the settlement, she had filled several pages with these new, more integrated drawings. Looking up at last, she found Sarah Dove standing quietly nearby, observing her work with keen interest.

"You have been learning from the ancestors today," the elder woman commented, nodding toward the sketchbook. "Your hand now speaks with two voices together."

Lydia realized, with surprise, that Sarah was right. Her technique had evolved, incorporating elements of the rock paintings' visual language without abandoning her formal training. The result was something new, a synthesis that honored both traditions.

"The rock paintings taught me to see differently," she acknowledged.

"As they have taught our people for generations." Sarah smiled, the expression softening the weathered contours of her face. "Come now. The evening meal awaits, and afterward, there will be a special ceremony to mark your departure."

Chapter 18

The firelight painted everyone's faces with flickering amber as Thomas raised his hands for silence. The evening meal had concluded, leaving behind a sense of contentment that settled over the gathering. Lydia sat cross-legged between Joseph and Little Crow, still savoring the rich flavors of the venison stew Sarah Dove had prepared with wild onions and roots that tasted of the earth itself.

"Tonight," Thomas announced, his voice carrying easily across the hushed circle, "we honor our guests before their journey tomorrow. Not as strangers who came to look upon us, but as friends who came to see with open hearts."

Murmurs of agreement rippled through the assembled community. Lydia felt a curious tightness in her throat, touched by the acceptance these people had shown her. Beside her, Joseph sat with quiet dignity, his shoulder occasionally brushing against hers as he shifted position, each brief contact sending warmth through her despite the evening's growing coolness.

Thomas nodded to several of the elders, who rose and disappeared briefly into the shadows. When they returned, they carried small bundles wrapped in soft leather. The first approached Lydia, an elderly man whose deeply lined face spoke of decades under the Montana sun.

"For the woman who sees with true eyes," he said, his English halting but clear. He extended his offering with both hands, a gesture of respect that Lydia mirrored as she accepted it.

Carefully unwrapping the leather, she revealed a small pouch made of finely tanned deer hide, adorned with intricate bead work in patterns of blue and white that reminded her of flowing water.

"Medicine bag," the elder explained. "To keep your seeing strong, even when you return to the stone cities."

"It's beautiful," Lydia said sincerely, running her fingers over the skilled bead work. "I'll treasure it."

Another elder approached Joseph, presenting him with a bundle that revealed a knife sheath decorated with porcupine quills dyed in brilliant reds and yellows.

"To replace the one you wore thin during the long winter," the man said with a hint of humor. "Maybe this one last longer."

Joseph accepted it with a deep nod of appreciation. "Craftsmanship like this deserves better care than I gave the last one," he acknowledged, examining the detailed quill work with obvious admiration.

Gifts continued to be presented. A small carved wooden flute for Lydia from Little Crow, a pouch of special tobacco for Joseph from Michael, each item clearly chosen with thought and meaning. The generosity overwhelmed Lydia, who had come expecting to be merely an observer and found herself instead welcomed as a participant in this community's life.

When the gift-giving concluded, Sarah Dove rose from her place beside Thomas and approached the fire. Her silver-streaked braids reflected the dancing flames, and her face held a solemn concentration that immediately commanded attention. The soft conversations around the circle quieted as she reached into a small pouch at her waist and took out a handful of something that she cast into the fire.

Sweet-smelling smoke billowed upward as the herbs caught fire, the aroma reminiscent of pine and sage with other elements Lydia couldn't identify. Sarah began to speak in her native tongue, her voice taking on a rhythmic quality that seemed to merge with the crackling of the flames.

Thomas translated quietly for their benefit. "She calls upon the ancestors to witness this gathering. She thanks them for guiding us to understand one another across the barriers of different ways."

Sarah continued, her hands moving in expressive gestures that seemed to shape her words into visible forms. The community watched with respectful attention, many nodding at particular phrases.

"She speaks now of visions that have come to her," Thomas explained, his voice dropping lower. "Dreams that show paths crossing and joining."

Lydia glanced at Joseph, finding his expression intense as he focused on Sarah's words. Something in Thomas's tone suggested these weren't merely traditional blessings, but something more specific.

Sarah turned suddenly, fixing her gaze directly on Lydia and Joseph. She addressed them specifically, her words flowing with increased urgency.

"My dreams have spoken of you both," Thomas translated, his eyes moving between them. "Not once, but many times since the winter moon. Two rivers from different mountains, flowing together to create something stronger than either alone."

Joseph shifted beside Lydia, his posture straightening. She felt a current of tension radiating from him.

Sarah moved toward them, gesturing for them to rise. Somewhat uncertainly, Lydia got to her feet, Joseph following suit. The elder woman positioned herself before them, eyes moving searchingly between their faces.

"She says your spirits recognized each other from the first meeting, though your minds argued against it," Thomas continued translating. "The man carved from stone and the woman who shapes stone with her vision—joined by purpose deeper than either understands yet."

Lydia felt heat rise to her cheeks, acutely aware of the entire community watching this unexpected turn in the ceremony. Joseph remained utterly still beside her, his breathing measured but slightly faster than normal.

Sarah reached out, taking Lydia's right hand and Joseph's left, bringing them together between her own weathered palms. The contact sent a jolt of awareness through Lydia. Joseph's hand warm and calloused against her skin, Sarah's fingers cool and surprisingly strong as they pressed their hands together.

"Among our people," Thomas translated, "when two souls are recognized as walking a shared path, the community acknowledges what the Creator has already joined in the world beyond sight."

Sarah spoke directly to Lydia now, her dark eyes holding a fierce intensity. "You came seeking images of a vanishing world. Instead, you found your place within it."

She turned to Joseph, continuing without waiting for Thomas to translate. "You sought redemption alone, believing yourself unworthy of companionship on that journey. The Creator thinks otherwise."

Releasing their hands but leaving them joined between her departed touch, Sarah reached again into her medicine pouch and withdrew a slender strip of soft, white-tanned leather decorated at each end with small blue beads and a single eagle feather.

"The binding cord," Thomas explained, his voice carrying a hint of surprise, "is used only in our most sacred ceremonies of connection. It symbolizes paths that the Creator has woven together through time."

Sarah gently wrapped the leather cord once around their still-joined hands, not tying it but allowing it to rest loosely against their skin. "Where this cord touches," she said through Thomas's translation, "truth must be spoken. The spirits of truth hover close."

She looked expectantly at Joseph, clearly waiting for him to speak. The silence around the fire grew profound, broken only by the soft popping of burning wood and the distant calling of a night bird.

Joseph cleared his throat, his gray eyes meeting Lydia's with an intensity that made her breath catch. "I came to Montana seeking escape," he said, his deep voice pitched low but carrying clearly in the hush. "From what I'd done. From who I'd been. I found instead a chance to build something new, but alone." His fingers tightened slightly around hers. "Until you arrived with your sketchbooks and Eastern ideas and somehow saw past every wall I'd built."

Lydia's heart thundered in her chest, her awareness narrowing to the warmth of his hand against hers and the raw honesty in his eyes.

"Your turn," Sarah prompted gently when Lydia remained silent. "Speak what the cord reveals."

Lydia took a steadying breath. "I came west seeking adventure and artistic opportunity, thinking I understood what that meant." Her voice grew stronger as she continued. "I found instead a world far more complex, more beautiful, and more challenging than I could have imagined. And a man whose integrity and quiet strength has changed how I see everything, including myself."

Something shifted in Joseph's expression, vulnerability breaking through his habitual reserve like sunlight through storm clouds. The moment stretched between them, weighted with unspoken meaning.

Sarah nodded, apparently satisfied, and began unwinding the cord from their hands. "The truth has been spoken and witnessed," Thomas translated. "What has been recognized cannot be unknown."

Rather than returning the cord to her pouch, Sarah folded it carefully and extended it toward them. "For you to keep," she said directly to Lydia. "Until the day comes when you choose to bind it permanently or release it back to the winds. The choice remains yours, but the recognition stands regardless."

Lydia accepted the cord with trembling fingers, acutely conscious of its symbolic weight. Joseph released her other hand, leaving a lingering warmth against her palm.

"Remember," Sarah continued, her voice taking on a rhythmic cadence that required no translation, "what is joined by the Creator is not easily separated. Like the rivers that meet and flow as one to the great waters, your paths have converged for a purpose beyond yourselves."

She returned to her place beside Thomas, and gradually the ceremony shifted into songs and stories, the focus moving away from Lydia and Joseph. But something fundamental had changed between them, an acknowledgment spoken aloud that could not be retracted or denied.

Little Crow appeared at Lydia's side, mercifully breaking the intensity of the moment. "I will play my flute," he announced, importantly. "The song about the eagle finding its mate after a long journey."

Despite her emotional turmoil, Lydia couldn't help smiling at the boy's earnest expression. "I'd like that very much."

As Little Crow retrieved his flute and took his place near the musicians, Joseph leaned closer to her. "I should explain," he said quietly, "what just happened isn't—"

"Something to discuss in the midst of all this," Lydia finished for him, surprising herself with her composure. "We'll have time tomorrow, on the trail."

He studied her face in the firelight, concern evident in his expression. "You're not upset?"

"Surprised," she admitted.

They settled back to watch the performances, maintaining a careful few inches of space between them. Yet, Lydia felt more acutely connected to him than if they'd been touching, an invisible current humming in the air between their bodies.

Little Crow's flute song rose above the gathering, sweet and plaintive in the night air. The melody spoke of yearning and discovery, separation and reunion. Though Lydia couldn't understand the cultural references embedded in the tune, its emotional resonance needed no translation.

As the evening progressed, she observed Joseph with new awareness. The firelight caught the angles of his face, throwing his strong features into relief against the darkness beyond. His attentiveness to the proceedings, the respect evident in his posture, the occasional smile that softened his usual gravity when Little Crow performed particularly well—all these details registered with heightened clarity.

Once, he caught her watching him and held her gaze steadily, neither challenging nor retreating from the moment of connection.

Chapter 19

The ceremony concluded with a final blessing from Thomas, thanking the ancestors for their guidance and the guests for bringing new perspectives to the community. As people began dispersing to their dwellings, Sarah approached Lydia.

"Walk with me before you sleep," she said, not a request but a gentle command.

Lydia glanced at Joseph, who nodded slightly.

Sarah led Lydia away from the central area, following a narrow path that wound between dwellings toward a small clearing at the settlement's edge. Above them, stars blazed in breathtaking profusion across the Montana sky, more brilliant than Lydia had ever seen in New York.

"You have questions," Sarah observed, stopping where the path opened to the clearing. "About the binding ceremony."

"Yes," Lydia admitted. "It seemed very... significant."

Sarah's weathered face creased in a smile. "Among my people, dreams carry messages from the spirit world. When the same dream comes many nights, it cannot be ignored." She gazed upward at the star-filled sky. "Three times I dreamed of two eagles circling high above Whispering Ridge, separate at first, then flying as one."

"And you believe those eagles represent Joseph and me?" Lydia asked, trying to understand.

"I know they do," Sarah replied with calm certainty. "Just as I know the river will continue flowing when I am gone, and the sun will rise tomorrow whether I witness it or not." She turned her penetrating gaze back to Lydia. "Some truths exist, whether we acknowledge them or not."

Lydia fingered the leather binding cord she'd tucked carefully into her pocket. "The ceremony... what exactly did it signify among your people?"

"Recognition, not obligation," Sarah clarified. "A naming of what already exists, like pointing to a star and giving it a name. The star remains unchanged, but our understanding of it grows."

This subtle distinction helped ease some of Lydia's uncertainty. "And the cord itself?"

"A reminder of connection that transcends distance. And some-times, a nudge for those who see truth but hesitate to embrace it."

Lydia couldn't help a small laugh. "A nudge indeed."

Sarah's expression grew more serious. "Joseph Calloway carries deep wounds from his past. Wounds that have begun to heal since you arrived." Her hand reached out, briefly touching Lydia's arm. "He believes himself undeserving of happiness because of actions long past. This is not truth."

"I sensed this," Lydia said quietly.

Sarah nodded, satisfaction in her eyes. "Good. You see with clear vision." She gestured toward the stars wheeling overhead. "Our lives are brief moments in the great circle of time. To waste them in needless separation when paths are meant to join—this is true foolishness."

The straightforward wisdom struck Lydia forcefully. How much time did people waste, herself included, pretending not to recognize connections when they appeared? How many opportunities passed by because fear or convention prevented their acknowledgment?

"Thank you for sharing your dreams and wisdom with me."

Sarah inclined her head in acknowledgment. "When you return to your world of tall buildings and many people, remember what you learned here. True seeing cannot be unlearned, though many try." Her dark eyes held Lydia's. "And what was recognized tonight will follow you both, whether you choose to bind the cord permanently or not."

They walked back toward the settlement in silence, Sarah Dove's words settling into Lydia's heart. By the time they reached the shelter she shared with Joseph, she felt both unsettled and strangely peaceful, as if contradictory currents flowed through her simultaneously.

***

Joseph waited outside, his tall figure outlined against the shelter's entrance. He straightened as they approached, watchfulness evident in his posture.

"Rest well," Sarah said to them both. "Tomorrow brings new journeys." With that, she moved away into the darkness, her footsteps whisper-quiet on the packed earth.

For a moment, Lydia and Joseph stood facing each other in the starlight, the changed awareness between them almost palpable.

"I should have warned you," he finally said, breaking the charged silence. "About Sarah's dreams and what they might lead to."

"You knew?" Lydia asked, genuinely curious rather than accusatory.

He shook his head. "Not specifically. But she mentioned dreams involving both of us yesterday. Among the Blackfoot, such dreams are taken seriously, especially coming from someone with Sarah's standing."

Lydia nodded, absorbing this. "She explained some of it to me just now. About recognition rather than obligation."

"Yes, exactly. It's important you understand that." He hesitated, seeming to struggle with his next words. "Whatever was said tonight doesn't bind you to anything you don't freely choose."

The careful way he distanced himself from the ceremony's implications stirred something protective in Lydia's heart. "And you?" she asked softly. "Does it bind you?"

In the starlight, his expression was difficult to read, but she sensed rather than saw his internal conflict. "My obligations to you were established the moment I agreed to be your guide," he said finally. "To ensure your safety and help you complete your commission successfully."

It was a careful answer that revealed nothing of his personal feelings. Lydia might have been discouraged if not for the way his voice had softened when he'd spoken during the ceremony, and the unmistakable tenderness in his eyes when their hands were joined.

"We should rest," she said, accepting that this wasn't the moment to press further. "Tomorrow will be a long day of travel."

Joseph nodded, holding the shelter's covering aside for her to enter. The small interior was dimly lit by a single oil lamp.

Lydia busied herself with preparing for sleep, removing her boots. Joseph moved to his area, his back turned to give her privacy, the line of his shoulders tense beneath his shirt.

As she settled onto her platform, arranging the blankets against the night's chill, Lydia realized she still held the leather binding cord Sarah had given her. She brought it out, studying it in the lamp's soft glow. The craftsmanship was exquisite—the leather beaten to buttery softness, the bead work precise and elegant, the single eagle feather attached with sinew so fine it was barely visible.

"May I see it?"

Joseph's quiet request startled her. He had moved closer without her noticing, now standing a few feet away, his expression unreadable in the dim light.

Lydia extended the cord toward him. "Of course."

He took it carefully, his fingers avoiding contact with hers, and examined it with evident appreciation. "Sarah made this herself," he said. "I recognize her bead work style."

"It's beautiful," Lydia agreed.

Joseph nodded, continuing to study the cord with unusual intensity, as if seeking answers in its craftsmanship. "The eagle feather signifies vision and courage," he explained. "The blue beads represent water—rivers flowing together."

"Like the two rivers in Sarah's dream," Lydia said softly.

His eyes lifted to her face, surprised. "She told you about that?"

"About the eagles too," Lydia confirmed. "Three identical dreams, she said."

Joseph returned the cord with careful precision, ensuring their fingers didn't touch in the exchange. "Sarah's dreams have proven remarkably accurate in the past," he said, his tone neutral. "During that winter I spent with them. She dreamed of buffalo returning to a specific valley weeks before it happened."

Lydia sensed he was deliberately focusing on the factual aspects of Sarah's abilities rather than their current implications. She decided not to push him further tonight, recognizing his need for distance to process what had occurred.

"Thank you for translating during the ceremony," she said instead, changing the subject slightly. "And for explaining the cultural significance afterward."

Relief flickered across his features. "Of course. That's why I was hired. To guide you through unfamiliar territory."

The statement was technically true, but felt suddenly inadequate. Lydia tucked the binding cord carefully into her small travel bag, aware of Joseph watching the gesture.

"We should leave at first light tomorrow," he said, returning to practical matters. "It will be a full day's ride. There's rain coming."

"How can you tell?" Lydia asked, genuinely curious.

"The way the night birds were calling earlier. The shift in the wind direction." He moved back toward his sleeping area. "And my shoulder aches where I broke it years ago. More reliable than any weather vane."

Lydia lay awake for some time, listening to Joseph's breathing gradually slow and deepen as he drifted into sleep. Outside, the night sounds of the settlement created a gentle backdrop of distant voices, and the soft rustling of wind through the nearby trees.

Her mind replayed the binding ceremony, the feel of Joseph's hand against hers, the intensity in his gray eyes when he'd spoken of seeing past his walls. Sarah's certainty about the dreams and their meaning. The surprising ease with which Lydia herself had accepted what might have seemed outlandish in any other context.

She reached in the darkness for her travel bag, fingers finding the leather cord by touch alone. Something about holding it provided comfort and clarity. Whatever happens tomorrow or in the days to come, something true had been recognized tonight. As Sarah had said, some truths existed, whether acknowledged or not.

Chapter 20

The small drum beat a steady rhythm as Lydia secured her last saddlebag, cinching it tight against Penny's flank. The farewell ceremony had begun at dawn, the entire Blackfoot community gathering despite the gray clouds massing on the horizon. Thomas stood at the center of the circle, his lined face solemn as he raised his hands toward the sky.

"May the Creator guide your path and keep your vision clear," he said, his words directed first at Lydia, then at Joseph. "Remember what you have witnessed here when you speak to those who have never seen our ways."

Joseph nodded, his expression grave as he adjusted Thunder's bridle. "Your hospitality won't be forgotten, Elder Thomas. Nor will your trust."

Sarah Dove approached Lydia, her weathered hands extended. In her palms rested a small bundle wrapped in soft deerskin.

"For your journey," she said, her voice low but strong. "Dried roots to make tea when sleep eludes you, and sage to clear troubled thoughts."

"Thank you," Lydia said, accepting the gift with both hands as she'd learned was proper. "For everything you've taught me."

Sarah's dark eyes held hers intently. "The teaching continues long after the teacher is gone from sight. Listen with your heart when your mind grows confused."

Little Crow pushed forward, clutching something in his hands. His face was a mixture of solemnity and barely contained excitement.

"I made this," he announced, opening his hand to reveal a small wooden carving. "For you to take."

Lydia bent down, examining the object in his palm. It was a wooden eagle, wings outstretched in flight, carved with remarkable skill for one so young. Every feather had been carefully rendered, the bird's-eye alert and watchful.

"So you remember what Grandmother saw in her dreams," Little Crow explained, his voice dropping to a whisper. "Two eagles flying together."

"It's beautiful, Little Crow. Did you carve this yourself?"

"My father taught me. I worked on it all night."

"Then I'll treasure it always," she promised, carefully wrapping the carving in her handkerchief and tucking it into her satchel where it would travel safely.

The boy beamed, then darted away to join the other children, who watched the proceedings with curious eyes. Lydia straightened, aware of Joseph's gaze on her from where he stood with Michael and several other men.

Michael stepped forward, his expression more grave than usual. "The Garrett brothers," he said to Joseph. "Fresh signs near the eastern ridge yesterday evening."

Joseph's posture stiffened. "How many?"

"Three riders. Following game trails that lead back toward the settlement." Michael's jaw tightened. "They're hunting where they shouldn't be."

"Watch yourselves," Joseph advised, his voice low but intent. "If they're armed and looking for trouble..."

Michael nodded once, his hand falling briefly to the knife at his belt. "We're always watching."

The implications of this exchange settled in Lydia's stomach like a stone. The carefree exploration she'd anticipated when first arriving in Montana Territory had revealed deeper complexities and genuine dangers. The beauty of this land came with shadows she couldn't have imagined from her New York home.

Thomas approached, extending his hand first to Joseph, then to Lydia. "When your pictures reach the people in the East, perhaps some will see beyond their preconceptions. All we ask is truth."

"You have my word," Lydia promised.

Sarah Dove joined them, her silver-streaked braids catching the early light. "Remember, daughter of the East, what was recognized cannot be unknown, even across great distance."

Despite her best efforts, Lydia felt heat rising in her cheeks. She nodded, unable to form an adequate response to the elder's forthright observation.

Thomas raised his hands once more, speaking in his native tongue. The gathered community responded in unison, the words unfamiliar to Lydia but their intent unmistakable. A blessing, a farewell, a connection that would remain even as physical distance grew.

Joseph mounted Thunder with ease, then reached down to assist Lydia onto Penny. His hand was warm and strong around hers, the brief contact sending a ripple of awareness through her.

As they rode from the settlement, Lydia turned in her saddle for one last look. Little Crow stood waving Sarah Dove beside him, her hand raised in a more restrained farewell. The small cluster of dwellings seemed to belong to the landscape, neither dominating nor submitting to the natural world, but existing in harmony with its rhythms.

She committed the image to memory, knowing no sketch could fully capture the feeling of this place and its people. Some truths required more than pencil and paper to convey.

***

The first hour of their journey passed in weighty silence. Joseph rode slightly ahead, his shoulders set in a rigid line that discouraged conversation. Occasional glances backward confirmed Lydia's well-being, but he offered nothing beyond these brief acknowledgments.

Lydia occupied herself, studying the changing landscape as they followed a game trail that wound through stands of lodgepole pine. The mountains loomed to their west, their peaks already obscured by the advancing clouds. Joseph kept watching with increasing frequency.

By mid-morning, the silence had grown from awkward to oppressive. Lydia urged Penny forward until she rode alongside Joseph.

"Those clouds seem to be moving faster than they were earlier," she observed, opting for neutral territory.

Joseph nodded, his expression preoccupied. "Storm's building. Bigger than I anticipated."

"Where are we headed next?" she asked.

His gaze remained fixed on the horizon as he answered. "There's a valley about twenty miles southeast of here. Rock formations unlike anything you've likely seen, red stone arches carved by wind and water over centuries. Thought you might want to sketch them."

"That sounds fascinating," she said.

Joseph finally met her eyes, his expression softening fractionally. "The Blackfoot call it the Valley of Standing Stones. Considered it a place of power. Can't say I disagree—there's something about it that affects even the most practical-minded visitor."

"Like Whispering Ridge," Lydia suggested.

"Similar, yes. Though more dramatic visually." He paused, studying the clouds again. "We might have to delay that visit, depending on how this weather develops."

A natural opening presented itself, and Lydia took it. "I'm concerned about what Michael mentioned. About the Garrett brothers."

Joseph's jaw tightened. "As am I. Those men have nursed their grudges for years. First against the buffalo hunters who came after them and took the profit they felt entitled to, then against settlers claiming land they wanted, and always against the Blackfoot for simply existing where they wanted to hunt."

"You think they might cause trouble for the settlement?"

"It's possible." His voice grew contemplative. "Thomas and his people have adapted remarkably well to changing circumstances. They farm now, raise some livestock, find ways to maintain their traditions while accommodating new realities. That resilience threatens men like the Garretts, who need someone to blame for their own failures."

"It seems universal, doesn't it? The need to find others at fault when life doesn't match our expectations."

Joseph glanced at her, surprise evident in his expression. "That's... insightful."

"I've seen it in different forms," she explained. "In drawing rooms rather than frontier territories, but the pattern remains similar. People establishing their superiority by designating others as somehow lesser."

"And where do you stand on such matters, Miss Hayes?"

"I believe God created all people with inherent worth and dignity," she said simply. "And that any system claiming otherwise serves human pride rather than divine truth."

For the first time that day, Joseph's expression truly softened. "Sarah Dove was right about you."

"In what way?"

"You see beneath surfaces." His eyes held hers for a moment longer than necessary before returning to the trail ahead. "It's a rare quality."

As they rode, Joseph pointed out wildlife signs she would have missed—a tree where a bear had marked its territory, tracks indicating a mountain lion's passage the previous night, the distinctive chewing pattern of beavers on streamside saplings.

Lydia asked questions that revealed her genuine interest, and gradually, Joseph's responses grew more detailed, his manner less guarded. They found common ground discussing the Blackfoot situation, sharing concern for Thomas's community and indignation at the violations of treaty boundaries.

"The irony," Joseph said as they paused to water the horses at a small stream, "is that many who support these land grabs consider themselves good Christian people. They simply fail to see the contradiction between their faith and their actions."

"That selective blindness troubles me deeply," Lydia admitted, watching Penny drink deeply from the clear water. "How easily we justify our desires by ignoring scriptural teachings that challenge them."

Joseph met her eyes. "You're not what I expected when I agreed to be your guide."

"And you're not what I expected either," she countered with a small smile. "Though I admit my preconceptions were rather vague and probably informed by dime novels."

A reluctant chuckle escaped him. "No fringed buckskin or dramatic shootouts, I'm afraid."

"Thank heavens for that."

The moment of levity dissipated as a distant rumble of thunder reached them. Joseph squinted at the sky, his expression growing serious.

"We need to keep moving," he said, swinging back into his saddle with swift efficiency. "That storm's picking up speed."

Chapter 21

By midday, the wind had strengthened significantly, gusting through the pines with enough force to send branches swaying. The temperature dropped noticeably, and the distant rumble of thunder had become a more frequent companion. Joseph's concern was evident in the tense set of his shoulders and his increasingly frequent glances toward the darkening western sky.

"This is developing faster than I anticipated," he finally admitted, reining Thunder to a halt on a rise that offered better visibility. "We won't reach the valley before it hits."

Lydia pulled her shawl tighter around her shoulders, the wind already carrying a damp chill that penetrated her clothing. "What should we do?"

Joseph surveyed their surroundings, mentally calculating distances and options. "There's an old trapper's cabin about an hour's ride east of here." He turned to meet her gaze directly. "It's rustic, but it's solid. We can shelter there until the storm passes."

"Lead on," Lydia said, suppressing a shiver as the first cold drops of rain spattered against her face.

Joseph's route changed, angling more directly east through stands of aspen, whose pale leaves shimmered nervously in the strengthening wind. The path narrowed in places, requiring them to ride single file through dense underbrush. Penny followed Thunder trustingly, seeming to sense the urgency behind their quickened pace.

The rain began in earnest twenty minutes later, light at first, then steadier as the wind drove it sideways. Joseph pulled his horse alongside Lydia's, reaching into his saddlebag.

"Here," he said, passing her a folded oilskin. "It's not fancy, but it'll keep you reasonably dry."

Lydia accepted it gratefully, struggling briefly with the unwieldy material as the wind snatched at its edges. Joseph dismounted without comment, stepping close to help arrange the weather protection over her shoulders. His hands moved with efficient care, securing the oilskin so it would stay in place while riding.

"Thank you," she said, startlingly aware of his proximity, the clean scent of him beneath the sharper smell of rain and horsehair.

His eyes flickered with concern. "It'll get worse before it gets better," he warned, adjusting his own protection before remounting. "Stay close behind me on this next stretch. The trail narrows between some rock outcroppings."

The rain intensified as they continued, driven by wind that seemed determined to push them off course. Joseph maintained a steady pace, neither rushing dangerously nor dawdling. Lydia's world narrowed to the mechanical process of riding, the rhythmic movement of Penny beneath her, the need to maintain proper posture despite growing discomfort, and the hypnotic sound of hooves on increasingly muddy ground.

They had just emerged from a dense stand of pine when Joseph reined Thunder to an abrupt halt. Lydia pulled up beside him, following his intent gaze to the ground before them.

Fresh tracks cut across their path—three horses, their hoof prints sharp-edged and clear despite the rain already filling them with muddy water.

"Garrett brothers?" she asked, recalling Michael's warning.

Joseph dismounted, crouching to examine the prints more closely. His expression darkened as he traced one particularly distinctive track. "Yes. The middle horse has a crack in the left front shoe. Same as I noticed near the settlement." He straightened, wiping muddy fingers on his trousers. "They passed through here less than an hour ago, more than likely, heading northeast."

"Toward the Blackfoot territory?"

"Circling it, more likely." He remounted with fluid grace despite the worsening conditions. "They're not fools enough to ride directly into the settlement, but they're watching, testing boundaries." The muscle in his jaw tightened. "We need to reach shelter. "

They pushed forward with increased urgency, the rain now falling in sheets that reduced visibility to mere yards. Thunder crashed above them, followed almost immediately by brilliant flashes of lightning that illuminated the landscape in stark relief.

Joseph kept them moving steadily, his broad shoulders hunched slightly against the driving rain. Lydia focused on maintaining her seat as Penny navigated the increasingly slippery terrain. Her hands, despite the protection of gloves, had grown numb with cold, and water had begun to seep through the seams of her oilskin.

"Not much further," Joseph called back to her, his voice nearly lost in the howl of the wind. "Next ridge."

They crested a small rise, and Joseph pointed ahead to where a dark shape emerged from the gray curtain of rain. A simple structure nestled against a rocky hillside, partially sheltered by overhanging pine boughs. The cabin was small but appeared sturdily built, its log walls darkened by years of exposure to Montana's unforgiving elements.

"Thank you, God," Lydia murmured, relief washing through her as they approached the shelter.

Joseph led them to a lean-to attached to the cabin's eastern wall. "Get inside," he directed, helping Lydia dismount with steady hands. "I'll see to the horses."

Rain streamed from the brim of his hat as he spoke, his face glistening with moisture. Despite her eagerness to escape the downpour, Lydia hesitated.

"Let me help with them. You shouldn't have to—"

"Lydia." His use of her first name, rare and deliberate, stopped her protest. "You're half-frozen. Get inside, see if the old fireplace is still usable. I'll join you shortly."

Something in his tone, concern layered over authority, convinced her not to argue. She nodded, gathering her satchel of art supplies protectively against her chest, and made her way to the cabin's entrance. The wooden door stuck initially, swollen from moisture, but yielded to a firm push of her shoulder.

The interior was dim and musty, a single small window providing minimal light in the storm-darkened afternoon. Lydia stood dripping just inside the entrance, allowing her eyes to adjust while taking stock of the space. A stone fireplace dominated one wall, its hearth swept clean despite the cabin's apparent abandonment. A rough-hewn table stood against the opposite wall, a single bench pushed beneath it. The only other furniture was a narrow platform bed frame in the corner.

Dust coated every surface, but the cabin appeared structurally sound. No obvious leaks in the roof, no signs of animal intrusion beyond some ancient spider webs festooning the ceiling corners. Considering its isolation and how long it had likely stood empty, the shelter was in remarkably good condition.

Lydia set her satchel on the table and moved to the fireplace, kneeling to examine it more closely. The chimney appeared clear, and a small stack of split wood remained in a box beside the hearth, dry and ready for use. Whoever had last occupied the cabin had left it prepared for the next visitor, an act of frontier courtesy that might now prove their salvation.

A sudden gust of wind rattled the small window, driving rain against the glass with renewed fury. Lydia shivered, her damp clothing clinging uncomfortably to her skin. She began methodically removing her outer layers, the oilskin first, then her sodden shawl, hanging them from pegs beside the door where they might begin to dry.

Joseph entered a few minutes later, carrying their saddlebags and his rifle. Rain dripped from his coat as he shouldered the door closed against the howling wind.

"Horses are secured and fed," he reported, surveying the cabin with a quick, assessing glance. "This place hasn't changed much since I last used it."

"You stayed here before?" Lydia asked.

Joseph nodded, hanging his dripping coat beside her things. "During my first winter in Montana Territory." A faint smile touched his lips. "Spent nearly a month here during the worst of February. Learned some valuable lessons about preparedness and solitude."

He moved to the fireplace, crouching to arrange kindling with practiced efficiency. "Chimney looks clear. We should have a fire going shortly."

"Let me find something to wipe down the table and bench," Lydia offered, already searching through her belongings for a suitable cloth. Finding a worn flannel piece of fabric she used for cleaning her drawing implements, she set about removing the accumulated dust while Joseph coaxed flames from his tinder.

They worked in silence, each focused on making the abandoned shelter more habitable. As warmth gradually began to emanate from the growing fire, Lydia discovered a small cupboard built into the wall beside the fireplace. Inside were basic supplies—a cast-iron skillet, two tin plates, a couple of rusting utensils, and, most interestingly, a leather-bound journal wedged at the back of the shelf.

"Joseph," she called, carefully extracting the book. "Look what I've found."

"Supplies left behind for weary travelers seeking refuge," he explained with a slight nod. "It's the unwritten code of the frontier. I've made use of these provisions myself, though I don't recall ever seeing that journal before."

The journal's cover was stiff with age, the leather cracked along its spine. Lydia opened it gently, revealing faded but legible handwriting that filled the first several pages.

"'Journal of William Thorne, Montana Territory, 1867-68,'" she read aloud. "That would be... six years ago?"

Joseph nodded, looking over her shoulder at the cramped handwriting.

Lydia skimmed the first entry, fascinated by this unexpected connection to the cabin's past. "'October 15, 1867. Snow will come soon. Set six traps along the eastern creek, caught two beaver. Their pelts will begin my winter collection. The silence here is complete when the wind stops. A man could hear his own thoughts too clearly in such quiet.'"

"He wasn't wrong about that," Joseph commented, returning to the fire to add another log.

A sudden crack from the ceiling drew their attention. A small but steady drip had begun in one corner, water finding its way through some previously undetected weakness in the roof.

"I'll see to that," Joseph said, and stepped outside, returning with a hollow section of birchbark folded into a makeshift bowl. He positioned it beneath the leak, then examined the ceiling carefully.

"Not serious," he announced. "Just a small gap in the chinking between logs."

Lydia had been leafing through more of William Thorne's journal, intrigued by his observations of solitary frontier life. "Listen to this entry from mid-winter," she said. "'January 20, 1868. Storm has raged for three days without ceasing. Drifts higher than my head against the north wall. I speak aloud sometimes just to hear a human voice, though only the fire answers. Read my Bible through twice since November. The Psalms bring particular comfort. A man faces his true nature in such isolation—all pretense falls away when there is no one to impress or deceive.'"

She looked up, finding Joseph watching her with an expression of unusual openness. "You must have experienced something similar during your winter here."

He nodded, returning to sit on the hearthstone, extending his hands toward the growing warmth. "There's truth in what he wrote. Isolation strips away distractions, forces you to reckon with yourself." His gaze shifted to the dancing flames. "For better or worse."

"And was it better or worse for you?" Lydia asked, setting the journal aside.

Joseph remained silent for a long moment, the firelight casting his features in warm relief against the dim interior. "Both," he finally answered. "There's pain in such honest self-examination, but also the beginning of healing. Like setting a broken bone. It hurts terribly in the moment, but creates the possibility of proper mending."

Lydia accepted this response, understanding instinctively that Joseph had shared more than he typically would.

"We should eat something," she suggested, moving toward their saddlebags. "I have some dried apples and jerky in my provisions that Sarah Dove insisted I take."

Joseph nodded, rising to contribute his own supplies. Together, they assembled a modest meal of dried meat, fruit, and hard biscuits, supplemented by coffee Joseph brewed in a small pot he positioned at the fire's edge.

Outside, the storm continued unabated, rain lashing against the single window and wind howling around the cabin's sturdy corners. Inside, the fire popped and hissed, casting dancing shadows across the log walls while providing blessed warmth to the small space.

Joseph sat on the hearthstone while Lydia took the bench, the arrangement providing necessary space in quarters that felt increasingly intimate as daylight faded.

"Will we need to stay the night?" Lydia asked, though the answer seemed obvious given the weather's intensity.

Joseph nodded, sipping his coffee. "This isn't passing quickly. Even if it eases by evening, the trails will be too treacherous to navigate safely in darkness." He hesitated, then added, "I hope that doesn't cause you undue concern."

"It's hardly your fault the weather turned," Lydia pointed out reasonably. "And I'd rather be here than caught out in that." She gestured toward the window, where a particularly fierce gust drove rain sideways against the glass.

Another silence stretched between them, more charged than the previous one.

Finally, Lydia gathered her courage. "I think we need to talk about what happened last night."

Joseph stiffened visibly, his expression closing like a door against the winter wind. "There's no obligation on your part, as I said previously. The ceremony was Sarah's recognition of... a possibility. Nothing more."

"Is that truly how you see it?" Lydia pressed gently. "Merely a possibility to be acknowledged, then set aside?"

His eyes met hers briefly before returning to the flames. "What I see or don't see is irrelevant. Some paths aren't available to me, regardless of what Sarah Dove's dreams suggested."

"Why not?"

The directness of her question seemed to startle him. Joseph set his cup aside, his hands coming together in a gesture that spoke of internal struggle. "Because some actions can't be undone, Lydia. Some debts can't be repaid."

"Your past as a buffalo hunter," she said, not a question but a statement of understanding.

He nodded once, jaw tight. "Not just any buffalo hunter. I was known for my efficiency. 'Calloway can drop thirty beasts in a morning, where other men get five,' they'd say. Like it was something to be proud of." Disgust colored his voice. "I didn't think beyond the profit. Didn't consider the consequences for the Blackfoot, the Crow, all the people who depended on those herds for everything from food to shelter."

"But you came to understand," Lydia said softly. "You changed."

"After the damage was done. After countless animals lay rotting on the plains, taken only for their hides and tongues, the rest left to waste." His voice had dropped to little more than a whisper. "After families went hungry because their primary food source was decimated by men like me."

Lydia considered his words carefully, recognizing the genuine remorse behind them. "There's a difference between acknowledging wrongdoing and refusing forgiveness, Joseph. One is honest reckoning; the other borders on pride."

His head came up sharply. "Pride?"

"Believing your sin is somehow greater than what God's grace can cover." She held his surprised gaze steadily. "As if your particular failings require a different standard than everyone else's."

For several heartbeats, they stared at each other across the small cabin, the only sounds the crackling fire and drumming rain. Then, unexpectedly, Joseph's expression softened.

"You don't pull your punches, do you?"

"Not when something matters," she replied simply.

He shook his head slightly, a reluctant smile touching the corner of his mouth. "Sarah Dove said you had wisdom beyond your years. I'm starting to believe her."

"It's not original to me," Lydia admitted. "My father's a minister as well as a business owner. I grew up hearing him counsel people who believed themselves beyond redemption for one reason or another. His answer was always the same—our capacity for sin, however terrible, remains smaller than God's capacity for grace."

Joseph absorbed this, his expression thoughtful. "That's a comforting theology."

"It's not meant to be comfortable," she corrected gently. "It's meant to be challenging. Because if we accept God's forgiveness, we're obligated to live differently as a result. To make amends where possible, certainly, but not to wallow in self-condemnation that ultimately serves no one."

After a moment's consideration, Joseph rose and moved to his saddlebag, retrieving something before returning to sit on the hearth. In his hands was a worn Bible, its cover softened by years of handling.

"This was my mothers," he explained, turning the book over in his calloused hands. "For years, I carried it but rarely opened it. Felt too hypocritical, I suppose. But during that winter I spent here, with nothing but time and silence, I finally read it through." His fingers traced the faded gilt edges. "Found myself returning to the Psalms, particularly those written by David, after his greatest failures. A man after God's own heart, yet capable of terrible wrongs when his desires overtook his principles."

"And finding his way back through honest repentance," Lydia added softly.

Joseph nodded, meeting her eyes. "I've been trying to live differently since then. To honor the land rather than exploit it. To deal fairly with everyone, including the Blackfoot, whose resources I once helped destroy." He drew a deep breath. "But personal redemption is one thing. Believing myself worthy of... of connection, of a future that includes more than solitary atonement—that's been harder to accept."

"May I show you something?" she asked.

At his nod, she retrieved her sketchbook from her satchel and carefully turned to a specific page. The drawing she sought showed Joseph seated by the council fire, his face illuminated by flames as he listened to Thomas speak. She had captured something essential in his expression, strength tempered by humility, alertness softened by respect, and the complexity of a man who had walked through fire and emerged purified rather than consumed.

She handed him the sketchbook.

Joseph studied the drawing for a long moment, his expression difficult to read in the cabin's dim light. "Is this how you see me?" he finally asked, his voice rough-edged with emotion.

"Yes," Lydia answered simply. "Not perfect. Not flawless. But fundamentally good, Joseph. Someone who has learned from mistakes rather than being defined by them."

He continued to study the image, seemingly transfixed by this external perspective of himself. "You have a gift," he said eventually, echoing his earlier observation. "For capturing essence rather than just appearance."

"That's what makes the difference between technical drawing and true art," she explained, watching his reaction closely. "Anyone can learn to reproduce what their eyes perceive. The artist's task is to reveal what might otherwise remain hidden—the spirit behind the form."

Joseph carefully closed the sketchbook and returned it to her, their fingers brushing briefly in the exchange. "Thank you," he said. "For showing me that."

"You're welcome." Lydia held his gaze.

The storm outside had settled into a steady rhythm, no longer gusting violently but still releasing a continuous cascade of rain against the cabin's roof and walls. Within their shelter, the atmosphere had similarly transformed—from charged tension to something more contemplative, a shared space where honesty seemed not just possible but natural.

"I've never had a real relationship with a man," Lydia found herself saying, surprising herself with the admission. "The men I met in New York society were... pleasant enough, I suppose. Well-mannered, appropriately attentive, utterly predictable in their interests and conversation."

Joseph listened attentively, neither pushing for more nor withdrawing from her unexpected confidence.

"I couldn't imagine sharing my real thoughts with any of them," she continued, watching the fire's dance rather than meeting his eyes. "My passion for art was tolerated as a charming feminine accomplishment, not taken seriously as a vocation. And whenever I expressed opinions on matters beyond household management or fashion, they'd exchange that particular glance men reserve for women they believe are overstepping."

"Their loss," Joseph commented quietly.

Lydia smiled, grateful for his understanding. "Their world felt suffocating. All those unwritten rules about proper behavior, acceptable topics, appropriate aspirations. I kept wondering if something was wrong with me for wanting more. For needing my life to matter beyond social appearances and advantageous matches."

"Nothing wrong with wanting substance over surface," Joseph observed. "Though I imagine that perspective wasn't popular."

"Not particularly," she agreed with a small laugh. "My mother worried constantly that I'd end up a spinster because I couldn't seem to maintain interest in suitable young men. My father, surprisingly, was more understanding. He's conventional in many ways, but he recognized something in me that needed more space than New York society permitted."

She glanced up, finding Joseph watching her with quiet intensity. "That's partly why I fought so hard for this commission. It wasn't just about artistic opportunity, though that mattered enormously. It was about proving to myself that I could exist beyond the narrow confines others had established for me."

"And have you?" Joseph asked. "Found that proof?"

Lydia considered the question seriously. "Yes, I believe I have. Though not in the way I anticipated." She met his eyes directly. "This journey has changed me, Joseph. The landscape, the Blackfoot community, working alongside you. It's all shifted something fundamental in how I understand myself and my purpose. I came to document Montana as a visitor. I've ended up participating in it instead."

Outside, thunder rumbled once more, but noticeably farther away than before. The worst of the storm had passed, though the rain continued to fall steadily.

Joseph rose to add another log to the fire, which had burned down to glowing embers. As he carefully rebuilt the flames, Lydia retrieved her Bible from her satchel. She opened it to the Psalms.

"Would you read aloud?" Joseph asked, noticing her absorption in the text.

Lydia looked up, momentarily surprised by the request, then nodded. "Of course." She began reading from the beginning of Psalm 103, her voice gaining confidence as she continued through the beautiful affirmation of God's forgiveness and compassion.

When she reached the verse about God removing transgressions as far as east from west, Joseph's expression shifted subtly, a tension visibly releasing around his eyes.

"That's the passage I was reading," he said when she finished, "the night before I left this cabin all those years ago. Like a message meant specifically for me."

The coincidence—or perhaps not coincidence at all—hung between them in the warm air.

"Sometimes Scripture finds us exactly when we need it," Lydia said.

Joseph nodded, his expression thoughtful as he stared into the flames. "I'd like to believe that's true."

Chapter 22

The morning sun struggled through dissipating clouds as Joseph secured the cabin door behind them. The storm had passed during the night, leaving behind a transformed land-scape—mud-slicked trails, swollen streams, and trees glistening with lingering droplets that sparkled like diamonds in the tentative sunlight.

"We should reach the Valley by midday if we keep a steady pace," Joseph said, adjusting Thunder's saddle cinch with practiced hands. "The rain will have made the colors more vibrant—the red stone takes on a deeper hue when wet."

Lydia secured her satchel of drawing supplies to Penny's saddle, carefully positioning it where the precious contents would remain protected. "Will the trails be passable? Everything looks quite muddy."

"The higher ground dries quickly," Joseph replied, offering his cupped hands to help her mount. "It's the low spots and creek crossings we'll need to watch for."

Lydia placed her boot in his interlaced fingers, noting how effortlessly he boosted her into the saddle. His strength never felt imposing, only reassuring, like a foundation one could build upon with confidence. As she settled into place, their eyes met briefly, and the quiet understanding they had shared in the firelight's glow the previous evening hummed between them, unspoken but undeniably present.

Joseph nodded. He swung easily onto Thunder's back, the horse prancing slightly with fresh energy after the night's rest.

"The cabin was quite nice for an abandoned trapper's shelter," Lydia remarked as they set off, following a narrow trail that wound between stands of aspens whose leaves trembled like nervous dancers in the morning breeze.

"Not abandoned—just awaiting its next visitor," Joseph corrected. "There's an unwritten code out here. You leave a place better than you found it, store dry wood for the next traveler, make sure there's coffee in the supply cache. It's how folks survive. No one makes it alone in Montana Territory."

"A practical application of 'do unto others,'" Lydia observed.

Joseph glanced back at her with the hint of a smile. "Never thought of it that way, but I suppose that's true. Though I suspect most frontiersmen would be startled to hear their habits described in biblical terms."

"Many of life's wisest practices have their roots in Scripture, whether people recognize it or not," Lydia said. "My father often pointed out how non-religious folk would stumble upon divine wisdom through practical experience, then declare it a personal discovery."

"Your father sounds like an insightful man," Joseph remarked, guiding Thunder around a particularly muddy patch.

"He is, though I don't always agree with him," Lydia admitted. "He sees much of the world, primarily through ledgers and accounts. Everything measured by practical return on investment. That's why my artistic ambitions troubled him. He couldn't calculate their value in dollars and cents."

Joseph considered this as they rode side by side where the trail widened. "Yet he allowed you to come west, despite his misgivings. That suggests he values something beyond financial profit, even if he doesn't readily admit it."

The observation surprised Lydia with its perceptiveness. "I never considered that. Perhaps you're right. But make no mistake, he did not want me coming west... he actually forbade it," She smiled, adjusting her hat against the strengthening sunlight. "It seems we both have fathers who shaped us in ways we're still discovering."

"You mentioned your father was a minister as well as a businessman," Joseph said. "Those seem like conflicting pursuits."

"He inherited the family shipping business but felt called to ministry in his thirties," Lydia explained. "Rather than abandoning one for the other, he found ways to integrate them. Sunday mornings in the pulpit, weekdays in the counting house. He believes commerce conducted ethically can be as much a calling as preaching."

"A practical theology," Joseph observed, his tone suggesting approval.

"Yes, though sometimes I wished for more... passion, I suppose. More evidence that faith transformed rather than merely informed his daily life." Lydia paused, concerned she might be speaking disrespectfully. "I love my father dearly, but his approach to faith often feels like a well-tailored garment he puts on, rather than something that flows from within."

Joseph nodded thoughtfully. "I've known men like that. Good men whose faith sits comfortably alongside their other concerns, rather than challenging them. It has its place, I suppose." He was quiet for a moment before adding, "My own father's faith was different—rawer, more immediate. He believed God spoke as clearly through a Montana thunderstorm as through any sermon."

"Like Sarah Dove's 'thin places' where the divine feels closer," Lydia suggested, recalling their conversation at Whispering Ridge.

"Similar, yes." Joseph guided Thunder around a fallen branch. "My father found God most readily in wild places, away from what he called 'the clutter of men's making.' Said it was easier to hear the Creator's voice when you weren't distracted by human noise."

"Is that another reason why you came west? To find that same connection?"

"Initially, no," he admitted. "I came because there was opportunity, adventure, profit to be made." His expression darkened slightly. "The spiritual awareness came later, after I'd contributed to the destruction I now regret."

Lydia sensed it was time to steer toward lighter territory. "What was your mother like? You mentioned the Bible we read from last night was hers."

The change of subject achieved its intended effect. Joseph's expression lightened noticeably.

"She was remarkable," he said, affection warming his voice. "Born in Boston, educated at a fine ladies' academy, then married my father and moved to a Missouri frontier cabin without complaint. She brought her books, her music, her refinement with her and somehow made them fit alongside the realities of frontier life."

"She sounds wonderful," Lydia said sincerely.

"She was." Joseph's eyes grew distant with memory. "She insisted on maintaining certain civilized practices, no matter how primitive our surroundings. Sunday dinner always required proper table settings. She read Shakespeare aloud during winter evenings. Taught me to appreciate beauty in unexpected places."

"Like mother, like son," Lydia observed with a smile. "You've been doing the same for me—showing me beauty I might have missed without your guidance."

Joseph looked momentarily startled by the parallel, then acknowledged it with a slight incline of his head. "I suppose that's true. Never considered the connection before."

They rode in companionable silence for a time, the trail gradually sloping upward as they approached a ridgeline. The vegetation changed subtly—pines replacing aspens, wildflowers dotting open meadows with splashes of purple and yellow. The air smelled fresher after the rain, carrying the scent of wet earth and sun-warmed pine needles.

"There," Joseph said eventually, pointing toward the horizon as they crested the ridge. "First glimpse of the Valley."

Lydia followed his gesture, her breath catching at the vista spread before them. In the distance, rising from the rolling landscape like sentinels from another age, stood a series of towering red stone formations. Even from this distance, she could see how they had earned their name—the structures resembled nothing so much as massive figures frozen in stone, their silhouettes dramatic against the clearing sky.

"Oh my," she whispered, already itching to capture the scene. "It's magnificent."

"This is just the beginning," Joseph promised. "It's unlike anywhere else I've encountered."

"How long until we reach them?"

"Couple of hours at most," Joseph said. "There's a good approach from the eastern side where we can make camp if you'd like to stay overnight. The formations are particularly striking at sunset and again at dawn."

"Yes, please," Lydia said immediately. "I'd hate to rush such an opportunity."

Joseph's smile broadened slightly. "I thought you might feel that way." He gestured forward. "Shall we continue?"

The trail descended through pine forests where birds called enthusiastically from rain-washed branches. Twice they crossed streams swollen with runoff, Joseph leading the way carefully through shallower crossing points he knew from experience. As the morning progressed, the temperature rose pleasantly, drying the mud on the trails and lifting a light mist from the sun-warmed earth.

They stopped briefly around mid-morning to rest the horses and enjoy a light meal of dried fruit and biscuits from their provisions. Joseph spread his coat on a fallen log to provide Lydia a dry place to sit, a small courtesy that touched her deeply.

"How did you first discover the Valley of Standing Stones?" she asked as they ate.

"During my buffalo hunting days," Joseph admitted, his honesty about his past coming more readily now. "We were tracking a herd that had moved south of their usual range. I separated from the main party to scout ahead and happened upon the Valley just as sunset was painting the stones." His expression grew contemplative. "It stopped me cold. Something about those ancient formations standing silent witness through centuries... it made our frantic pursuit of immediate gain seem suddenly petty and shortsighted."

"A moment of perspective," Lydia suggested.

"More like a moment of reckoning," Joseph corrected. "Not religious conversion. That came later, but the beginning of questioning." He brushed crumbs from his trousers, his eyes distant with memory. "I've returned many times since then."

"And now you're sharing it with me," Lydia said, her voice soft with appreciation.

Their eyes met.

"Yes," he said simply. "I am."

They remounted and continued their journey, the red stone formations gradually growing larger as they approached. The landscape opened before them, transitioning from forested highlands to a more arid terrain where juniper and sage replaced the taller pines. The air grew warmer, carrying the fragrant scent of sun-baked sage and mineral-rich earth.

By early afternoon, they were entering the Valley proper, riding between the first of the massive stone pillars. Lydia rode with her head tilted back, marveling at formations that towered hundreds of feet above them. The rain had indeed intensified the colors, turning the sandstone to deep rust and burgundy hues, with streaks of ochre and cream where mineral deposits had leached through the porous rock.

"It's like riding through a natural cathedral," she observed, her voice hushed with awe.

Joseph nodded, understanding her reverence. "The Blackfoot believe these formations were once giants who challenged the Creator and were turned to stone as punishment for their pride." He gestured toward a particularly tall spire. "That one they call The Chief, for the way the top resembles a proud head with a stern profile."

Lydia studied it with an artist's eye. "I see it! And that one there, it looks like a woman with her arms raised."

"The Weeping Woman," Joseph confirmed. "According to legend, she was the Chief's wife who begged the Creator for mercy and was frozen in the act of pleading."

They continued deeper into the Valley, Joseph naming formations while Lydia absorbed everything with eager attention. The trail wound between towering monuments of stone, sometimes narrowing into passages barely wide enough for their horses to navigate single file, then opening to circular clearings where multiple formations could be viewed from a central vantage point.

By mid-afternoon, they reached what Joseph described as the Valley's heart, a broad, sandy expanse surrounded by the tallest formations, with a small spring-fed pool nestled against the western edge.

"This is where we'll camp," he announced, dismounting near the water source.

Lydia slid from Penny's back, her legs stiff from the long ride, but her spirit buoyed by their magnificent surroundings.

"The light is perfect right now," she said, glancing at Joseph. "Would you mind if I started sketching while you make camp?"

"Go ahead," he encouraged, already beginning to unsaddle the horses. "No need to wait on my account."

Lydia retrieved her satchel, selecting her best drawing paper and several pencils of varying hardness. She hesitated, looking around at the overwhelming array of potential subjects.

"Where would you suggest I begin?" she asked Joseph. "There's so much to capture."

He paused in his work, studying the surrounding formations with a familiarity born of many visits. "That grouping to the southeast," he finally suggested, nodding toward three spires of varying heights that framed a fourth, more weather-worn formation. "The interplay of light and shadow there is particularly striking this time of day. The

Blackfoot call it The Family—father, mother, daughter, and grandfather."

Lydia followed his guidance, finding a comfortable spot on a sun-warmed boulder. Opening her sketchbook, she began blocking in the major shapes, establishing proportions, before focusing on details. The familiar process of observation and translation to paper centered her, bringing a deep satisfaction that pushed aside all other concerns.

Time slipped away as she worked, her pencil capturing the towering red stones with their weather-carved textures, the dramatic shadows cast by the westering sun, the sense of ancient permanence these formations evoked. She was so absorbed that she started slightly when Joseph's voice came from behind her.

"You forgot to eat," he said, extending a tin-plate with dried meat, berries, and a piece of journey bread.

Lydia blinked, suddenly aware of her surroundings again. The sun had moved significantly since she began drawing, and Joseph had efficiently established their camp, a small fire already burning.

"Thank you," she said, accepting the plate gratefully. "I lose track of everything when I'm drawing."

"I noticed," he said, the observation free of judgment. He glanced at her sketch, appreciative respect evident in his expression. "May I join you?"

"Of course."

He settled on a nearby rock, his own plate in hand.

The late afternoon sunlight bathed the red stone formations in increasingly dramatic illumination as they ate. Birds called from hidden crevices in the rock faces, their songs echoing slightly in the natural amphitheater created by the surrounding formations.

"I've been thinking about what Sarah Dove said," Joseph said suddenly, his voice carefully neutral. "About recognizing what already exists."

Lydia's heart quickened, but she maintained an outward calm, waiting for him to continue rather than rushing to fill the silence.

"There's truth in her observation," he admitted, setting his empty plate aside. "Something has... changed between us that wasn't there when we first met in Bozeman."

"Yes," Lydia agreed simply, holding his gaze steadily.

Joseph looked away, his profile strong against the backdrop of red stone. "I told myself it was professional respect. Then friendship. Both true, but incomplete." His hands came together, fingers interlaced tightly. "I find myself thinking about you. Noticing how the light catches your hair, how your expression changes when you're concentrating on a drawing, how your mind works differently than anyone else I've known."

"I think about you too," she said. "More than I probably should."

He turned back to her, his gray eyes intense. "I'm not free to offer what you deserve, Lydia. You have a life waiting in New York, opportunity, family, culture, everything Montana Territory lacks."

"That's not a decision for you to make on my behalf," she pointed out gently. "And you assume I value those things more than I might value... alternatives."

"What alternatives?" he asked, a hint of rough vulnerability entering his voice. "A life of frontier hardship? Isolation from everything familiar? Constant struggle against elements and circumstances most Eastern women can't even imagine?"

"Perhaps those hardships look different to me," Lydia suggested. "Perhaps isolation from societal expectations feels more like freedom.

Perhaps the struggle against honest natural elements seems preferable to navigating the treacherous undercurrents of New York."

Joseph shook his head not dismissively, but with genuine concern. "You've been here during the gentle season. You haven't experienced Montana winters, where temperatures drop so low breath freezes in your lungs. Or summer droughts when dust coats everything and water becomes precious. Or the loneliness when snow cuts you off from human contact for weeks at a time."

"You survived those challenges," Lydia observed. "Others have too."

"It's different when it's all you've known."

"Like Sarah Dove?" Lydia asked pointedly. "Who told me she was born in Texas and chose to follow her heart west?"

Joseph looked startled. "When did Sarah tell you that?"

"The morning we left. She told me privately," Lydia replied. "She said you weren't the first person to underestimate a woman's capacity for adaptation when her heart was engaged."

"She's a forthright woman."

"She is," Lydia agreed. "And wise."

The sun continued its westward journey, lengthening shadows and intensifying the red-gold glow of the stone formations. Lydia retrieved her sketchbook, working quickly to capture the changing light while their conversation continued.

"I'm not asking you for promises, Joseph," she said, her pencil moving across the paper with sure strokes. "I'm only suggesting that you stop constructing barriers based on assumptions about what I want or need. Let me make those determinations for myself."

He watched her draw, his expression thoughtful. "Fair enough," he acknowledged after a moment. "But I have another concern that's harder to address."

"Which is?"

"The stain of my past actions," he said bluntly. "The blood on my hands from the buffalo hunts, the damage done to the Blackfoot and other tribes. That can't be erased, regardless of how I've tried to live since then."

Lydia paused in her drawing, considering her response carefully. "When King David took another man's wife and arranged his death, did God abandon him?"

Joseph's eyebrows rose at the unexpected scriptural reference. "No, but—"

"When the Apostle Paul—then Saul—hunted Christians and participated in Stephen's stoning, did God declare him beyond redemption?"

"That's different," Joseph protested. "Those were biblical figures specifically chosen—"

"When Peter denied Christ three times after promising absolute loyalty, did Jesus reject him?" Lydia continued, gentle but persistent.

Joseph fell silent, the weight of these examples settling between them.

"The Bible doesn't hide the failures of even its greatest figures," Lydia said quietly. "It showcases them alongside God's unfailing grace, precisely to prevent the kind of thinking you're engaged in now—the belief that some sins are beyond forgiveness or that past mistakes permanently disqualify us from future blessing."

"You should have been the minister in your family," Joseph said, a hint of reluctant humor lightening his expression.

Lydia smiled, returning to her drawing. "I'm merely repeating truths I've heard all my life. The difference is that I believe them, not just as abstract theology, but as practical reality." Her pencil captured the lengthening shadows cast by The Family formation. "God's forgiveness is real, Joseph. The question is whether you'll accept it or continue punishing yourself for actions He's already forgiven."

For several minutes, Joseph sat in silence while Lydia worked. The Valley grew quieter as evening approached, the daytime birds yielding to the first calls of nighthawks and owls. The air cooled slightly, carrying the scent of sage and the distant fragrance of pine from the surrounding highlands.

Finally, Joseph spoke again, his voice carrying a new quality—more open, less guarded. "When I first met you in Bozeman, I saw only what I expected to see, an Eastern lady with romantic notions and impractical expectations. It took me far too long to recognize the substance beneath the surface." His gaze was direct, honest. "I was wrong about you, Lydia Hayes. Profoundly wrong."

"First impressions are rarely complete," she offered.

"Mine was worse than incomplete. It was willfully blind." He leaned forward slightly, his expression earnest. "You possess a rare combination of artistic vision and practical wisdom. You see beauty where others miss it, yes, but you also see truth... including truths people try to hide from themselves."

Lydia felt a blush warming her cheeks at his praise. "I simply pay attention," she demurred.

"It's more than that," Joseph insisted. "It's a gift. One I've benefitted from, even when I resisted it."

The sun had begun to set in earnest now, the western sky ablaze with colors that reflected off the red stones, transforming the entire valley into a breathtaking tableau of crimson, gold, and deepening purple shadows. Lydia set aside her drawing implements, overwhelmed by the beauty that exceeded her ability to capture it.

"I've never seen anything like this," she breathed, rising to her feet to better appreciate the spectacle.

Joseph stood as well, moving to stand beside her. "Nor have I, despite visiting many times. Each sunset here is unique, never the same combination of light, cloud, and color twice."

They stood shoulder to shoulder, watching nature's magnificent display. The silence between them felt comfortable, expectant.

"Thank you for bringing me here," Lydia said eventually, her voice soft in the gathering dusk. "For sharing something that clearly means a great deal to you."

Joseph turned slightly toward her, his expression open in a way she hadn't seen before. "I knew from the moment we crested that first ridge that you would understand this place, as few others have. That you would see beyond the obvious beauty to the deeper significance these ancient stones represent."

"What significance do they hold for you?" she asked, genuinely curious.

He considered the question, watching as the last direct sunlight gilded the top of The Chief formation. "Perspective," he said finally. "These stones have stood witness to countless human dramas—Blackfoot ceremonies, trappers passing through, buffalo herds migrating, cavalry patrols scouting—yet remain fundamentally unchanged. They remind me that most human concerns, including my own, are temporary."

"That could be depressing or comforting, depending on how you look at it," Lydia observed.

"Exactly," Joseph agreed, a small smile touching his lips. "I find it mostly comforting."

Chapter 23

The light continued to fade, the sunset's brilliant display gradually yielding to the deeper blues of approaching night as Lydia continued to draw. Joseph moved toward their campfire, stirring it to life and adding more wood to combat the evening chill.

"We should eat before it gets completely dark," he suggested, returning to practicalities. "I promised you sunset and sunrise among the stones, and both are better appreciated with a full stomach."

They prepared a simple meal together. Joseph brewed coffee in a small pot nestled at the fire's edge, while Lydia sliced dried meat and fruit onto their tin plates. As they ate, the first stars appeared overhead, brilliant pinpricks of light in the darkening sky.

"The stars seem closer here," Lydia observed, tilting her head back to better view the emerging constellations. "More immediate somehow."

"Less competing light," Joseph explained. "And clearer air. Makes them appear sharper, more defined."

He pointed out constellations as they became visible. Ursa Major, with its distinctive dipper shape, Cassiopeia's crooked W, the three perfect points of Orion's belt. Lydia listened attentively, appreciating both the knowledge itself and Joseph's evident pleasure in sharing it.

After they finished eating, Joseph surprised her by retrieving something from his saddlebag. A small wooden box that opened to reveal his harmonica, its metal surface glinting in the firelight.

"Would you mind?" he asked, uncharacteristically hesitant. "Music seems fitting for such an evening."

"I'd love to hear you play again," Lydia encouraged.

He settled on a rock near the fire; the instrument held confidently between calloused hands. After a moment's consideration, he began a slow, plaintive melody that seemed to capture the essence of the Valley—its ancient beauty, its solitude, its enduring presence. The notes floated on the night air, somehow both melancholy and uplifting simultaneously.

Lydia listened, entranced by this new dimension of Joseph's character. His music carried the same quiet strength as his other actions—understated yet deeply felt, technically skilled yet focused on expression rather than display. When the final notes faded into the night stillness, she found herself reluctant to break the spell with words.

"That was beautiful," she finally said, her voice hushed. "Did you compose it?"

Joseph shook his head. "An old Ozark tune my mother used to play on her piano. 'Mountain Hymn,' she called it. She said it reminded her of God's faithfulness through changing seasons."

"It feels appropriate here," Lydia observed.

Joseph nodded, his fingers absently tracing the harmonica's edge. "She would have loved this place," he said.

"Tell me more about her," Lydia invited, sensing his need to share these memories.

As the fire burned lower and the stars wheeled overhead, Joseph spoke of his mother with rare openness—her love of literature and music, her unwavering faith despite frontier hardships, her gentle insistence that beauty mattered even in practical circumstances. His voice carried profound respect, tinged with lingering grief for her premature death.

"She gave me this the week before she died," he said, holding up the harmonica. "Said music would be a companion when words failed and life grew too heavy to bear alone."

"Wise advice," Lydia said softly.

"She was full of wisdom I was too young to fully appreciate," Joseph admitted. "Including her final counsel to me, which I've only recently begun to truly understand."

"What was that?"

Joseph's gaze moved from the fire to meet Lydia's eyes directly. "'Don't measure your worth by your mistakes, Joseph,'" he quoted, "'but by your response to them. God specializes in creating beauty from our broken pieces when we surrender them honestly.'"

The words hung in the night air, their relevance to Joseph's current struggles unmistakable. Lydia recognized the significance of his sharing something so personal, understanding it represented more than casual conversation.

"She sounds remarkable," Lydia said with genuine appreciation. "I wish I could have met her."

"She would have liked you," Joseph replied with quiet certainty. "Your forthright nature, your willingness to look beyond surfaces. Those were qualities she valued highly."

The compliment, indirect yet deeply meaningful coming from Joseph, warmed Lydia more than the campfire's glow. They sat in companionable silence for a time, the crackling flames and distant call of a hunting owl the only sounds in the vast stillness of the Valley.

Eventually, Joseph rose to add more wood to the fire. "We should rest soon," he suggested. "Dawn comes early, and you'll want to be ready when the first light hits the stones. It's a sight worth waking for."

He moved to check on the horses, ensuring they were secure for the night, while Lydia prepared for sleep, washing with precious water from the spring and changing into her sleeping attire behind the privacy of a large boulder. By the time she returned to the campfire, Joseph had arranged their bedrolls on opposite sides of the fire, maintaining proper distance while ensuring both benefited from the fire's warmth.

"Thank you for sharing this place with me... and for sharing your memories," Lydia said, settling onto her bedroll with her blanket wrapped around her against the increasing night chill.

Joseph nodded, his expression thoughtful in the firelight. "Thank you for listening," he replied. "Not just with your ears, but with understanding."

Lydia sensed Joseph had more to say. She waited patiently, watching the play of firelight and shadow across his strong features.

"I've been carrying my past like a burden I'm obligated to bear alone," he finally said, his voice low but clear in the night stillness. "Believing isolation was my penance, that connections with others were luxuries I had no right to pursue."

Lydia listened attentively, recognizing the cost of such openness to a man accustomed to guarding his thoughts.

"But this past week with you have challenged that belief," he continued. "Made me question whether solitude is truly what God requires of me. Whether turning away from..." he hesitated, searching for the right words, "...from possibility is actually faithful or merely fearful."

"And what have you concluded?" Lydia asked.

Joseph's eyes met hers across the campfire, gray depths reflecting orange flames. "That I've been hiding behind righteousness when the real barrier was fear. Fear of disappointment. Fear of loss. Fear of hope itself." His voice dropped even lower. "Fear of allowing myself to care for someone who might eventually see all my flaws and find me wanting."

The confession, simple yet profound, touched Lydia deeply. "Vulnerability is frightening," she acknowledged. "For everyone, not just you. But without it, we miss the deepest connections God designed us to experience."

Joseph nodded slowly. "My mother used to quote from Ecclesiastes—'Two are better than one, for if either falls, the other can help their companion up.' I understood that practically, in terms of frontier survival, but I'm beginning to see its broader application."

Above them, the stars continued their stately progression across the night sky, indifferent to human concerns yet somehow comforting in their constancy. The Valley's stone formations stood as dark silhouettes against the star-scattered backdrop, their massive presence felt rather than seen in the darkness.

"What happens when your commission is complete?" Joseph asked suddenly. "When you've gathered all the sketches you need for National Geographic?"

The question carried weight beyond its practical implications. Lydia considered it carefully before answering.

"Officially, I return to New York with my portfolio, work with the magazine's engravers to transfer my sketches to plates for printing, and resume my previous life." She paused, watching the firelight play across Joseph's attentive face. "But I'm no longer certain that's what I want."

"What do you want, Lydia?" he asked, the directness of his question matched by the steadiness of his gaze.

"To follow where God leads," she answered honestly. "Even if that path differs from what I originally planned. Even if it means disappointing others' expectations." She drew a deep breath, matching his courage with her own. "I came west seeking professional opportunity, but I've found something I wasn't looking for... a sense of belonging I never experienced in New York."

"Here? In Montana Territory?" Joseph sounded genuinely surprised.

"Not just the place," Lydia clarified, her heart beating faster. "Though I've come to love the landscape and its people. But belonging can attach to a person as much as a location."

The implication hung between them, clear but not demanding an immediate response. Joseph's expression shifted subtly—surprise yielding to something deeper, more complex, a recognition that matched the one Sarah Dove had named around the council fire.

"I can't offer certainty," he said finally, his voice rough-edged with emotion. "Or comfort, or luxury, or many of the things you've known."

"I'm not asking for those things," Lydia replied simply.

"What are you asking for?"

"Honesty. The courage to explore whatever this connection between us might become, without artificial barriers of your creation or mine." She smiled slightly. "The rest we can discover together, if you're willing."

For a long moment, Joseph remained silent, firelight casting his features in warm relief against the surrounding darkness. When he finally spoke, his voice carried a new quality—tentative yet resolute, as if testing unfamiliar ground he nevertheless intended to traverse.

"I am willing," he said. "More than willing. Drawn in a way I've never experienced before." His hands came together, fingers interlacing tightly. "You've awakened something I thought permanently dormant, Lydia. A capacity for connection I believed I'd sacrificed along with my other mistakes."

"Nothing is permanently lost that God wishes to restore," she said softly.

Joseph nodded, acceptance of this truth visible in his expression. "Then perhaps this is part of that restoration, not something I've engineered or deserve, but grace extended where I least expected it."

The fire popped suddenly, sending a shower of sparks spiraling upward into the night. Both watched their brief, bright journey before returning to each other's gaze.

"We should rest," Joseph said eventually, practical concerns reasserting themselves. "You'll want to be awake before first light for those sunrise sketches."

Lydia nodded, settling more comfortably onto her bedroll. "Goodnight, Joseph. And thank you for your honesty."

"Goodnight, Lydia," he replied, his voice warm with unspoken feeling. "Sleep well."

As she drifted toward sleep, Lydia's last conscious awareness was of Joseph adding another log to the fire, his movements careful and quiet, his attention to her comfort constant even in this simple act. In that moment of twilight consciousness, a certainty settled over her—whatever path lay ahead, it would be traveled together, not alone.

The Valley of Standing Stones kept silent witness to this unspoken understanding, its ancient presence a reminder that while individual lives might be brief against the backdrop of geological time, the connections formed between souls could transcend such limitations. This created something as enduring as the red stone formations themselves.

Chapter 24

Dawn broke in a gentle whisper of pink and lavender across the eastern sky as Lydia's eyes fluttered open. For a moment, she remained perfectly still, absorbing the extraordinary beauty surrounding her. The massive stone formations stood like sentinels against the brightening horizon, their red-hued surfaces still dark but beginning to catch the first hints of morning light along their highest edges.

She sat up quickly, not wanting to miss a moment of the spectacle Joseph had promised. Across the dying embers of their fire, his bedroll lay empty, neatly folded. A steaming cup of coffee sat waiting on a flat rock beside her, evidence of his thoughtfulness.

"You're awake," Joseph's voice came from behind her. "Perfect timing."

Lydia turned to find him standing a few yards away, already dressed for the day, watching the horizon with quiet anticipation. He gestured toward an outcropping of stone that offered an unobstructed view of the Valley.

"That's the best vantage point," he said, extending a hand to help her up. "If you hurry, you'll catch the first light striking The Chief."

Lydia grabbed her shawl against the morning chill, wrapped it around her shoulders, and accepted Joseph's hand. His grip was warm and steady as he helped her to her feet.

"What about my coffee?" she asked, glancing at the steaming cup.

"Bring it," he suggested. "The sunrise won't wait, even for coffee."

Lydia retrieved the cup and followed Joseph to the outcropping, careful of her footing on the uneven ground. The stone felt cool beneath her bare feet, still holding the night's chill despite the approaching day.

"Here," Joseph said when they reached the perfect spot, a natural shelf of stone that provided both comfortable seating and a commanding view of the Valley. "Watch."

They settled side by side on the smooth rock surface, shoulders nearly touching. Lydia cradled her coffee between her palms, grateful for its warmth as she fixed her gaze on the massive formation Joseph had identified as The Chief.

The sky continued to lighten, colors intensifying from pale lavender to deeper rose along the horizon. Then, with perfect dramatic timing, the first direct ray of sunlight crested the eastern ridge and struck the highest point of The Chief. The effect was instantaneous and breathtaking—the stone seeming to ignite from within, transforming from dark silhouette to vibrant, living red that almost appeared to pulse with internal fire.

"Oh!" Lydia gasped, nearly spilling her coffee in her excitement. "It's as if it's coming alive!"

Joseph nodded, his own gaze fixed on the spectacle. "Watch," he repeated softly.

As the sun continued its rise, the light traveled downward across The Chief's face, revealing intricate textures and variations in color that had been invisible in shadow. Bands of cream and ochre appeared among the dominant red, creating natural striations that enhanced the formation's resemblance to a stern, weathered face.

Then, one by one, the surrounding formations caught the light—The Weeping Woman next, then The Family grouping—each transformation equally dramatic as stone after stone awakened to the new day.

"It's like watching a painting being created before my eyes," Lydia whispered, transfixed by the unfolding display.

"Reminds me of some Scripture verses," Joseph observed quietly. "About truth being revealed and darkness giving way to light."

Lydia glanced at him, intrigued by this spiritual reflection. "Ephesians? 'Everything exposed by the light becomes visible.'"

He nodded, a small smile touching his lips. "My mother's favorite passage. She would quote it whenever I tried to hide something from her, which was pointless, as mothers seem to have a special ability to see what children prefer to keep hidden."

"Mine too," Lydia agreed with a soft laugh. "Though she applied it more to misplaced hairpins than matters of character."

They fell silent again, watching as the Valley continued its morning transformation. Birds began to call from hidden nests within the rock formations, their voices echoing slightly in the still air. A desert hare darted between sparse brush at the base of The Weeping Woman, pausing briefly to assess potential danger before continuing on its morning rounds.

"My sketchbook," Lydia said suddenly, reluctant to leave yet knowing she needed her materials.

Joseph reached behind a rock where he'd placed her satchel of drawing supplies without her noticing. "Thought you might need it."

The simple thoughtfulness of this gesture touched Lydia deeply. "Thank you," she said, accepting the familiar leather case. Their fingers brushed in the exchange, a brief contact that nevertheless sent a ripple of awareness through her.

Joseph cleared his throat slightly. "I'll let you work," he said, rising from the stone shelf. "Need to see to the horses."

"You don't have to go," Lydia said, surprising herself with her boldness. "I don't mind company while I draw."

He hesitated, clearly tempted by the invitation. "You're sure?"

"You might notice details I would otherwise miss."

Joseph settled back beside her. Lydia opened her sketchbook to a fresh page and selected several pencils from her case, arranging them within easy reach.

As she began to work, blocking in the major shapes with swift, confident strokes, she was acutely aware of Joseph's quiet presence beside her. Unlike many observers who felt compelled to offer unnecessary commentary or questions that disrupted concentration, he simply watched, his silence comfortable and attentive.

The Valley continued to transform as the sun rose higher, shadows shifting and colors deepening. Lydia worked quickly, capturing the essential quality of the light and the magnificent scale of the formations. Her pencil moved across the paper with practiced ease, laying down lines that caught not just the appearance but the feeling of this extraordinary place.

"There," she said eventually, adding a final detail to the foreground. "It's just a preliminary sketch. I can refine it later or perhaps do a more finished piece with color."

She turned the sketchbook toward Joseph, offering him a clear view of her work. His expression as he studied it was gratifying, not polite appreciation, but genuine understanding of what she had accomplished.

"It's beautiful," he said, his finger hovering just above the paper.

Their eyes met, and something profound passed between them.

"We should eat," Joseph said after a moment, breaking the intensity of the connection. "The day's warming up, and we have much to explore if you want to see more of the Valley before we move on."

Lydia nodded, gathering her drawing materials and following him back to their campsite. The morning had fully arrived now, the eastern sky a clear, pale blue that promised heat later in the day.

Joseph had already prepared a simple breakfast before waking her. They ate in silence, both still half-absorbed in the beauty of the sunrise they had witnessed.

"What would you like to see next?" Joseph asked as they finished their meal. "There's a series of smaller formations to the north with interesting features, natural arches, balanced rocks, and even some ancient pictographs the Blackfoot created generations ago."

"The pictographs sound fascinating," Lydia replied. "Are they far?"

"About an hour's ride," Joseph said, calculating distances in his head. "We could visit there this morning, return here for midday when the heat is strongest, and then explore the southern formations this afternoon."

"That sounds perfect," Lydia agreed. She hesitated, then added, "I'll need a few minutes to... prepare for the day."

Joseph understood immediately. "Of course. I'll see to breaking camp while you have privacy."

He moved away toward the horses, giving Lydia space to collect her personal items and retreat behind the large boulder that had served as her changing area the previous evening. She quickly washed using water from her canteen, changed into fresh clothing, and arranged her hair as neatly as possible, given the limited resources of camp life.

When she emerged, Joseph had already packed most of their supplies and extinguished the fire. He looked up from adjusting Thunder's saddle cinch, and something in his expression as he took in her appearance made her heart beat faster.

"Ready for adventure?" he asked, his voice carrying a warmth that hadn't been there during their first days of travel together.

"Always," she replied with a smile.

Chapter 25

The ride to the pictographs took them through a narrower section of the valley, where the towering formations closed in on either side, creating a natural corridor of red stone. The morning air remained pleasantly cool despite the increasing height of the sun, and Lydia found herself studying every detail of their surroundings with an artist's hungry eye.

Joseph rode beside her where the trail allowed, pointing out features of interest. A perfectly balanced boulder perched improbably atop a slender column, a natural window eroded through solid stone that framed a perfect view of distant mountains. A small spring that emerged mysteriously from seemingly solid rock before disappearing again beneath the sandy soil.

"How did you first discover the pictographs?" Lydia asked as they navigated a particularly narrow passage.

"By accident," Joseph admitted. "During that first visit years ago. I was seeking shelter from a sudden thunderstorm and found an overhang that provided decent protection. While waiting out the rain, I noticed markings that were clearly man made."

"Why show them to me?" Lydia asked, genuinely curious.

"Because you'll see them differently. Not as curiosities or primitive scrawls, but as communication across time."

The insight revealed how thoroughly Joseph had come to understand her perspective, and Lydia felt a surge of appreciation for this man who continuously surprised her with his depth.

"I'm honored," she said simply.

They emerged from the narrow passage into a more open area where several massive boulders had fallen from the surrounding cliffs, creating a natural amphitheater of stone. Joseph dismounted, securing Thunder to a stunted juniper that had somehow established itself in this harsh environment.

"We'll walk from here," he explained as he helped Lydia down from Penny's back. "The approach is too narrow and rough for horses."

He led her toward what appeared to be a solid wall of red stone, but as they drew closer, Lydia could see a narrow fissure partially hidden by brush and shadow. Joseph pushed aside a gnarled branch, revealing the opening.

"Watch your step," he cautioned, taking her hand to guide her through the gap. "The footing's uneven here."

His hand was warm and strong around hers, providing steady support as they navigated the uneven ground.

The fissure opened into a protected alcove, a natural half-cave carved into the cliff face by ancient waters or wind. The overhanging rock created a welcome shade, and the temperature dropped noticeably as they stepped fully into the protected space.

"There," Joseph said quietly, gesturing toward the back wall of the alcove.

Lydia followed his indication and gasped softly. The smooth red stone surface was covered with intricate paintings—not crude marks, but sophisticated images rendered in black, white, and ochre pigments that had somehow withstood the passage of time. Hunters pursuing buffalo, stylized human figures in ceremonial poses, spirals and geometric patterns with meanings she could only guess at, and, most dramatically, a series of hand prints pressed directly against the stone surface.

"These are extraordinary," she breathed, moving closer to study the artistry. "How old do you think they are?"

"Thomas believes they date back many generations," Joseph replied, standing beside her as she examined the paintings. "Perhaps two hundred years or more. He said this place was sacred to the Blackfoot long before white settlement."

Lydia reached toward one of the handprints, her fingers hovering just above the ancient mark without touching it. "Someone stood exactly where I'm standing now, centuries ago, and pressed their hand against this stone. A direct connection across time."

"That's what I thought you'd understand," Joseph said, his voice soft with approval.

They spent nearly an hour in the alcove, Lydia sketching the most significant images while Joseph explained what little he knew of their meanings, based on conversations with Thomas during previous visits. The hand prints, he said, represented a direct transfer of spirit between person and place, a way of marking one's presence in a sacred location. The hunting scenes commemorated successful expeditions that had fed the community. The spirals might represent journeys or the passage of seasons.

"I wish I could speak with whoever created these," Lydia said as she completed her final sketch. "To understand their thoughts as they worked, what they hoped to communicate to future viewers."

"Isn't that the mystery of all art?" Joseph asked. "Even when the artist stands before you explaining their work, something essential remains un-communicated except through the work itself."

The observation startled Lydia with its perception. "Yes, exactly. There's always something beyond words, something that can only be expressed through the created thing itself." She looked at him with newfound appreciation. "You understand art better than most collectors I've met in New York."

"I understand very little about formal art," he demurred. "But I recognize truth when I encounter it, whether in words, music, or images."

They emerged from the alcove into the full brightness of mid-morning, blinking as their eyes readjusted to the intense light. The temperature had risen significantly during their time examining the pictographs, the sun now high enough to eliminate most shadows from the Valley floor.

"We should head back to our campsite," Joseph suggested. "The heat will be considerable midday, and there's shade near the spring."

As they rode, Lydia reflected on the unexpected depth of her experiences in Montana Territory. She had come seeking picturesque landscapes and frontier color for her National Geographic commission, expecting a straightforward artistic assignment. Instead, she had found herself immersed in a complex world of cultures in collision, environmental change, and personal transformation.

And Joseph, most surprising of all, was so different from her initial impression of the taciturn and judgmental guide she had met in Bozeman. His knowledge, his integrity, his genuine respect for the land and its peoples, and his emerging willingness to reveal his own struggles and hopes had all combined to create something Lydia had never anticipated: a profound connection that transcended their different backgrounds.

They reached their campsite as the sun approached its zenith. Joseph helped Lydia dismount, his hands lingering slightly at her waist for a heartbeat longer than strictly necessary. The subtle contact sent a flutter of awareness through her that had nothing to do with the day's increasing heat.

"I'll fetch fresh water from the spring," he said, releasing her and reaching for their canteens. "You might want to find some shade. The temperature will keep rising for another couple of hours."

Lydia nodded, already feeling perspiration beading along her hairline. She moved toward a broad, flat boulder positioned perfectly beneath an overhanging rock formation that provided substantial shade. Spreading her shawl across the stone surface to protect against its residual heat, she settled onto this natural bench and opened her sketchbook to review her morning's work.

Joseph returned a few minutes later with filled canteens, the water deliciously cool from its underground source. He handed one to Lydia before taking a seat on a nearby rock, removing his hat to wipe his brow.

"I've been thinking about what comes next," he said after they had both refreshed themselves with long drinks of water.

"The southern formations this afternoon?" Lydia asked, assuming he meant their immediate plans.

"No... I mean yes, that too, but I was thinking further ahead. Your commission work. You've documented several things so far. Do you have enough material for National Geographic's needs?"

"Possibly, though I could happily continue sketching Montana's wonders for months without exhausting its possibilities."

"Would you consider visiting someplace just for your personal enjoyment? Not so much for National Geographic, but for yourself."

"What did you have in mind?"

"There's a place further north. It's a valley surrounded by mountains, with lakes so clear you can count pebbles twenty feet down. The Blackfoot considers it sacred ground." He paused, gathering his thoughts. "I promised Thomas years ago that I would never bring outsiders there, but he specifically mentioned to me before we left that you might be an exception."

"That's... a remarkable honor," Lydia said, genuinely moved by the trust this represented. "I'd love to see this place."

"That's what I hoped you might say," he admitted, his voice rougher than usual.

Joseph rose from his seat, moving to stand before her. He extended his hand, not in the practical assistance he had offered countless times during their travels, but as a more meaningful gesture, an invitation to connection.

Lydia placed her hand in his without hesitation. His fingers closed gently around hers, and with careful respect, he drew her to her feet so they stood facing each other in the dappled shade.

"May I..." he began, then stopped, seeming to search for the right words. "Would it be presumptuous to—"

"Yes," Lydia interrupted softly, understanding his unspoken question. "It would be entirely welcome."

With that permission granted, Joseph leaned forward slowly, giving her every opportunity to reconsider. When she didn't move away, he closed the remaining distance between them and pressed his lips to hers in a kiss that held both tenderness and restraint.

The contact lasted only a few heartbeats, proper and respectful, yet Lydia felt it echo through her entire being.

When Joseph drew back, his eyes searched hers with quiet intensity. "I've wanted to do that since the cabin in the storm," he admitted. "Perhaps even earlier, though I wasn't ready to acknowledge it then."

"I'm glad you waited until now," Lydia replied honestly. "Until we both understood what it might mean."

He nodded, still holding her hand between both of his. "I don't take this lightly, Lydia. What's growing between us... it's unlike anything I've experienced before."

"For me as well," she assured him.

Eventually, Joseph released her hand with evident reluctance. "We should rest during the worst of the heat," he suggested, practical concerns reasserting themselves. "The southern formations will be best viewed when the sun begins to descend."

They settled in the shade, Joseph propped against his saddle, Lydia seated on her shawl-covered rock. Despite the day's growing heat, a sense of peace pervaded their small camp.

Lydia watched Joseph as he dozed lightly, his hat pulled low over his eyes. This man, so different from anyone in her New York circle, had become central to her thoughts in ways she couldn't have imagined when they first met. His strength, his integrity, his fierce protectiveness of the land and its people, and most compelling of all, his capacity for growth and change, all combined to create someone uniquely valuable to her.

Was this love? The question formed unbidden in her mind. Not the romanticized version from novels, filled with dramatic declarations and impossible perfection, but something more substantial—a growing certainty that her life was better with him in it than without him. That his perspective completed hers in essential ways. That their differences strengthened rather than undermined their connection.

She had no immediate answer, but the question itself felt significant—a milestone in her internal journey as meaningful as any physical landmark they had visited together.

Chapter 26

The sudden splash of cold water against Lydia's legs made her gasp as Penny stepped deeper into the stream crossing. The mare snorted, clearly enjoying the relief from three days of dusty travel since leaving the Valley of Standing Stones.

"Careful there," Joseph called from several paces ahead, where Thunder stood midstream, water swirling around the stallion's muscular legs. "It drops off unexpectedly on your right."

Lydia guided Penny slightly leftward, following the invisible path Joseph seemed to intuit even beneath the rushing water. The stream was wider than the others they'd crossed, fed by mountain snowmelt.

"Is this part of the watershed for the lake in the valley we are heading toward?"

Joseph nodded, waiting until she drew alongside him before continuing forward. "One of many tributaries. The mountains gather water from dozens of streams like this one, channeling it all to the valley." He gestured toward the distant peaks that had been growing larger on the horizon with each passing day. "We're getting close. Should reach the ridge overlooking the valley by nightfall."

The anticipation that had been building inside Lydia intensified. Three days of travel since Joseph had first mentioned this special place. Three days of growing closeness between them, and many conversations that stretched long into evening hours.

"Tell me more about it. You've been remarkably secretive about what makes it so special."

"Some things defy description, Lydia. They need to be experienced." He adjusted his hat against the afternoon sun. "But I promise it'll be worth every mile of dust we've eaten to get there."

They climbed steadily through a landscape that transitioned from open grassland to scattered pines and eventually into a proper forest of lodgepole and ponderosa. The air grew cooler and tinged with the sharp scent of resin as the trees closed around them, providing welcome shade from the persistent summer heat.

Near a small clearing, Joseph raised his hand, signaling a halt. "Let's rest the horses a bit. There's a steep climb ahead."

Lydia dismounted gratefully, stretching her legs while Joseph loosened the saddle cinches to give the horses comfort during their break. Three days in the saddle had conditioned her muscles significantly since her first awkward rides, but the long hours still took their toll.

"You're becoming quite the horsewoman," Joseph observed, offering her a canteen. "Penny's taken a shine to you."

As if confirming his assessment, the mare nudged Lydia's shoulder gently, seeking attention. Lydia laughed, stroking the horse's velvety muzzle. "The feeling's mutual. I'll miss her terribly when..." The words trailed off, the unspoken future hanging between them.

Joseph's eyes met hers, holding a question neither had directly addressed since leaving the Valley of Standing Stones. Their relationship had shifted perceptibly after that first careful kiss, becoming something deeper and more intentional, yet the practicalities of what might come next remained largely undiscussed.

"There's something I want to show you here," he said, instead of pursuing the delicate topic. He extended his hand. "It's just beyond those trees."

Lydia placed her hand in his, now familiar with the pleasant roughness of his calloused palm against her softer skin. He led her through a screen of young pines into another clearing where a massive, lightning-scarred ponderosa stood alone, its enormous trunk splitting into three distinct leaders about fifteen feet above the ground.

"The Blackfoot call this the Grandfather Tree," Joseph explained. "It's a landmark for travelers heading to the sacred valley."

Lydia approached the ancient pine, placing her hand against its rough bark. "How old do you think it is?"

"Thomas believes it was already ancient when his grandfather's grandfather was a boy," Joseph replied, coming to stand beside her. "Lightning struck it at least twice, but it survived. The Blackfoot say it's protected by particular spirits. Thomas says travelers traditionally leave a small offering here before proceeding to the valley. A gesture of respect and gratitude for safe passage."

"What kind of offering?"

"Something personal. Something that represents the traveler's journey or purpose."

Lydia considered this, then reached into her satchel. After a moment's deliberation, she withdrew a small piece of charcoal she used for sketching, one that had captured dozens of Montana scenes over the past weeks.

"Would this be appropriate?" she asked, holding it out for Joseph's consideration. "It represents my seeing, my way of understanding this land."

His expression warmed with approval. "Perfect."

Lydia knelt at the base of the enormous tree, placing the charcoal carefully in a natural hollow between two massive roots.

Joseph watched her with evident appreciation, then reached into his shirt pocket and withdrew something small that Lydia couldn't immediately identify. He knelt beside her and placed it next to her charcoal—a harmonica reed, she realized, recognizing the thin strip of metal.

"A piece of your past," Lydia observed.

"And maybe a symbol of something new." His voice carried a significance that made her heart beat faster. "Music yet to be played."

Joseph cleared his throat. "We should continue if we want to reach the overlook by nightfall."

They returned to the horses. As Joseph helped Lydia mount, his hands lingered at her waist a moment longer than necessary. The small intimacy sent warmth spreading through her despite the forest's cool shade.

"The trail gets narrower from here," he warned as they set off again. "Stay close behind me."

True to his word, the path soon constricted into a winding animal track that climbed steadily upward through increasingly dense forest. Pine boughs brushed against Lydia's shoulders as Penny picked her way carefully behind Thunder. The horses' breathing grew more labored as the incline steepened, and conversation became impractical over the sound of their exertion.

For nearly two hours, they climbed steadily, the forest eventually thinning as they approached alpine elevations. The trees became smaller and more wind-sculptured, and gaps in the forest revealed tantalizing glimpses of snow-capped peaks ahead.

"Almost there," Joseph called back. "Just around this ridge."

The trail curved sharply around an outcropping of gray stone, then suddenly opened onto a natural plateau that stopped Lydia's breath in her chest. Before them stretched a panoramic view of a perfect alpine valley cupped in the embrace of towering mountains. Far below, nestled in the valley floor like scattered jewels, several lakes of varying sizes gleamed in the late afternoon sun, their surfaces an impossible blue that rivaled the sky itself.

"Joseph," Lydia whispered, no other words adequate to express her reaction.

He dismounted and came to help her down, his expression a mirror of her own awe, despite having seen this view before. Together, they stood at the edge of the plateau, absorbing the magnificent vista spread before them.

"Now I understand why the Blackfoot considers it sacred," Lydia said finally. "It feels like looking directly at God's handiwork before human interference."

"That's exactly what Thomas said you would understand," Joseph replied softly. "Why he agreed you should see this place?"

The wind coursed up from the valley below, carrying the scent of pine and clean water and something indefinable that seemed to speak of pristine wilderness. Lydia breathed deeply, feeling something in her spirit expand in response to this magnificent landscape.

"We'll make camp here for tonight," Joseph said, reluctantly turning from the view to practical matters. "The descent to the valley is too steep to attempt in fading light. Tomorrow morning, we'll follow the switchback trail down to the lakes."

They established camp efficiently after so many nights on the trail together, falling into familiar patterns without the need for discussion. Joseph tended the horses while Lydia gathered wood for their fire. She arranged stones for a fire ring while he prepared a simple meal from their provisions.

As twilight descended, they sat side by side near the fire's warmth, their shoulders touching comfortably while they ate from tin plates. The valley below had transformed with the changing light, shadows deepening among the trees while the lakes still caught the last gleams of sunset.

"I wonder how many people have seen this view," Lydia mused, setting aside her empty plate.

"Very few, I'd imagine," Joseph replied. "Maybe a handful of trappers over the years. Thomas has kept it as protected as possible."

"I'm honored he trusted me to see it."

"He saw something in you, Lydia. The same thing I've come to see, a respect for this land. A willingness to understand it on its own terms rather than imposing outside expectations."

"That means a great deal coming from you."

They fell silent, watching darkness claim the valley as stars emerged overhead in breathtaking profusion. The sound of nighthawks calling in their distinctive diving pattern echoed from the slopes below, while the wind whispered continuously through the surrounding pines.

"The Blackfoot have a creation story about this valley," Joseph said eventually, his voice taking on the cadence of storytelling. "Thomas shared it with me during my first winter in Montana Territory, when I was still struggling with the consequences of my buffalo hunting days."

"Will you tell me?" Lydia asked, drawing her blanket closer around her shoulders against the growing night chill.

Joseph nodded, adding another small log to their fire before continuing. "The story says that in the early days, after Old Man—that's their name for the Creator—had made the mountains and forests, he realized something was missing. The land was beautiful but incomplete. So he cupped his hands together and filled them with tears of joy over his creation."

The fire crackled, sending sparks spiraling upward toward the star-scattered sky as Joseph continued.

"When Old Man opened his hands, those tears became the lakes of this valley, the purest water in all creation because they came directly from the Creator's happiness. He declared this place sacred, a reminder of his love for all he had made."

"That's beautiful," Lydia said softly.

"Thomas says the water in these lakes holds healing properties, not just for the body but for the spirit. The Blackfoot have traditionally brought those who are troubled in heart or mind here to find peace."

Lydia contemplated this, watching the flames dance between them and the darkened valley beyond. "Is that why you came here before? To heal?"

Joseph was quiet for so long that Lydia wondered if he would answer. When he finally spoke, his voice carried a vulnerability she had rarely heard from him.

"Yes. I was... lost. Directionless." He stared into the flames, remembering. "Thomas brought me here. Had me stay for nearly a month, alone with the mountains and lakes and my own thoughts."

"Did it help?"

"It saved me," he said simply. "Not immediately, not completely—that kind of healing takes time. But it began here."

Lydia reached for his hand in the firelight, intertwining her fingers with his. The simple contact conveyed understanding words couldn't adequately express.

"I've wanted to bring you here since the moment I recognized what was happening between us," Joseph admitted. "This place... it means everything to me. There's never been anyone else I wanted to bring here."

Eventually, Joseph spoke again, his voice thoughtful. "Tomorrow we'll descend to the valley floor. The largest lake, the one that looks almost perfectly round from up here, is called Spirit Water by the Blackfoot. Thomas says it's where the barrier between worlds is thinnest."

"Between worlds?"

"Between the physical world, we perceive with our ordinary senses and the spiritual reality that underlies everything. Like Sarah Dove's 'thin places,' but more powerful." He turned to look at her directly. "It's a place for decisions, Thomas says. For clarity about one's path forward."

"I would like that clarity," she acknowledged. "About many things."

Joseph nodded. "It's getting late. We should rest if we want an early start tomorrow."

They prepared for sleep with the practiced efficiency of experienced travelers, banking the fire for the night and arranging their bedrolls on opposite sides of the glowing embers. As had become their custom, Joseph read aloud from his mother's Bible before they retired, his deep voice giving resonance to familiar verses.

"'The Lord is my shepherd; I shall not want,'" he read from Psalm 23. "'He maketh me to lie down in green pastures: he leadeth me beside the still waters...'"

The ancient words seemed particularly appropriate given their destination the following day. Lydia closed her eyes, letting the Scripture and Joseph's voice wash over her as the fire crackled softly and night insects chirped from the surrounding vegetation.

"'Surely goodness and mercy shall follow me all the days of my life: and I will dwell in the house of the Lord forever,'" Joseph concluded, closing the Bible reverently.

"Amen," Lydia murmured.

"Sleep well, Lydia," he said softly from across the fire.

"You too, Joseph."

Despite her physical fatigue from the day's journey, sleep proved elusive as Lydia lay gazing at the star-filled sky above their camp. Her mind replayed moments from their journey together. Joseph's initial skepticism in Bozeman, his gradual warming, the flash of impressed surprise when she'd demonstrated unexpected competence, the growing respect and eventual tenderness that had transformed their relationship.

"Lord," she prayed silently, "grant me wisdom to see clearly what path You've set before me. And courage to follow it wherever it leads."

Eventually, lulled by the night sounds and the distant murmur of water far below in the valley, Lydia drifted into sleep.

Chapter 27

Morning arrived with the cheerful calling of mountain bluebirds and the gentle touch of sunrise painting the surrounding peaks with rosy light. Lydia woke to find Joseph already up, tending a small fire where coffee brewed in their battered pot.

"Good morning," he greeted her, his expression brightened by the anticipation of their day's journey. "Sleep well?"

"Eventually," she admitted, sitting up and running fingers through her loose hair. "My mind was too full for easy sleep."

He nodded, understanding. "The mountain air will do that—sharpen thoughts, clarify impressions."

They shared a simple breakfast while watching sunlight gradually fill the valley below, transforming shadowed forests to vibrant green and setting the lakes sparkling like scattered sapphires. The morning air carried a crisp edge, a reminder of their elevation.

"The trail down is steep but well-established," Joseph explained as they prepared to break camp. "The Blackfoot have used it for generations. Just stay close behind me and let Penny set her own pace. She'll follow Thunder's lead."

An hour later, they were descending a series of switchbacks cut into the mountainside. The trail was indeed steep, requiring complete concentration from both riders and horses. Conversation became impractical over the sound of hooves on stone and the occasional dislodged pebble clattering down the slope below.

Lydia focused on maintaining her balance as Penny navigated the sharp turns of the switchbacks, trusting the sure-footed mare to find secure footing. Joseph remained vigilant ahead, occasionally calling back warnings about particularly tricky sections.

The descent took most of the morning; the sun climbing higher as they made their way down the mountainside. The air gradually warmed and softened as they lost elevation, transitioning from the crisp mountain atmosphere to something richer with the scent of meadow flowers and lakeside vegetation.

Finally, the trail leveled out as they reached the valley floor. Joseph reined Thunder to a halt, waiting for Lydia to join him on the broad, grassy expanse that stretched toward the nearest lake.

"We made it," he said, satisfaction evident in his voice. "Welcome to Creator's Tears Valley."

From ground level, the valley revealed details invisible from their overlook the previous evening. The forest floor was carpeted with wildflowers in riotous profusion—lupine in shades from the deepest purple to pale lavender, bright yellow arnica, delicate columbine in blue and white, and dozens of other varieties Lydia couldn't name. Between stands of pine and aspen, natural meadows created sun-drenched openings where deer grazed, lifting their heads curiously as the riders approached before bounding unhurriedly into the sheltering trees.

They rode across a meadow toward the nearest lake, a medium-sized body of water fringed with reeds and wildflowers. As they drew closer, Lydia gasped at the unprecedented clarity of the water. Just as Joseph had promised, the lake was so transparent that rocks and fallen branches on the bottom were perfectly visible, despite being many feet below the surface.

"It's like looking through clear glass," she marveled.

"Wait until you see Spirit Water," Joseph replied. "It's the largest and clearest of all the lakes here."

They continued through the valley, alternating between forest paths and open meadows. Joseph pointed out features of significance—a stand of aspen trees where the Blackfoot traditionally harvested bark for medicinal purposes, a natural stone formation resembling a seated figure that marked the boundary of particularly sacred ground, and a small spring bubbling from beneath a moss-covered boulder that Thomas claimed had never run dry, even during the most severe droughts.

By midday, they approached the shores of Spirit Water. The lake was indeed nearly circular, its surface an impossible blue that seemed to both reflect and transcend the sky above. Mountains cupped the water in a protective embrace, their reflections creating perfect mirror images on the lake's glassy surface.

Joseph dismounted near the shore, helping Lydia down with his customary care. They stood for a long moment in silence, absorbing the profound tranquility of the setting.

"It feels different here," Lydia said eventually.

Joseph nodded understanding. "Thomas says the veil between seen and unseen is particularly thin here. That those who come with honest hearts can sometimes glimpse deeper realities."

They secured the horses in a small meadow with good grazing, then Joseph led Lydia along the lakeshore to a natural clearing where several large, flat rocks provided perfect seating overlooking the water.

"This is where Thomas brought me," Joseph explained, indicating one particularly large stone warmed by the midday sun. "He told me to sit, to watch, and most importantly, to listen, not just with my ears but with my heart."

Lydia settled on the sun-warmed stone, arranging her skirt comfortably around her. "And what did you hear?"

Joseph sat beside her, close enough that their shoulders almost touched. "At first, nothing beyond the ordinary sounds of wind and water." His expression grew reflective. "But on the third day, after hours of frustrated waiting, I finally stopped trying so hard. Stopped expecting some dramatic revelation and simply...opened myself to whatever might come."

"And then?"

"Then I heard it, not an audible voice, but a certainty that seemed to rise from somewhere beyond myself. A conviction that my past actions, however regrettable, didn't define my future unless I allowed them to." His voice softened with remembered emotion. "That forgiveness wasn't something I needed to earn, but something already extended, waiting only for me to accept it."

"That's beautiful."

"It changed everything," he confirmed simply. "Set me on the path to becoming the man I am now, however imperfectly I walk it. I've forgotten that God will and has forgiven me. You've reminded me of that and made me realize once again that I am forgivable."

They sat in companionable silence for a time, watching an osprey circle high above the lake before diving with startling precision to emerge with a fish clasped in its talons. A gentle breeze rippled the lake's surface, sending soft waves lapping against the shore at their feet.

Joseph reached into his saddlebag, which he'd brought from the horses, and withdrew a small bundle wrapped in clean cloth.

"Thomas asked me to bring something here, and to share it with you if you agreed to come," he explained, carefully unwrapping the bundle to reveal several pieces of what appeared to be dark bread. "It's wasna—a traditional Blackfoot travel food made from dried berries, meat, and fat. Sharing it at Spirit Water is part of their ceremony for significant moments."

He offered a piece to Lydia with evident reverence. She accepted it carefully, noting the rich, complex aroma of berries and something savory beneath.

"We eat it together," Joseph explained, "as a symbol of sharing not just food but purpose and path."

The simple ritual carried a weight beyond its physical elements. Lydia understood intuitively that this represented more than just a cultural experience Joseph was sharing; it was an invitation with deeper significance.

They ate the dense, surprisingly flavorful food in silence, watching the play of light on the lake's surface. The taste was unlike anything Lydia had experienced—sweet from dried berries but with a savory undertone from the meat, rich with an almost buttery quality from the rendered fat.

"It's sustaining," Joseph explained when they had finished. "Provides strength for long journeys."

The implication hung unspoken between them.

"Joseph," Lydia said finally, turning to face him directly. "I think it's time we spoke plainly about what comes next."

His gray eyes met hers steadily, unafraid of the conversation, yet allowing her to lead it. "I agree."

"My commission from National Geographic will come to an end," she began, organizing her thoughts carefully. "I have more than enough material to fulfill their expectations already. Under normal circumstances..."

"Yes?"

"Joseph, nothing about this journey has been what I expected."

She looked out over the impossibly clear water, gathering courage for what she needed to express next. "I came west seeking artistic opportunity and perhaps a brief adventure before returning to my prescribed life in New York. I never anticipated..." She paused, searching for adequate words. "I never anticipated finding something that would make returning to that life seem hollow by comparison."

Hope filled Joseph's eyes, though he remained silent, allowing her to continue without interruption.

"The land itself has changed me," Lydia continued. "Montana's beauty, its rawness, its honesty. The Blackfoot people's relationship with the land, so different from anything I've known. And you, Joseph." She met his gaze directly. "How you've shown me a different way of seeing and being in the world."

"What are you saying, Lydia?"

"I'm saying I don't want to leave," she answered simply. "Not Montana, and certainly not you."

Joseph closed his eyes briefly, as if absorbing the impact of her statement. When he opened them again, they shone with an intensity that took her breath away.

"I've been afraid to hope for that," he admitted, his voice barely above a whisper. "Afraid to believe someone like you could choose this life... choose me over everything waiting for you in New York."

"Someone like me?"

"Educated, cultured, connected to a world I can't offer you," he clarified. "My life here is good but simple, Lydia. Hard sometimes. Far from the comforts you've known."

"Those 'comforts' often felt more like constraints," she countered. "And I've found more genuine stimulation, for my mind, my heart, and my spirit here with you, than in years of New York society."

She reached for his hand, intertwining their fingers with deliberate purpose. "I'm not naïve, Joseph. I understand what choosing Montana means. The winter cold you've described, the isolation, and the physical demands. But I also understand what it offers. Authenticity, purpose, connection to land and people and God Himself in ways I never experienced back east."

Joseph's hand tightened around hers. "And what about your family? Your career? The recognition your talent deserves?"

"My family will adjust," she said with more confidence than she entirely felt. "As for my career, I see possibilities here too. The West is changing rapidly, these landscapes, these communities deserve documentation by someone who respects them. Perhaps National Geographic would welcome more commissions, or I could explore other publishing opportunities."

She looked out over the perfect circle of Spirit Water, drawing strength from its serene presence. "I don't pretend it will be simple or without sacrifice. But nothing worthwhile ever is."

Joseph was silent for a long moment, processing her words. When he finally spoke, his voice carried a profound tenderness that made her heart swell.

"Since that first night at the Blackfoot settlement, when Sarah Dove spoke of paths joining, I've been fighting against hope," he admitted. "Telling myself it was impossible that someone like you belonged in a different world. That whatever we felt was temporary... beautiful but ultimately impractical."

He shifted to face her more directly, still holding her hand between both of his. "But every day since then has proven me wrong. Every conversation, every shared experience, has shown me that what exists between us transcends practical considerations. That it's not something either of us created, but something we discovered. A path already laid out, waiting only for us to recognize and walk it."

"Yes," Lydia whispered.

Joseph's expression shifted, growing more solemn yet suffused with quiet joy as he took both her hands in his.

"Lydia, there's something I need to ask you." His voice was steady but carried an undercurrent of emotion rarely displayed so openly. "Would you be willing to travel back to the Blackfoot village?"

"Of course," she replied, curious about his specific request. "I'd welcome the chance to see Thomas and Sarah Dove again."

Joseph nodded, his thumbs gently stroking the backs of her hands. "I was hoping we might ask them to acknowledge what's grown between us. To offer their blessing over our union."

Understanding dawned in Lydia's eyes as the significance of his request became clear.

"You should know," he continued carefully, "the Blackfoot don't perform a Christian ceremony as you might be accustomed to. They offer words of wisdom and respect... a blessing that acknowledges what already exists rather than creating something new."

"Like the binding ceremony Sarah performed," Lydia recalled softly.

"Yes, but more..." He searched for the right word. "More definitive. If Thomas agrees to bless us, we could exchange our own vows there, among people who have come to respect and care for you. We would be married in our hearts, in the eyes of their community, and in God's sight."

His gray eyes held hers steadily as he continued. "Then later, after this journey has ended, we could go to Bozeman and make it official before the law with a proper minister. But I find myself wanting this first step to happen in a place that's been significant to our journey together."

Lydia considered his words, deeply moved by the thought behind them. The traditional girl from New York might have balked at such an unconventional proposal, but she wasn't that girl anymore. Montana had changed her, Joseph had changed her, and her own choices had led her to this moment.

"I would be honored," she said finally, her voice clear and certain. "To exchange our promises before Thomas and Sarah feels right. As if we're acknowledging that our bond was formed here, in this land, through these experiences we've shared."

Relief and joy mingled in Joseph's expression. "You're sure?"

"Yes. I've chosen a different path," Lydia said simply. "One that feels truer to who I've become." She smiled, a sudden thought occurring to her. "Though we might need to consider a more conventional ceremony later."

Joseph laughed, the sound echoing across the still water. "I suppose I should be prepared to face your family, eventually."

"They'll come to love you," Lydia assured him, though she wasn't entirely certain how her father would react to her choice. That was a bridge to cross later.

"When would you want to return to the settlement?" she asked, practical considerations entering her thoughts.

"We could begin our journey back tomorrow," Joseph suggested. "It would take us three days, possibly four, depending on the weather." He hesitated. "Though perhaps we should continue exploring today. Spirit Water deserves more than a brief visit."

Lydia nodded in agreement. "I'd like that." She glanced at her satchel. "And I should make at least one sketch to commemorate this place. It feels important to preserve this moment."

They spent the remainder of the day beside the sacred lake, Lydia sketching while Joseph occasionally played soft melodies on his harmonica.

As evening approached, they made camp near the lakeshore, dining on provisions while watching the sunset transform the mountains into silhouettes of deepening purple against a flame-colored sky. Their conversation flowed easily between practical planning and deeper sharing, weaving together dreams and realities with the natural rhythm of two souls finding their shared path.

That night, as stars emerged in breathtaking profusion above Spirit Water, they sat side by side before their small fire, shoulders touching, connected by the certainty of their shared future. No formal vows had yet been spoken, no rings exchanged, yet both felt the profound shift that had occurred, a covenant already formed in their hearts, awaiting only formal acknowledgment.

"Tomorrow we begin the journey back," Joseph said softly, his voice blending with the gentle lapping of water against the shore. "But something tells me we've already started a much longer journey together."

Lydia leaned her head against his shoulder, content in a way she had never imagined possible when she first arrived in Montana Territory. "Yes," she agreed simply. "We have."

Chapter 28

The pungent scent of smoke reached them first.

Lydia's hand tightened instinctively on the reins, and Penny stopped, ears pricked forward. Ahead of her, Joseph had already halted Thunder, his posture alert and tense as he scanned the horizon.

"That's not a cooking fire," he said, his voice tight with concern.

They had been riding since dawn, anticipation building as they approached the Blackfoot settlement. The journey back from Creator's Tears Valley had been filled with quiet contentment, plans shared between them as easily as water flowing downhill. But now, cresting the final ridge that would bring them within sight of the settlement, everything changed.

Dark smoke billowed upward, an ominous smudge against the otherwise perfect Montana sky.

"Joseph—" Lydia began, fear constricting her throat.

"Stay close," he cut in, his jaw set in a hard line. He urged Thunder forward, picking up pace.

Lydia followed, her heart pounding against her ribs. As they rounded the bend in the trail, the settlement came into view below them. Relief washed through her as she realized the buildings still stood intact. The smoke wasn't coming from the settlement itself, but from the eastern edge of the Blackfoot territory, where the forest met meadowland.

Joseph pointed. "Deliberate burning. Someone's set fire to the eastern grazing lands."

His face had transformed, all the softness of recent days replaced by hard vigilance. This was Joseph, the protector, Joseph the frontiersman, who understood threats and how to meet them.

They descended quickly, Thunder and Penny responding to their riders' urgency. As they approached the settlement, figures emerged from the dwellings. Michael, Thomas's son, ran toward them, his expression grim.

"Calloway!" he called. "You've returned at a critical time."

Joseph dismounted in one fluid motion, meeting Michael halfway. The men clasped forearms in greeting.

"The fire—" Joseph began.

"Garrett brothers," Michael confirmed, his voice tight with anger. "Three days ago. They came with torches in the night. We drove them off before they could reach the settlement, but they fired the eastern grasslands where our horses graze. We've been fighting to contain it since."

Lydia dismounted, her legs stiff after hours in the saddle. "Was anyone hurt?" she asked, stepping forward to join the men.

Michael's expression softened slightly at seeing her. "No serious injuries. Running Elk suffered burns on his hands while rescuing a foal trapped by the flames. Little Crow's mother is tending to him."

Joseph's face darkened. "This is retaliation. For what, I don't know, but the Garretts don't act without purpose, twisted as it may be."

A commotion from the settlement drew their attention. Several Blackfoot men were gathering, carrying water containers and tools. Among them moved Thomas, his silver-streaked hair gleaming in the afternoon sun, calling directions with the calm authority of a natural leader.

"They're starting another fire break," Michael explained. "The wind shifted an hour ago, pushing the flames back toward the hunting grounds."

Joseph nodded decisively. "We'll help. Lydia, perhaps you could—"

"I'm coming too," she interrupted, her tone brooking no argument. "I can carry water, help with the smaller tasks."

Joseph studied her face for a moment, and something in her expression must have convinced him. "Stay close to me or Michael," he said finally. "Wildfire is unpredictable and dangerous."

Michael led them quickly to the settlement, where Thomas greeted them with solemn dignity despite the crisis. The elder's weathered face showed signs of exhaustion, but his eyes remained alert and determined.

"Joseph, Lydia," he acknowledged. "Your return brings strength when it is most needed."

"We came seeking your blessing," Joseph said, his voice dropping, so only Thomas could hear. "Instead, we find you under attack."

Thomas's expression shifted, understanding dawning in his eyes as he looked between them. "The Creator's timing is never without purpose," he replied. "Perhaps your journey was meant to bring you here exactly when you were most needed."

Sarah Dove emerged from a nearby dwelling, carrying a bundle of cloth strips. Her silver-streaked braids hung loose down her back, and her face lit with recognition when she saw them.

"The travelers have returned," she said, approaching them with purposeful strides. Her sharp eyes took in their closeness, the changed way they stood together. "With answers found, I see."

Lydia felt heat rise to her cheeks but met the older woman's gaze steadily. Sarah nodded once, satisfaction evident in her expression.

"There will be time for that conversation," she said. "But now, we must protect what is ours." She handed the cloth strips to Lydia. "For masks against the smoke. Soak them in water before covering your face."

The settlement bustled with organized activity. Women prepared food and water for the firefighters, children filled containers from the stream, and men gathered tools and discussed strategy. Despite the danger, there was no panic, only determined cooperation.

Joseph conferred briefly with Thomas and the other men about the fire's progression and containment efforts. Lydia soaked cloths as Sarah had instructed, handing them to those preparing to face the flames.

Little Crow spotted her and darted across the central area, his young face smudged with ash but his eyes bright with excitement.

"You came back!" he said. "Just like Grandmother saw in her dreams!"

"We did," Lydia confirmed, smiling despite the circumstances. "Though I wish it were under better conditions."

The boy nodded solemnly. "The bad men came with fire. But we are fighting it together." He lowered his voice to a conspiratorial whisper. "I've been helping carry water. Father says I'm quick as a fox between the stream and the fire line."

"I'm sure you are," Lydia agreed. "But be careful, promise me?"

Little Crow drew himself up proudly. "I am careful. Grandmother says a warrior must be both brave and wise."

A call went up from the edge of the settlement. The next group was ready to depart for the fire line. Joseph appeared at Lydia's side, his face set with determination.

"I'm going with them," he said. "Michael knows these lands better than most. We'll create a wider fire break to prevent the flames from reaching the hunting grounds."

Lydia nodded, swallowing her fear. "Be careful."

His eyes softened momentarily. He touched her cheek with calloused fingers, a brief, intimate gesture. "I will. Stay here and help Sarah. She knows what needs doing."

Then he was gone, striding toward the gathered men. Lydia watched them depart, a knot of worry forming in her stomach. The danger was real—wildfires could shift with the wind, trapping even experienced frontiersmen.

Sarah Dove appeared beside her, her presence somehow reassuring. "Come," she said. "We prepare food for when they return. And while our hands work, we can speak of what has changed between you and Joseph Calloway."

Chapter 29

The kitchen area buzzed with activity as women prepared large quantities of food for the returning firefighters. Lydia was assigned to cutting dried meat into strips, which would be added to a hearty stew simmering in a large pot over the central fire.

Sarah Dove worked beside her, her skilled hands moving with practiced efficiency. "So," she said without preamble, "you have recognized what I saw from the beginning."

Lydia glanced up. "Yes. Though the path wasn't as straightforward as you might have anticipated."

Sarah's weathered face creased in a smile. "The most important paths rarely are. They wind and twist, testing our determination to follow them." She added herbs to the pot, the fragrant steam rising between them. "Tell me about the sacred valley. Did you drink from Spirit Water?"

"We did," Lydia confirmed. "It was... transformative. Like nowhere, I've ever been."

"The lakes there hold ancient wisdom," Sarah nodded approvingly. "Did Joseph ask you the question that was in his heart?"

Lydia's hands stilled on the cutting board. "He asked if we might return here to receive your blessing." She met the elder woman's gaze directly. "We hoped you and Thomas might acknowledge our union before we make it official in Bozeman."

Sarah's expression warmed with genuine pleasure. "So he found his courage at last. Good." She stirred the pot thoughtfully. "When the fire danger has passed, we will speak with Thomas. Such a blessing is not given lightly, but I believe he will agree."

A woman called to Sarah from across the cooking area, and she moved away to address some question about the food preparation. Lydia continued her work, mind divided between concern for Joseph and processing Sarah's words.

The afternoon stretched on; the sun beginning its westward descent. Periodically, messengers returned from the fire line with reports: the containment was progressing, the wind had shifted favorably, and more hands were needed in the southern sector.

Lydia worked alongside Morning Sky. As they packed water containers for the next group heading to the fire line, Morning Sky spoke hesitantly.

"The pictures you made before... of our people, our ways... did they reach the important people in the East?"

Lydia paused in her work. "Not yet. I must return to the Bozeman area to send them to National Geographic. But they will be published, I promise you that."

Morning Sky nodded, her dark eyes serious. "My grandfather believes your pictures might speak louder than our words. That they might show the truth of who we are, not who others claim we are."

"That's my hope as well," Lydia assured her. "To show the dignity and wisdom of your community, your connection to this land."

"And then what will you do? Return to your eastern cities?"

The question was asked without judgment, simple curiosity. Lydia found herself responding with equal directness.

"No. I've decided to stay in Montana. With Joseph."

Morning Sky's expression brightened. "This is good news! Sarah Dove said it would happen this way." She tied off a water bag with practiced movements. "You will face challenges together, I think. Both from your people and from those like the Garrett brothers who want only destruction."

"We're prepared for that," Lydia said, realizing as she spoke that they had indeed discussed the difficulties they might face. Joseph had been characteristically forthright about the hardships of ranching life, the isolation of Montana winters, and the potential disapproval from her family. Lydia had been equally honest about her determination to pursue artistic opportunities despite geographical limitations, and her concerns about fitting into the frontier community.

Their conversations had been refreshingly direct, no sugar-coating of realities or false promises. That honesty felt more romantic than any flowery declarations could have been.

Morning Sky tilted her head, studying Lydia with surprising perception. "Yes, I see that you are." She smiled. "You have changed since you first came to us. Your eyes see differently now."

"Montana has changed me," Lydia acknowledged. "For the better, I believe."

As the afternoon progressed into evening, the settlement maintained its state of alert readiness. A meal was served to those who remained behind, with portions set aside for the firefighters. Lydia ate little, her stomach tight with concern for Joseph and the others at the fire line.

As twilight descended, Sarah Dove approached Lydia where she sat near the central area, a sketch pad open on her lap. She had been drawing the surrounding scene, women preparing supplies, children carrying water, the organized response to crisis and capturing the resilience of the community.

"Come with me," Sarah said. "There is a place from which we can see the fire line. Thomas's messenger says they have nearly contained the eastern front."

Lydia followed eagerly, relief flooding through her at this news. Sarah led her to a small rise at the northern edge of the settlement, from which they could see across the darkening landscape to where the fire line glowed orange against the gathering night.

"They've been successful," Sarah observed, pointing to where a long, dark strip separated the smoldering burned area from the untouched grassland beyond. "The fire break is holding."

In the distance, Lydia could make out tiny figures moving along the containment line, some carrying torches to complete controlled burns, others beating out stray embers that threatened to cross the barrier. The wind now seemed to be working in their favor, pushing the remaining flames back into already-burned areas.

"Will they return tonight?" Lydia asked, scanning the distant line for any figure that might be Joseph.

"Some will. Others will maintain watch through the night," Sarah replied. "Fire can hide in root systems and flare again with the morning breeze."

They stood in silence for a time, watching the distant battle against the flames. The stars emerged overhead, contrasting with the orange glow on the horizon. Despite the circumstances, Lydia found the scene hauntingly beautiful. The vast, star-scattered Montana sky, the silhouettes of distant mountains, and the evidence of human determination against destructive forces.

"I must ask you something," Sarah said finally, her voice serious in the darkness. "The path you have chosen with Joseph… are you certain of it? Not just in your mind, but in your spirit?"

"Yes," she answered. "More certain than I've been of anything."

"Even knowing that your city life must be left behind? That your family may not understand?"

"Even then," Lydia confirmed. "What I've found here, it's worth any sacrifice."

Sarah nodded, satisfaction in her posture. "Good. Because the blessing Thomas may give requires truth in your hearts, not just your words." She turned to face Lydia directly, her expression visible in the combined light of stars and distant fire. "Joseph Calloway carries wounds that run deep. You have begun their healing, but that work is not complete."

"I know," Lydia said softly. "He's told me about his past, his regrets."

"Not all of them, I think," Sarah said cryptically. "But that is for him to share when he is ready." She placed a weathered hand on Lydia's arm. "You bring him balance he has long needed. And he offers you roots where before you had only branches reaching for light."

The metaphor struck Lydia as particularly apt. Her life in New York had been all about reaching for recognition, for independence, and for purpose, without the grounding stability she now felt with Joseph.

Their conversation was interrupted by movement below, at the settlement's edge. A group of men were returning from the fire line, their figures dark silhouettes against the night sky. Lydia's heart leapt, eyes searching the approaching group for Joseph's familiar form.

Sarah noticed her eagerness and smiled. "Go. Meet them. They will be hungry and weary."

Lydia needed no further encouragement. She made her way quickly down the slope, hurrying toward the returning firefighters. As she drew closer, relief washed through her as she recognized Joseph among them, his tall frame unmistakable despite the ash and dirt that covered him from head to toe.

The returning men were greeted with water, food, and quiet gratitude from those who had remained behind. There were no dramatic celebrations or effusive thanks—just the practical, mutual support of a community that understood their interdependence.

Joseph accepted water from a young boy, drinking deeply before catching sight of Lydia. His expression lightened immediately, fatigue giving way to evident pleasure at seeing her. He handed the empty water container back to the child and crossed to where she stood.

Up close, his exhaustion was even more apparent. His face was streaked with soot, his eyes reddened from smoke, and his clothing showed signs of hard work against the flames. But his smile was genuine as he reached for her.

"You're safe," she said, taking his hands in hers, not caring about the dirt and ash.

"We contained the eastern front," he confirmed. "Michael and some others will keep watch through the night, but the immediate danger has passed." His voice was raspy from smoke, and he cleared his throat. "The Garrett brothers knew what they were doing. They set the fire where the wind would drive it toward the heart of the Blackfoot hunting grounds. If it had reached the pine forest beyond the grasslands, it could have burned for weeks."

Lydia shuddered at the thought. "Thank God you stopped it."

"It was a community effort," Joseph said, his gaze moving over the settlement. "Every person here played their part." His eyes returned to her. "Including you, I'm told. You worked without rest since we arrived."

"Nothing compared to what you faced," she demurred.

He shook his head, rejecting her dismissal. "Every contribution matters in a crisis. That's something I've learned from the Blackfoot. No role is insignificant when survival is at stake."

Thomas approached them, his dignity undiminished by the ash that covered his clothing and skin. "Joseph, our thanks for your skilled assistance. The fire break strategy prevented much greater losses."

"You would have managed without me. Your people know this land and how to protect it."

Thomas acknowledged this with a slight nod. "Nevertheless, your return was timely. Sarah tells me you bring news of a personal nature as well, but that can wait until tomorrow, after rest has restored us all." His dark eyes moved between them thoughtfully. "For tonight, we have prepared the guest dwelling for both of you. It offers more privacy than the communal sleeping areas."

Joseph glanced at Lydia, a question in his eyes. She understood immediately—they were unmarried, and Joseph was concerned about proprieties.

"We would be honored," she said to Thomas, answering Joseph's unspoken concern as much as accepting the elder's offer. "Though we'll need separate sleeping areas, of course."

Thomas's eyes crinkled slightly at the corners, the Blackfoot equivalent of an amused smile. "Of course. Sarah Dove has arranged it appropriately." He gestured toward a dwelling at the eastern edge of the settlement. "Rest now. Morning will bring clearer minds for important discussions."

As Thomas moved away to speak with other returning firefighters, Joseph turned to Lydia. "I should clean up before anything else. I'm hardly fit company in this state."

"The stream is quiet now," she suggested. "Most have finished their evening washing."

He nodded gratefully. "I'll join you at the dwelling shortly. It's the one with the painted entrance—blue handprints on either side of the doorway."

Lydia watched him move away toward the stream, his exhaustion evident in the set of his shoulders despite his attempt to hide it. Her heart swelled with a complex mixture of emotions—pride in his courage, relief at his safety, and a deepening love that seemed to grow stronger with each shared experience.

She made her way to the designated dwelling, easily identifying it by the distinctive blue handprints that framed its entrance. Inside, she found a space both simple and welcoming. The single room was divided by a hanging woven blanket that created two distinct areas. On each side, sleeping pallets had been prepared with clean furs and blankets. A small fire burned in a central stone circle, providing warmth and modest light.

Sarah had clearly prepared the space with care. Fresh water waited in ceramic vessels, along with clean cloths for washing. A plate of dried fruits and meat had been left on a small woven mat, along with two cups and a pitcher of what smelled like herbal tea.

Lydia gratefully used some water to wash away the day's dirt and smoke from her face and hands. She had just finished braiding her hair when Joseph appeared at the entrance, silhouetted against the night sky.

"May I enter?" he asked formally, respecting her privacy.

"Of course," she replied, smiling at his consideration.

He stepped inside, closing the dwelling's entrance flap behind him. He had clearly made good use of the stream; his face and hands were clean, his hair damp, and he had changed into a clean shirt she recognized from their packs. The transformation was remarkable, though fatigue still shadowed his eyes.

"You should eat something," Lydia suggested, gesturing to the plate Sarah had left.

Joseph sank down near the fire with a barely suppressed groan of weariness. "I'm not sure if I have the energy to chew," he admitted with a rueful smile.

"Then at least drink this," she insisted, pouring some of the herbal tea into one of the cups. "Sarah Dove seems to know exactly what's needed, and I suspect this has properties to ease smoke-strained lungs."

He accepted the cup gratefully, inhaling the steam before taking a cautious sip. "Mint and something else... likely willow bark. Sarah's knowledge of medicinal plants is unmatched in these parts."

The small fire crackling softly between them. Despite the day's chaos and danger, Lydia felt a profound sense of peace.

"I spoke with Sarah while you were gone," she said eventually. "About our request for a blessing."

"What did she say?"

"That she believes Thomas will agree once the fire danger has fully passed." Lydia watched his face in the flickering light. "She seemed... pleased about our decision."

A smile touched his lips, softening the lines of exhaustion. "Sarah has been hoping for this outcome since our first visit, I think. She sees things others miss."

"She also sees things that haven't happened yet," Lydia pointed out. "Her dreams about us joining paths proved remarkably accurate."

"Thomas says she has the gift of 'seeing beyond,' as his people call it." Joseph set down his empty cup. "I was skeptical when I first came to Montana, but I've witnessed too much to dismiss it entirely."

Lydia nodded thoughtfully. "My father would call it heathen superstition, I suspect. But I've seen enough to believe God works through many channels we don't fully understand."

"Speaking of your father," Joseph said carefully, "have you considered how you'll inform your family of your decision to stay? They'll be expecting your return once your commission is complete."

It was a question Lydia had been pondering herself. "I'll need to write to them, of course. Explaining will be... challenging." She sighed. "My mother will be heartbroken, I think. She's always envisioned a certain life for me, appropriate marriage, children, and maintaining our family's social position in New York."

"And instead, you're choosing a former buffalo hunter with a ranch in Montana Territory," Joseph observed, his tone revealing lingering doubts about whether he was worthy of such a choice.

Lydia met his gaze directly. "I'm choosing the man I love, Joseph. A man of integrity, courage, and profound connection to this land. A man who sees me, truly sees me, as I am, not as someone to be molded into a proper society wife."

"Lydia," he said, his voice rough with emotion. "I—"

"You don't need to say it back," she interrupted gently. "Not until you're ready."

He shook his head, moving to kneel beside her. "That's just it. I am ready. More than ready." He took her hands in his, his touch gentle despite the callouses earned from years of ranch work. "I love you. Have loved you since before I could admit it, even to myself. You entered my life like a sudden spring after the longest winter, bringing light and color where I'd grown accustomed to shadows."

The poetry of his words surprised her. This man, so often cautious with language, now spoke with an eloquence born of genuine feeling.

"When we first met in Bozeman, I saw only what I expected to see. An Eastern woman with romantic notions and impractical expectations," he continued. "But you challenged every assumption, showed me depths of courage, insight, and faith I never anticipated. You saw beauty where I had forgotten to look for it. You offered grace where I believed only judgment was deserved."

He raised one hand to gently touch her cheek. "I love you, Lydia Hayes. And I find myself continually astonished that you could love me in return."

Lydia leaned into his touch, her heart so full it seemed impossible to contain the feeling. "I do love you, Joseph. With a certainty that surprises me sometimes."

His thumb traced the curve of her cheek, his eyes intent on hers in the firelight. "May I kiss you? Properly this time, not with the hesitation of uncertainty between us."

"Please," she whispered.

His lips met hers with gentle certainty, a kiss that conveyed reverence and passion in equal measure. Lydia's hands moved to his shoulders, feeling their solid strength beneath the clean fabric of his shirt. The kiss deepened, speaking of promises and possibilities, before Joseph pulled back slightly, resting his forehead against hers.

"We should remember we're guests in Thomas's community," he said, his voice husky. "And that certain traditions of propriety still apply."

Lydia nodded, appreciating his respect, even as part of her wished to continue the moment indefinitely. "You're right, of course."

Joseph reluctantly moved back, though he kept hold of one of her hands. "It won't be long before we can be properly married. First with Thomas's blessing here, then legally in Bozeman."

"And then?" Lydia asked, curious about his vision for their future.

"Then we build our life together," he said simply. "The ranch needs work, improvements I've put off too long. The main house could use expansion if you're to have proper space for your art. Perhaps we could add a north-facing room with good light for your drawing..." He trailed off, suddenly self-conscious. "I'm getting ahead of myself."

"No," Lydia said warmly. "I like hearing your plans. They're becoming our plans now."

His expression brightened at this affirmation of their shared future. "There's good land to the east of my current boundaries. I've had my eye on it for expansion. With more cattle, we could build something truly sustainable, something to pass on someday."

The implication—children, a legacy beyond themselves—remained unspoken but understood between them. Lydia felt a quiet thrill at the thought of building not just a life with Joseph, but a family, a true home rooted in the Montana soil.

"I'll need to return east briefly," she pointed out. "To deliver my commission work to National Geographic and collect my personal belongings. And to face my family in person... they deserve that much."

Joseph nodded, his thumb tracing circles on the back of her hand. "Would you want me to accompany you? To meet your family, stand beside you as you explain your decision?"

The offer touched her deeply. "Would you be willing to do that? New York would be as foreign to you as Montana was to me initially."

"I won't pretend the prospect isn't intimidating," he admitted with a wry smile. "But facing your father's likely disapproval seems a small price to pay for supporting you through what won't be an easy conversation."

Lydia considered the image. Joseph Calloway in her father's formal parlor, so utterly different from the elegant young men of New York society who had occasionally called upon her. The contrast would be stark, dramatic even. Yet somehow, she couldn't imagine any of those polished gentlemen showing the steadfast courage Joseph offered now.

"I'd be honored to have you with me," she said. "Though I should warn you, my mother will likely subject you to intense scrutiny and thinly veiled interrogation about your prospects and intentions."

Joseph chuckled, the sound warm in the quiet dwelling. "I've faced Blackfoot warriors and grizzly bears. Surely, I can survive a New York society matron."

"Don't be too certain," Lydia teased, glad to see his sense of humor returning despite his evident exhaustion. "My mother can be formidable when she believes her daughter's future is at stake."

Their conversation drifted to more immediate plans, how long they might stay with the Blackfoot community, when they would return to Joseph's ranch, and what preparations would be needed for their journey to Bozeman.

Eventually, Joseph's fatigue became impossible to ignore. His responses slowed, and he struggled to keep his eyes fully open despite his evident desire to continue their conversation.

"You need to rest," Lydia said gently. "The fire line took everything you had today."

He nodded reluctantly. "You're right. Though I find I'm reluctant to end this evening, perfect as it has been despite the circumstances that brought us here."

"There will be many more evenings," she promised. "A lifetime of them."

His smile at these words was worth every mile of their journey, every challenge they had faced or would face in the future. "A lifetime," he repeated, as if testing the weight and wonder of the concept. "I look forward to each one."

With obvious reluctance, he rose and moved to his side of the dwelling's dividing blanket. "Good night, Lydia," he said, his voice carrying a tenderness that wrapped around her like a physical embrace. "Sleep well."

"Good night, Joseph," she replied. "I thank God you came back safely to me today."

After he had disappeared behind the dividing blanket, Lydia prepared for sleep, her mind full of the day's events and the evening's revelations. From the crisis of the wildfire to the quiet intimacy of their conversation, it had been a day of extremes.

As she settled onto her sleeping pallet, she could hear Joseph's breathing already deepening into sleep on the other side of the divider. The sound brought unexpected comfort—the simple, human evidence of his presence nearby.

Lydia closed her eyes, feeling Montana's soil beneath her through the layers of furs and blankets. This land that had seemed so foreign when she first arrived now felt like home in the deepest sense of the word. Not because of familiar surroundings or comfortable routines, but because here she had found her truest self, and the man with whom she would build a future.

Chapter 30

Morning arrived with the gentle sounds of the settlement coming to life. Quiet conversations, children's laughter, and the domestic noises of breakfast preparations. Lydia woke feeling refreshed despite the unfamiliar sleeping arrangements. She braided her hair neatly and straightened her clothing as best she could, aware they would likely meet with Thomas early.

When she emerged from behind the dividing blanket, she found Joseph already awake and alert, stoking the small fire back to life. He looked considerably better than the previous evening, the night's rest having restored much of his usual vitality.

"Good morning," he greeted her, his eyes warming appreciatively as they took in her appearance. "Did you sleep well?"

"Surprisingly so," she admitted. "And you seem recovered. The rest did you good."

"Sarah's tea helped considerably," he acknowledged. "My lungs feel clearer this morning, and the worst of the fatigue has passed."

A soft call came from outside their dwelling. "Visitors approach," a woman's voice announced formally.

"Enter," Joseph responded, rising to his feet.

The entrance flap opened to reveal Sarah Dove carrying a basket covered with a cloth. Behind her stood Little Crow, his young face eager and excited.

"Morning meal," Sarah Dove announced, entering and setting the basket near the fire. "Thomas asks that you join him afterward, at the council circle. He wishes to speak with you both."

Little Crow darted forward. "Grandfather says there will be a special ceremony," he blurted, earning a gentle but reproving look from his grandmother.

"Little Crow, some matters are for elders to discuss first," she reminded him.

The boy looked momentarily abashed, but recovered quickly. "But I already know! I heard Grandmother telling Mother that the binding cord would be needed again, but permanent this time." He looked at Lydia with innocent directness. "Are you going to stay with us and be Joseph's wife? Mother says you draw pictures better than anyone she's ever seen, and that you understand our ways."

Sarah sighed, though a smile tugged at the corners of her mouth. "The boy hears everything, even when he pretends to be sleeping." She shooed him toward the entrance. "Go help your mother now. Tell her these two will come to the council circle after their meal."

Little Crow departed reluctantly, casting curious glances back at them until the entrance flap fell closed behind him.

Sarah turned to them, her expression becoming more serious. "Thomas spent much of the night in prayer and meditation after the fire danger passed. He believes your arrival at this precise time was significant. That your union represents something important not just for you, but for the community."

Joseph and Lydia exchanged glances, surprised by this pronouncement.

"In what way?" Joseph asked carefully.

Sarah opened the basket, revealing freshly baked bread, dried berries, and what appeared to be honey in a small clay pot. "That is for Thomas to explain, not me." She arranged the food on a clean cloth near the fire. "Eat, prepare yourselves. Important words await."

After she had gone, Joseph turned to Lydia with a raised eyebrow. "It seems our blessing may be more significant than we anticipated."

"Little Crow mentioned the binding cord 'permanent this time,'" Lydia recalled. "What do you think that means?"

Joseph's expression grew thoughtful as he broke the bread and offered her a piece. "During traditional Blackfoot marriages, a binding cord is sometimes wrapped around the couple's joined hands during their vows. It symbolizes their paths being permanently woven together." He poured tea from a small pot Sarah had included in the basket. "The temporary binding Sarah performed during our first visit was a recognition of possibility. A permanent binding would be a formal acknowledgment of commitment."

Lydia accepted the tea, considering this. "So Thomas intends to perform a traditional Blackfoot marriage ceremony for us?"

"It appears so," Joseph confirmed. "Though we should hear his explanation before making assumptions." He hesitated, studying her face. "Would that be acceptable to you? Understanding that we would still be legally married in Bozeman afterward?"

"More than acceptable," she assured him. "I find it deeply meaningful that Thomas would honor us this way. That he would include us in his people's traditions."

Relief and pleasure mingled in Joseph's expression. "I feel the same." He reached across the space between them to take her hand. "To be blessed by both cultures, Blackfoot and Christian, feels right. A reflection of how our journey together has bridged different worlds."

They ate quickly but gratefully, aware that Thomas was waiting. The bread was still warm, clearly freshly baked that morning, and the honey added a perfect sweetness to complement the tartness of the dried berries.

As they left the dwelling, Lydia was struck by the changed atmosphere in the settlement compared to the previous evening. Despite the recent fire emergency, a sense of quiet anticipation had settled over the community. People they passed offered smiles and respectful nods, clearly aware of the ceremony that would likely take place.

The council circle was located in a flat, open area at the center of the settlement. Thomas sat on a woven mat, his silver-streaked hair gleaming in the morning sun. Beside him, several elders had gathered, including Morning Sky's grandfather and two older women Lydia recognized from previous cooking preparations. Sarah Dove sat slightly apart, arranging various items on a beautifully tanned deerskin.

As Joseph and Lydia approached, Thomas rose to greet them, his movements deliberate and dignified despite his advanced years.

"Welcome," he said, extending his hands in formal greeting. "Please, sit with us."

He indicated two mats positioned directly across from his own. Joseph and Lydia settled themselves as directed, aware of the ceremonial atmosphere that filled the space.

Thomas studied them for a long moment before speaking. "Last night, as our people fought the flames that threatened our lands, I was reminded of an ancient teaching. Our elders say that in times of greatest danger, the Creator often provides unexpected strength." His gaze moved between them. "Your arrival precisely when needed was not coincidence."

Lydia felt Joseph tense slightly beside her, attentive to Thomas's words.

"When you first came to us," Thomas continued, addressing Lydia, "you were a visitor seeking images for your eastern papers. We saw your respect, your willingness to learn rather than judge. When you defended our right to our treaty lands, you became more than a visitor."

He turned to Joseph. "And you, who once walked a path of destruction, returned to walk a path of protection. Yesterday, your knowledge helped save our hunting grounds from the flames."

Thomas gestured to the gathered elders. "We have spoken together this morning. When Sarah Dove told us you seek blessing for your union, we understood more clearly what the Creator intends."

Sarah moved forward, placing the deerskin with its arranged items between them and Thomas. Lydia could now see what had been prepared: the white leather binding cord, now elaborately decorated with additional bead work and feathers; two small pouches of different colors; a beautifully crafted pipe; and a shallow bowl containing what appeared to be sacred herbs.

"Among our people," Thomas explained, "marriage is not merely the joining of two individuals but the strengthening of the entire community. When two rivers flow together, all who live along the new river benefit from its increased strength."

He leaned forward, his expression intensifying. "The Garrett brothers and others like them seek to destroy what remains of our way of life. Their fire was aimed at our very survival. I believe the Creator has joined your paths not only for your happiness, but for a greater purpose."

Joseph spoke respectfully. "What purpose do you see, Elder Thomas?"

"A bridge between worlds," Thomas replied without hesitation. "Your union represents something new, yet anchored in respect for what has come before. As the old ways of the buffalo hunts fade and new patterns emerge, we need those who understand both worlds, who can speak truth that others will hear."

Lydia felt the weight of these words settle around them. This was far more than a simple blessing; Thomas was describing a role, a responsibility that extended beyond their personal relationship.

"Sarah Dove's dreams have shown this path," Thomas continued. "A future where your joined strength creates protection for this land and its people." He gestured toward the binding cord. "If you accept this understanding of your union, we offer our most sacred blessing."

Joseph and Lydia exchanged glances, a silent communication passing between them. They had come seeking a simple acknowledgment of their commitment. Thomas was offering something more profound, a place within the community's future, and a shared purpose that transcended cultural boundaries.

"We would be honored," Joseph said, his voice steady and sure. "Though I must ask if this changes your people's expectations of our lives after. We still intend to live at my ranch, to build our life there."

Thomas nodded understanding. "The river must follow its natural course. We ask only that you remember this connection. That your hearts remain open to our people's needs as the world continues to change around us."

"That we can promise," Lydia affirmed.

Thomas seemed satisfied with their response. He gestured to Sarah Dove, who began preparing the ceremonial elements with practiced movements.

"Normally, such a joining would involve many preparations and the entire community," Thomas explained. "But circumstances call for adaptation. The essence remains the same, the Creator's recognition of two paths becoming one."

Sarah lit a small bundle of sage and cedar, the fragrant smoke rising between them. Thomas took the bundle and moved it in a circular pattern that encompassed both Joseph and Lydia.

"This smoke carries our prayers upward," he explained. "It cleanses the space between us and opens our hearts to truth."

What followed was unlike any wedding ceremony Lydia had ever witnessed. Thomas spoke in his native tongue, translated occasionally when he wished for them to understand specific elements. The elders joined in at certain points, their voices rising in harmonized chants that seemed to vibrate with ancient power.

The binding cord was central to the ritual. Thomas instructed Joseph and Lydia to join their right hands, palm to palm. Unlike the previous ceremony where Sarah had simply laid the cord across their hands, Thomas now wrapped it three times around their joined wrists, securing it with an intricate knot that left the decorated ends hanging free.

"Three circles," he explained. "For past, present, and future. The cord joins your life paths, as the Creator has already joined your spirits."

Sarah Dove brought forward the two small pouches. "Earth from your ranch," she said to Joseph, "and clay from the sacred valley's shore," she added to Lydia. "Gathered during my own journeys, saved for this moment."

Thomas instructed them to each take a pinch from both pouches and combine them in their free hands. "Two lands becoming one," he said as they mixed the soils together. "A symbol of worlds joining."

The mixture was returned to the earth at their feet, a small but powerful gesture of commitment to the land itself.

The ceremonial pipe was lit, and Thomas drew deeply before passing it to Joseph, who followed the elder's example. When it came to Lydia, she hesitated only briefly before accepting it. The smoke was surprisingly mild, aromatic with herbs she couldn't identify. She understood this was not merely a ritual but a spiritual sealing of promises.

After the pipe had been passed among all present, Thomas returned to the binding cord still wrapped around their joined hands. He spoke directly to them now, his voice carrying the weight of formal acknowledgment.

"Before the Creator and this community of witnesses, your paths are now recognized as one. What was begun in your hearts is now visible to all. The journey ahead will know both sunshine and storm, calm waters and dangerous rapids. Remember always that two trees growing side by side withstand winds that would topple either alone."

He addressed the gathered elders. "Do you acknowledge this union and offer your blessing?"

Each elder spoke in turn, formal words in their native language that needed no translation. Their expressions and tones conveyed approval, blessing, and welcome.

Thomas returned his attention to Joseph and Lydia. "Now you must speak your promises to each other. Not words learned from others, but truth from your own hearts. The cord binds your hands as a symbol, but only your freely given words can truly bind your lives."

Joseph's gray eyes met Lydia's, steady and certain. His voice, when he spoke, carried a depth of emotion that made her heart swell.

"Lydia Hayes, you came into my life unexpectedly, challenging every wall I had built around myself. You saw beauty where I had forgotten to look, possibility where I saw only limitation." His fingers tightened gently around hers beneath the binding cord. "I promise to love you through all seasons, to protect and respect you, to walk beside you rather than ahead or behind. I promise to build with you a life rooted in faith, honesty, and mutual purpose." He paused, his voice roughening slightly. "I once believed my path must be traveled alone as penance for past mistakes. You've shown me a better truth. That redemption lies not in isolation but in connection, in using what remains of our days to create something worthy of the grace we've been given."

Tears pricked at Lydia's eyes as she absorbed the profound simplicity of his vows. When it was her turn to speak, she drew a steadying breath.

"Joseph Calloway, when I first came west, I was seeking new landscapes to capture with my art. Instead, I found a new landscape within myself." Her voice grew stronger as she continued. "You've shown me a way of being in the world that values substance over appearance, integrity over convenience, and genuine connection over social advantage. I promise to stand beside you through whatever challenges we face, to build our home on foundations of faith and respect. I promise to remember always that our joining is not just for our happiness, but for a purpose greater than ourselves." She smiled through gathering tears. "I came to Montana seeking artistic inspiration. I found instead the other half of my heart."

Thomas nodded approvingly at their words. He placed his weathered hands over their bound ones.

"What has been joined by the Creator and acknowledged by this community is a bond that transcends mere words or ceremonies. It exists now in the fabric of your lives." He began unwinding the binding cord, but instead of removing it completely, he tied the ends together, creating a continuous circle. "Keep this as a reminder of what has been sealed today. In times of difficulty, let it remind you of promises made and strength found in union."

He handed the now-circular cord to Lydia, who accepted it with reverent care.

"You are now joined in the eyes of our people and before the Creator," Thomas concluded. "May your path together bring strength to both your hearts and to the wider circles of community your lives will touch."

As the ceremony concluded, Lydia became aware of a small crowd that had gathered at a respectful distance. Sarah had mentioned the private nature of this initial ceremony, but it seemed news had spread throughout the settlement. Little Crow stood at the front, barely containing his excitement, while behind him gathered many members of the community they had come to know.

Joseph's hand, now free of the binding cord but still holding hers, squeezed gently. "It seems we have witnesses after all," he murmured.

Thomas rose to his feet, turning to address the gathered community. "The joining has been completed," he announced. "Tonight we will feast to honor this union that strengthens all our lives."

A murmur of approval ran through the crowd. People came forward to offer congratulations and express joy at their union. Michael clasped Joseph's arm in the traditional greeting of equals, while Morning Sky approached Lydia with a small gift, a beaded bracelet she had apparently worked on through the night.

"To remember us," she said simply as she tied it around Lydia's wrist.

The remainder of the day passed in a blur of activity. Despite the recent fire crisis, the community insisted on preparing a celebration feast for that evening. Lydia found herself welcomed into the women's cooking preparations not as a visitor to be taught, but as a new member with skills to contribute. She helped grind corn and prepare bread dough, her artistic hands proving adept at shaping the traditional pattern Sarah Dove demonstrated.

Joseph, meanwhile, was invited to join the men, checking the fire lines one final time. Lydia watched him ride out with Michael and several others, her heart swelling with pride at his easy acceptance among these people who had once been strangers to them both.

As the women worked, conversation flowed around Lydia, sometimes directed at her, sometimes simply including her in its natural rhythm. She noticed Sarah Dove watching her occasionally, satisfaction evident in the elder woman's expression.

"You were right," Lydia said quietly when they found themselves working side by side. "About everything you saw in your dreams."

Sarah nodded, her hands continuing their practiced motions with the bread dough. "The Creator shows what is needed, not always what is expected. Your path with Joseph serves many purposes beyond your own happiness."

"Thomas spoke of being a bridge between worlds," Lydia recalled. "That seems a significant responsibility."

"It is," Sarah agreed. "But one you are both prepared for, each in your own way. Joseph, with his understanding of the land and its changes, you with your ability to capture truth in ways others will see and believe."

The realization settled over Lydia. Her artistic talent wasn't merely a personal passion or professional pursuit; it could serve a greater purpose in documenting and preserving cultural truth at a time of profound transition. The sketches she had made of the Blackfoot community, showing their dignity, their connection to the land, and their complex cultural practices, could speak to Eastern audiences in ways written reports or politics never could.

By evening, the celebration was ready. The entire community gathered around an enlarged central fire, with Joseph and Lydia given places of honor near Thomas and the other elders. The meal was abundant despite the community's recent challenges. Venison and rabbit, corn cakes, dried berries reconstituted into sweet sauces, roots, and herbs prepared in traditional ways.

Little Crow appointed himself their personal guide to the feast, explaining each dish's significance with the solemn importance of a child entrusted with cultural knowledge. "This sauce is made from chokecherries gathered when the moon was full," he informed them seriously. "Grandmother says it brings sweetness to the journey ahead."

After the meal, music and storytelling began. Several men played drums, while others produced flutes carved from various woods, each with its distinctive voice. Little Crow proudly joined the musicians with his flute, his earnest concentration bringing smiles to many faces.

Thomas told stories of the community's history, of challenges faced and overcome through generations. Joseph surprised Lydia by adding his harmonica to the musical interludes, the instrument's voice blending unexpectedly well with the traditional sounds.

As the evening progressed, Sarah Dove appeared at Lydia's side with a small leather pouch. "For your journey tomorrow," she explained, handing it to Lydia. "Herbs for tea that will ease the body after long riding, and something special." She leaned closer, lowering her voice. "A small bundle of sage and sweet grass. When you reach Joseph's ranch, your ranch now, burn it in the four directions around your home. It cleanses the space for your new beginning together."

Lydia accepted the gift with heartfelt thanks, touched by the practical and spiritual thoughtfulness it represented.

The celebration continued until the moon rose high above the settlement.

Chapter 31

Lydia woke to the sound of birdsong filtering through the dwelling's smoke hole, her fingers already reaching for the circular binding cord she'd kept beside her sleeping pallet. The smooth, beaded leather felt warm against her skin, as though it had absorbed some essential energy from yesterday's ceremony. On the other side of the divider, she heard Joseph stirring, the quiet rustling of blankets and the deep inhale that signaled his awakening.

"Lydia?" His voice, sleep-roughened but gentle, carried across the space between them. "Are you awake?"

"Yes," she replied, sitting up and quickly plaiting her loosened hair. "Good morning."

"Good morning," he echoed, and she could hear the smile in his voice. "Wife."

The word sent a flutter through her chest. Wife. Not yet by the laws of Montana Territory or the standards of New York society, but in every way that mattered to her heart and to the community that had embraced them.

"Husband," she returned, testing the word and finding it felt perfectly natural, as though she'd been meant to address him this way all along.

The dividing blanket rustled, and Joseph's hand appeared at its edge, reaching around rather than through, respecting the boundary still necessary until their Christian ceremony in Bozeman. Lydia reached out, lacing her fingers with his.

"Did you sleep well?" he asked.

"Better than I've ever slept," she admitted. "I feel... at peace."

His thumb traced small circles against her palm. "I know what you mean. It's as though something that was unsettled has finally found its proper place."

A call from outside interrupted their quiet moment. "Morning comes! The sun waits for no one, not even newly joined paths!"

Lydia recognized Sarah Dove's voice, practical yet warm with humor. Joseph chuckled, releasing her hand.

"Sarah has always believed sleeping past sunrise is a waste of good daylight," he explained. "We'd better ready ourselves, or she'll come in and rouse us properly."

They dressed quickly on their respective sides of the divider. Lydia donned her riding clothes, the split skirt and practical blouse that had become her standard attire during their journey. She tucked the binding cord carefully into her satchel, nestling it between sketchbook pages for safekeeping.

When she emerged from behind the divider, Joseph stood waiting. He looked more handsome than ever, his tall frame outlined by morning light filtering through the entrance flap, his gray eyes warm with an emotion that needed no verbal expression.

"Ready for our journey to Bozeman, Mrs. Calloway?" he asked, extending his hand.

She placed her hand in his. "More than ready, Mr. Calloway."

Outside, the settlement bustled with morning activity that seemed to center around their departure. Women moved purposefully between dwellings carrying bundles, while men prepared their horses and checked saddle cinches. Children darted about, their excitement palpable.

"What's happening?" Lydia asked as they stepped into the cool morning air.

Sarah Dove approached, carrying a bundle wrapped in deerskin. "Preparations for your journey," she explained. "Among our people, when paths join, the community provides what is needed for the road ahead."

"That's not necessary," Joseph protested gently. "You've done so much already."

Thomas appeared beside his wife, his dignified presence commanding respectful attention. "It is necessary," he corrected. "Not because you lack, but because it strengthens the bonds between us. To refuse would deny us the blessing of giving."

Joseph inclined his head in acceptance. "Thank you. We're honored."

Over a breakfast shared with Thomas, Sarah, and several elders, the couple learned the extent of the community's generosity. They were being given provisions for their journey to Bozeman, but more significantly, several items meant to establish their life together once they reached Joseph's ranch.

"From the women, cooking vessels and a wedding blanket," Sarah explained, gesturing to where Morning Sky and others were carefully packing a distinctive, intricately woven blanket into a bundle. "Many hands worked late to finish it, each woman adding her own pattern section for prosperity and many children."

Lydia felt her cheeks warm at this last comment, but accepted the gift with genuine gratitude.

"The men have prepared these," Michael added, showing them finely crafted leather saddlebags decorated with geometric designs. "For carrying what matters most between dwellings."

Little Crow could barely contain himself, hopping from foot to foot beside his grandfather. "Tell them about my gift!" he urged, tugging at Thomas's sleeve.

Thomas smiled indulgently. "Patience, young one. Everything in its proper time."

As they finished their meal, Joseph leaned closer to Lydia. "This level of generosity is extraordinary," he murmured. "It speaks to how deeply Thomas believes in the significance of our union."

"It humbles me," she admitted. "When I first arrived in Montana Territory, I never imagined being welcomed this way into a community so different from my own."

"Not so different in the ways that truly matter," Joseph observed. "Faith, family, connection to something larger than oneself, these values transcend the boundaries we humans so often create."

Their conversation was interrupted as Michael approached with Thunder and Penny, both horses brushed to gleaming perfection and adorned with beaded decorations on their bridles.

"For the journey of newly joined paths," he explained, handing the reins to Joseph. "May they carry you safely to your next dwelling place."

As Joseph inspected the horses, Lydia felt a tug at her skirt. Little Crow stood beside her, holding something behind his back, his expression a mixture of pride and shyness.

"When you have children, you must bring them here so I can teach them to carve and play the flute."

"We will," Joseph promised, coming to stand beside Lydia. He placed his hand on the boy's shoulder. "And perhaps you'll visit our ranch someday, when you're older."

"I would like that," Little Crow said solemnly. "Grandmother says I will travel far one day."

Sarah Dove's eyes sparkled with mysterious knowledge as she joined them. "The boy has his own path to follow, in time. But for now—" she turned to Joseph and Lydia, "—you must begin yours. The journey to Bozeman is long, and it's best to cover a good distance before the heat of day."

Final preparations moved swiftly. Their horses were loaded with provisions and gifts, with Thomas personally overseeing the distribution of weight for the animals' comfort. As they prepared to mount, the elder raised his hands for attention.

"Before our friends depart, we offer one final blessing," he announced to the gathered community.

At his signal, several men brought forward a small fire in a portable stone container. Thomas took a handful of herbs from a pouch at his waist and cast them into the flames. Sweet-smelling smoke billowed upward.

"Stand together," he instructed Joseph and Lydia.

They obeyed, standing side by side before the elder. Thomas used an eagle feather to direct the fragrant smoke toward them, first over their heads, then across their bodies, while speaking words in his native language that needed no translation to communicate their reverent intent.

"May the Creator guide your steps in all seasons," he said in English. "May your dwelling be filled with enough—enough food to satisfy, enough warmth for comfort, enough love to sustain through difficulty, and enough wisdom to walk in balance."

"And enough children to carry your legacy," Sarah Dove added with twinkling eyes, causing ripples of appreciative laughter among the community.

Joseph's hand found Lydia's, warm and steady. "Thank you," he said, his voice carrying clearly to all gathered. "For your wisdom, your acceptance, and your belief in what we might become together."

Lydia nodded her agreement, too moved for words. This place, these people, had transformed her understanding of community, of connection to the land, and of her own purpose. The changes would remain part of her always, no matter where her path with Joseph might lead.

As they prepared to mount their horses, Morning Sky stepped forward with one last gift, a small leather pouch on a cord.

"Medicine bag," she explained, placing it over Lydia's head. "Protection for the journey ahead. My grandmother says all good marriages need both blessing and protection." Her eyes crinkled with humor. "Especially when the bride is as strong-willed as this one."

Joseph chuckled. "Wise grandmother."

With final embraces and well-wishes, they mounted their horses. The entire settlement gathered to witness their departure, forming an honor line along the path that would lead them back toward Bozeman.

"Tell my story," Thomas called as they began to move away. "Show our truth to those who would not hear it otherwise."

"I will," Lydia promised, commitment settling deep in her heart. Her art would serve not just beauty but truth, capturing the dignity and complexity of lives too often reduced to simplistic stereotypes by those who had never bothered to truly see.

Little Crow ran alongside their horses for several yards, his young legs keeping pace with surprising stamina. "Remember to put the eagles I carved for you somewhere high," he instructed breathlessly. "So they can see the sky!"

"We'll place them in the perfect spot," Joseph assured him, reaching down to ruffle the boy's hair. "Now return to your grandmother before she worries."

The boy reluctantly fell back, waving vigorously until they crested the first rise that would take them out of sight of the settlement.

As the sounds of the community faded behind them, Joseph and Lydia settled into the comfortable rhythm of travel that had become second nature during their weeks together. The Montana landscape stretched before them, vast and magnificent beneath the clear morning sky, promising adventure and challenge in equal measure.

"Three days to Bozeman, if weather permits," Joseph estimated, guiding Thunder alongside Penny so they could ride together where the trail allowed. "Are you nervous about the Christian ceremony?"

Lydia considered the question honestly. "Not about the ceremony itself," she decided. "But about what comes after. There will be telegrams to send to my family, explanations to make to National Geographic..."

"Second thoughts?" Joseph asked, his tone carefully neutral, though Lydia could detect the hint of uncertainty beneath.

"Not one," she assured him firmly. "I'm precisely where I'm meant to be, Joseph. With exactly whom I'm meant to be with. The rest is just... details to be managed."

Relief softened his features. "I'm glad. Because I've been thinking about our future at the ranch, and I have some ideas I'd like to share with you."

As they rode through the morning, Joseph outlined his vision for their life together. The ranch house would need expansion—a proper studio with north-facing windows for Lydia's art, additional bedrooms for the family they hoped to have, and perhaps a larger kitchen where they could welcome neighbors and friends.

"The land east of the current boundary has good water access," he explained, his hands gesturing expressively as he described terrain features. "Perfect for expanding the herd, eventually. And there's a stand of old-growth pines that would provide excellent building material."

Lydia listened, offering suggestions and questions that revealed her growing understanding of ranch operations. Her artistic eye envisioned improvements to the house, while her practical nature—nurtured through their journey—considered the work and resources each change would require.

"We'll need to be patient," Joseph acknowledged. "Build our dream in stages as resources permit. But I want you to know I'm committed to creating a home that supports your art as much as my ranching."

"And I want a home that supports both," Lydia countered. "Not competing priorities, but complementary parts of our shared life."

They stopped at midday beside a small stream, dismounting to rest the horses and share a simple meal from their provisions. Sitting side by side on sun-warmed rocks, they continued their planning, dreams taking shape through shared conversation.

"I've been thinking about my commitment to Thomas," Lydia said, breaking a piece of journey bread to share with Joseph. "About documenting their community truthfully."

"What are you considering?" Joseph asked.

"Beyond the National Geographic commission, I'd like to create a more comprehensive portfolio. Paintings, perhaps, not just sketches. Something that captures what I've learned about the Blackfoot, not as subjects of anthropological curiosity, but as people adapting to profound change while maintaining their essential dignity and values."

Joseph nodded thoughtfully. "It would be important work. Especially as more settlers arrive and pressure on traditional lands increases."

"Would you help me?" Lydia asked. "Your understanding of both worlds would be invaluable."

"Of course," he agreed without hesitation. "Though I suspect you already see more clearly than most who've lived here far longer."

As they prepared to continue their journey, Joseph helped Lydia mount, his hands lingering at her waist slightly longer than necessary. The simple contact sent warmth through her despite the afternoon heat.

"Three more nights," he murmured, his voice low enough that only she could hear. "Then no more dividing blankets between us."

Lydia felt her cheeks flush, but she met his eyes steadily. "Three nights," she agreed. "Though I suspect they'll pass quite slowly."

His laugh, rich and unreserved, carried across the open landscape. It struck Lydia how rarely she'd heard that sound during their early days together, how Joseph's natural reserve had gradually yielded to genuine joy in her presence. The transformation seemed emblematic of their entire journey together—barriers lowered, truth acknowledged, connection deepened through shared experience.

They rode through the afternoon, the familiar Montana landscape taking on new significance as Lydia viewed it through the lens of permanence rather than temporary visitation. These mountains, valleys, and rivers would form the backdrop of her life with Joseph. The thought filled her with quiet exhilaration.

As evening approached, they made camp in a protected hollow beside a small creek. The routine of setting up camp had become so familiar that they moved in efficient tandem, each anticipating the other's needs without discussion. Joseph tended the horses while

Lydia gathered wood and started a small fire. They prepared a simple meal from their provisions, supplemented by fresh berries Joseph had spotted and gathered along the trail.

As twilight deepened into night, they sat beside the fire, shoulders touching. Joseph removed his mother's Bible from his saddlebag, opening it to a passage that seemed particularly meaningful.

"'And now these three remain: faith, hope and love. But the greatest of these is love,'" he read, his deep voice giving the familiar words renewed significance. "I've always appreciated this verse, but never understood its depth until recently."

"How do you see it now?" Lydia asked, watching the firelight play across his strong features.

"Before, I recognized it intellectually as truth. Now—" his eyes met hers across the small space between them "—I understand it experientially. Faith sustains us through uncertainty, hope gives us courage to continue when the path seems unclear, but love..." He paused, searching for the right words. "Love transforms everything it touches. It makes burdens lighter when shared, joys deeper when celebrated together, and even ordinary moments somehow sacred."

Lydia's heart swelled at this unexpected eloquence from her usually taciturn companion. "Joseph Calloway, you've been hiding a poet's soul beneath that practical exterior."

He chuckled softly. "Don't tell the neighboring ranchers. They'd never let me hear the end of it."

As the night deepened around their small campfire, they talked of practical matters—the telegram they would send to her parents once they reached Bozeman, the minister Joseph knew who could perform their Christian ceremony, the supplies they would need for the ranch. But beneath these logistics ran a current of deeper connection, of shared understanding that transcended the words themselves.

Eventually, Joseph rose reluctantly. "We should rest. Tomorrow will be another full day of travel."

Following their established pattern, they prepared their bedrolls on opposite sides of the fire, maintaining the propriety both still valued despite their Blackfoot marriage ceremony. As Joseph spread his blanket, Lydia watched him with quiet appreciation. This man, so different from anyone she had known in New York, had become the center of her world through a journey neither could have anticipated.

"Joseph," she said softly as he turned to bid her goodnight. "I want you to know something."

He paused, waiting attentively.

"When I first came west, I was seeking adventure, artistic opportunity, perhaps a brief taste of independence before returning to the life expected of me." She met his eyes across the fire between them. "I never imagined finding someone who would see me so completely, who would value both my strengths and my struggles."

Joseph's expression softened. "God's plans often surprise us," he observed. "Especially when we think we've already determined our own path."

"Yes," she agreed. "And I'm profoundly grateful for His unexpected direction."

"As am I," Joseph replied, his voice deepening with emotion. "Sleep well, Lydia. Tomorrow brings us one day closer to beginning our life together."

"Goodnight, Joseph."

Despite her physical fatigue from the day's journey, Lydia lay awake for some time, listening to the night sounds of Montana Territory—the distant call of a hunting owl, the soft rustle of wind through surrounding grasses, the occasional snap from their dying fire. The vastness of the star-scattered sky above made her feel simultaneously small and significant, a paradox she was learning to embrace.

The next two days followed a similar pattern, each mile bringing them closer to Bozeman and their Christian wedding ceremony. Joseph grew increasingly animated as they approached familiar territory, pointing out landmarks and sharing stories connected to each location. Lydia found his enthusiasm endearing, recognizing it as an expression of his desire to integrate her fully into the world he loved.

"There," he said on the afternoon of their third day, pointing toward a distant cluster of buildings. "Bozeman. We should arrive before sunset."

Lydia studied the growing settlement with new eyes. When she had first arrived weeks ago, Bozeman had seemed disappointingly primitive compared to her New York expectations. Now, after experiencing the true wilderness of Montana Territory, the small frontier town appeared positively civilized, with its wooden sidewalks and actual glass windows.

"Will Martha Tipton be surprised to see us returning together?" she asked, recalling the observant hotel owner who had first introduced them.

Joseph chuckled. "Martha is rarely surprised by anything. She probably predicted our outcome the moment she saw us arguing in her dining room."

As they rode into town in the golden light of late afternoon, Lydia felt curious gazes following their progress. Their appearance told a story even without words, their matched travel-stained clothing, the beaded decorations on their horses' bridles, and the unmistakable closeness in how they rode side by side.

Joseph led them directly to a modest white clapboard building with a small cross mounted above its entrance. "Reverend Hollister's church," he explained. "He's a good man, practical but devout. I thought we might speak with him first about the ceremony."

Lydia nodded agreement, suddenly feeling a flutter of nerves. The Blackfoot ceremony had felt organic, a natural extension of their journey together. This more conventional step, with its connections to her past life and family expectations, carried a different emotional weight.

Joseph sensed her hesitation. "Second thoughts?" he asked quietly as they dismounted.

"Not about marrying you," she clarified quickly. "Just... awareness of worlds colliding. My New York past meeting my Montana future."

Understanding softened his expression. "We'll navigate it together," he promised. "One step at a time."

The reverend proved to be exactly as Joseph had described—a practical man of faith with kind eyes and a no-nonsense manner. He listened to their unusual situation with interest rather than judgment.

"So you've had a traditional Blackfoot ceremony, and now seek a Christian blessing on your union," he summarized, stroking his neatly trimmed beard. "Unusual, but not unprecedented on the frontier. Many couples find themselves far from conventional churches when love finds them."

"It's important to us that our marriage be recognized both by the Blackfoot community who have become our friends, and by the laws and faith traditions we both value," Joseph explained.

Reverend Hollister nodded approvingly. "A thoughtful approach. I'd be pleased to perform the ceremony. When did you have in mind?"

Joseph looked at Lydia for her preference.

"Tomorrow, if possible," she said with newfound decisiveness. "We've waited long enough."

The reverend's eyes twinkled with amusement. "Tomorrow it is, then. Say, noon? That will give word time to spread so any in town who wish to witness can attend."

That settled, they thanked the minister and returned to their horses. Their next stop was Martha Tipton's hotel, where they would spend their last night before becoming legally married.

Martha's reaction to their return confirmed Joseph's prediction. The capable hotel owner took one look at them standing together in her lobby and broke into a broad smile.

"Well, well," she said, hands on her ample hips. "If this isn't exactly what I expected when I introduced you two." Her sharp eyes noted the beaded decorations on their clothing, the subtle changes in how they stood together. "Though I'm guessing there's quite a story behind how you got from bickering in my dining room to returning as a couple."

"More than we could possibly relate in one evening," Joseph acknowledged with a smile. "Though we're happy to share the abbreviated version over dinner, if you're interested."

"Oh, I'm interested all right," Martha assured them. She reached behind the counter and produced two room keys. "But I'm assuming you'll be wanting separate rooms just one more night." She placed significant emphasis on the last three words, her expression knowingly amused.

Lydia felt heat rise to her cheeks, but Joseph handled the moment with easy grace. "Indeed, Mrs. Tipton. We'll be married by Reverend Hollister tomorrow at noon."

"Wonderful!" Martha exclaimed. "I'll spread the word. Bozeman sees too few proper weddings, and folks will be delighted to celebrate with you." She handed them their keys. "Now, go get cleaned up from your journey. Dinner's at six, and I expect that abbreviated story you promised."

In her room, the same one she'd occupied during her first stay in Bozeman, Lydia noted with amusement, she unpacked her few belongings and gratefully used the basin of warm water Martha had sent up to wash away the trail dust. Changing into the one clean dress she had with her, she felt the curious sensation of straddling two worlds. The dress, with its eastern styling and fitted bodice, belonged to her past life; yet the woman wearing it had been fundamentally changed by Montana's vast landscapes and the man she would marry tomorrow.

When she descended to the dining room, she found Joseph already waiting, similarly transformed by clean clothing and freshly trimmed hair. His eyes widened appreciatively as she approached.

"You look beautiful," he said, rising to hold her chair. "Though I've grown rather fond of your practical riding attire as well."

"And you look quite handsome yourself," she returned, noting how the simple act of a haircut and clean shirt highlighted his strong features. "Though I suspect you're as uncomfortable in what, I assume, is a borrowed shirt complete with a collar, as I am in these stays."

His genuine laugh drew curious glances from other diners. "Another thing we agree on," he said as he took his seat across from her. "Perhaps our house rules should include sensible clothing within our own four walls."

"A fine first decree for our household," Lydia agreed with a smile.

Martha joined them as promised, bringing a bottle of her "special occasion" cider and three glasses. "On the house," she announced, pouring generously. "Now, I want to hear everything. How did you go from this man complaining about escorting an Eastern lady through the wilderness to returning as a couple about to be married?"

Over a leisurely dinner, they shared the highlights of their journey, the ranch, the Valley of Standing Stones, their growing understanding of each other, the Blackfoot community, and eventually, their decision to build a life together in Montana Territory.

Martha listened with evident fascination, occasionally interrupting with perceptive questions. When they described the Blackfoot wedding ceremony, her eyes grew misty, though she quickly blinked away the emotion.

"That's quite a story," she said when they'd finished. "More romantic than any novel I've read, and all the better for being true." She raised her glass. "To unexpected journeys and the courage to follow where they lead."

They touched glasses, the simple toast capturing the essence of their experience together. After dinner, they lingered over coffee, discussing practical aspects of their future plans.

When they finally bid Martha goodnight and climbed the stairs to their separate rooms for the last time, Joseph paused at Lydia's door.

"Tomorrow," he said softly, taking her hands in his.

"Tomorrow," she echoed, the single word carrying a world of anticipation.

He lifted her hands to his lips, pressing a kiss to each palm before releasing them. "Sleep well, Lydia. I'll see you at the church."

In her room, Lydia opened her satchel and carefully removed her mother's Bible, the binding cord from the Blackfoot ceremony, and the wooden eagles Little Crow had carved. She arranged them on the small table beside her bed, tangible reminders of the journey that had brought her to this moment. From her window, she could see the Montana stars, brilliant and countless, against the black velvet sky. The same stars that had witnessed their conversations around countless campfires, their gradual discovery of each other, and finally, their commitment to a shared future.

"Thank You, God," she whispered, the simple prayer encompassing more gratitude than elaborate words could express.

Chapter 32

Morning brought clear skies and a flurry of activity at the hotel. Word of the wedding had indeed spread quickly through Bozeman, and Martha had taken it upon herself to arrange certain details the couple hadn't considered. Flowers for the church, a special luncheon to follow the ceremony, even a small cake commissioned from the wife of the general store owner.

"You can thank me by naming your first daughter Martha," the hotel owner declared when Lydia expressed gratitude for these unexpected arrangements. "Now, let's get you ready. A bride deserves some fussing over, even on the frontier."

With Martha's experienced assistance, Lydia's travel-worn appearance was transformed. Her hair was arranged in an elegant twist, adorned with small white flowers from Martha's personal garden. Her dress, though simple by New York standards, had been skillfully pressed to remove travel wrinkles.

"Something old, something new, something borrowed, something blue," Martha recited, producing a delicate lace handkerchief. "This was my mother's—that's your 'old.' Tuck it in your sleeve for luck."

Lydia accepted the handkerchief, touched by the thoughtful gesture. "What about the others?"

"Your dress is borrowed from your old life," Martha said with practical wisdom. "The flowers in your hair are newly picked this morning. And for blue—" She hesitated. "I'm not sure..."

"I have that covered," Lydia smiled, retrieving the beaded bracelet Morning Sky had given her. The predominant color in its intricate pattern was a deep, rich blue. "A gift from a friend in the Blackfoot settlement."

Martha nodded approval. "Perfect. Now, it's almost time. Are you ready?"

Lydia took a deep breath, centering herself in the certainty of her choice. "More ready than I've ever been for anything."

A knock at the door announced the arrival of their escort, the town's mayor, who had volunteered to walk the bride to the church in the absence of her father. He was a jovial man with impressive whiskers and a formal black coat somewhat at odds with the frontier setting, but his gallant manners reminded Lydia pleasantly of home.

The short walk to the church provided a moment of reflection. Bozeman's citizens paused in their daily activities to offer smiles and good wishes as she passed, many planning to attend the ceremony. This place, initially so foreign to her sensibilities, now felt welcoming in its straightforward acceptance of her choice.

The church, small and unassuming from the outside, had been transformed within by Martha's organizational skills and the contributions of local women. Wildflowers adorned the simple wooden pews, and extra chairs had been brought in to accommodate the unexpectedly large turnout.

And there, waiting at the altar beside Reverend Hollister, stood Joseph. His expression as he watched her walk toward him contained such naked emotion that Lydia felt tears threaten. This man, who had once hidden his feelings beneath layers of stoic reserve, now allowed his love to show plainly for all to witness.

The ceremony itself was both familiar in its traditional structure and uniquely personal. Reverend Hollister had thoughtfully incorporated elements that acknowledged their unusual journey, references to God's guidance through wilderness, the joining of different worlds through love, and the building of new traditions while honoring established ones.

When the time came to exchange vows, Joseph spoke first, his voice steady and clear.

"Lydia, when you arrived in Montana Territory, I saw only what I expected to see, an Eastern woman with unrealistic expectations of the frontier. I was wrong in ways I'm still discovering." His gray eyes held hers with unwavering focus. "You've shown me that some barriers exist only in our minds, that forgiveness is possible, even for mistakes I thought unforgivable, and that God's grace often arrives in forms we least expect."

He took her hands in his. "I promise to love you through all seasons of our life together. To protect without constraining, to support your gifts and dreams as fervently as my own, to face whatever challenges arise as true partners. With God as my witness, I commit myself to you fully and without reservation, from this day forward."

Lydia blinked back tears as she prepared to speak her own vows, her heart so full it seemed impossible to express.

"Joseph, I came west seeking new landscapes to capture with my art. Instead, I found the landscape of my own heart transformed." Her voice grew stronger as she continued. "You've taught me to see beneath surfaces, to value substance over appearance, to recognize God's handiwork in places I might otherwise have overlooked."

She squeezed his hands gently. "I promise to build our life together on foundations of faith, respect, and mutual purpose. To face hardships with courage and celebrate joys with gratitude. To remember always that our union is both gift and responsibility, blessed by God and witnessed by communities that span different worlds. With full awareness of the path ahead, I give you my heart, my loyalty, and my future."

The exchange of rings followed. Simple bands purchased that morning from Bozeman's jeweler, yet meaningful in their unadorned integrity. When Reverend Hollister pronounced them husband and wife, Joseph's kiss was both reverent and possessive, signaling to all present the depth of his commitment.

The celebration that followed at the hotel exceeded anything Lydia could have imagined in this frontier setting. Martha had outdone herself, transforming the dining room with bunting and flowers, providing a feast that featured the best local ingredients prepared with surprising sophistication.

Townspeople they had never met offered heartfelt congratulations and practical gifts, handmade quilts, preserves, tools for the ranch, and items for their home. The genuine warmth of this community, so different from the formal social obligations of New York, touched Lydia deeply.

"Your first time experiencing frontier hospitality at its finest," Joseph observed as they took a moment alone between well-wishers.

"When resources are limited, generosity becomes even more meaningful."

"It's wonderful," Lydia agreed. "Though I'm finding myself eager for the celebration to end, so we can begin our journey home."

Joseph's eyes darkened at her emphasis on the final word. "Home," he repeated. "Yes, I'm rather eager for that myself."

The festivities continued through the afternoon. Lydia sent a telegram to her parents, announcing her marriage and promising a longer letter to follow with full explanations. Joseph arranged for supplies they would need at the ranch to be delivered once they returned. And finally, as evening approached, they thanked their hosts and prepared to depart.

"You're welcome to stay at the hotel tonight," Martha offered with a knowing smile. "Your room is prepared—one room, this time."

Joseph glanced at Lydia, leaving the decision to her.

"Thank you, but we'd prefer to begin our journey," Lydia replied. "There's a perfect camping spot about two hours' ride from here, if I recall correctly. We'll reach it before dark."

Joseph's smile confirmed her memory and approved her choice.

They departed amid cheers and well-wishes, riding side by side through Bozeman's main street toward the open country beyond. As the buildings fell away behind them and the vast Montana landscape opened before them, Lydia felt a profound sense of rightness settle in her soul.

"Happy?" Joseph asked, guiding Thunder closer to Penny, so their legs almost touched as they rode.

"Completely," she assured him. "Though I'll be happier still when we reach our campsite."

His deep chuckle sent warmth through her despite the cooling evening air. "We've had practice setting up camp, certainly. Though I suspect tonight's arrangements might differ slightly from our previous experience."

"No dividing blanket necessary," Lydia agreed, her cheeks warming at the implication.

They rode in companionable silence as the sun began its descent, painting the Montana sky in spectacular hues of gold and crimson. The familiar landscape seemed transformed once again, now viewed through the lens of their shared future.

"There," Joseph pointed as they crested a small rise.

The location was perfect, a sheltered hollow beside a clear running stream, with adequate grazing for the horses and natural windbreaks provided by surrounding cottonwoods. They dismounted and began setting up camp with their usual efficiency, though each casual touch between them now carried new significance.

Joseph built a small fire while Lydia arranged their bedrolls—together this time, on a soft patch of grass beneath the spreading branches of the largest cottonwood. As darkness settled around them, they shared a simple meal from their provisions, sitting side by side with shoulders touching.

"I was thinking about tomorrow," Joseph said, staring into the dancing flames. "If we start at first light, we should reach the ranch by mid-afternoon."

"Our home," Lydia said softly, testing the words.

Joseph turned to her, the firelight catching the certainty in his gray eyes. "Our home," he confirmed. "The beginning point for whatever lies ahead."

He took her hand, his fingers intertwining with hers with familiar ease. "I can't promise it will always be easy, Lydia. Montana changes quickly, weather, circumstances, opportunities, and challenges. But I can promise we'll face whatever comes together."

"That's all I need," she assured him. "Not promises of perfection, but commitment to partnership through whatever we encounter."

The fire danced between them, casting a golden light on their faces as the Montana night deepened around their small camp. The vast sky above them shimmered with countless stars, a celestial canopy celebrating their union as completely as the community they'd left behind in Bozeman.

Joseph raised their intertwined hands, pressing a gentle kiss to Lydia's fingers. "I've been thinking about what Thomas said, about being a bridge between worlds. It's a responsibility I never sought, but one I find myself embracing now."

"As do I," Lydia agreed, her voice soft in the stillness. "My art can speak truths that politics and policies often obscure. The dignity of the Blackfoot people, the beauty, and vulnerability of this land, these deserve to be seen through honest eyes."

"Your eyes," Joseph affirmed. "Which somehow manage to be both gentle and unflinching at once."

Their conversation ebbed and flowed like the nearby stream, discussing practical plans for the ranch, dreams for their future, and reflections on the journey that had brought them together. As the fire burned lower, their words grew fewer, replaced by touches and glances charged with anticipation.

Finally, Joseph stood and extended his hand to Lydia. "Mrs. Calloway," he said, his voice deepening. "I believe it's time we retired for the evening."

Lydia placed her hand in his, allowing him to draw her to her feet. "I believe you're right, Mr. Calloway."

They moved together toward their shared bedroll beneath the sheltering cottonwood. Above them, a shooting star streaked across the vast Montana sky, a brilliant benediction on the night that would truly begin their life together.

Epilogue

Three months later, Lydia stood on the porch, watching the first snow of winter descend in gentle swirls across the ranch yard. She had just finished a letter to her parents, describing the changes underway at the ranch and the upcoming publication of her Montana sketches in National Geographic. Their response to her marriage had been predictably mixed, her mother's initial dismay gradually softening through correspondence, her father's concern about her future balanced against his reluctant respect for Joseph's forthright letters about their plans.

The screen door opened behind her, and Joseph emerged carrying two steaming cups. "Thought you might want some coffee," he said, offering one to her. "It's getting colder."

"Thank you." She accepted the cup gratefully, warming her hands around its earthenware sides. "I was just thinking about how much has changed since I first arrived in Montana."

Joseph leaned against the porch railing beside her, his shoulder touching hers in casual intimacy. "Having second thoughts about winter on the frontier?" he asked, only half-joking. He knew the months ahead would test her adaptation to ranch life more severely than the gentle seasons they had shared thus far.

"Not one," she assured him firmly. "Though I reserve the right to complain occasionally when the temperature drops below zero."

His chuckle vibrated through the shoulder pressed against hers. "Fair enough. And I reserve the right to remind you that you chose this life with your eyes wide open."

"That I did," she agreed, smiling up at him.

The past three months had been filled with steady work and quiet joy as they established their life together. The north-facing room Joseph had promised was now framed and partially enclosed, awaiting final completion when spring allowed. Her sketches of the Blackfoot settlement and Montana landscapes had been sent east, where the editors at National Geographic had responded with enthusiastic approval and requests for more work.

Most precious of all, their relationship had deepened through the daily rhythms of shared life. Morning coffee while planning the day's work, Joseph's patient teaching about ranch operations, Lydia's growing competence with tasks once foreign to her, and nights spent in each other's arms. They discovered the profound intimacy possible between two people fully committed to one another.

"I received word from Thomas yesterday by way of a traveler passing through," Joseph said, interrupting her reflections. "The Garrett brothers have moved on. Apparently Idaho Territory offered opportunities they found more appealing."

"That's a relief," Lydia acknowledged. The threat those men represented to the Blackfoot community had remained a lingering concern.

"Indeed. Though Thomas says we should remain vigilant. The pressure on treaty lands continues from other quarters." Joseph sipped his coffee thoughtfully. "He also sent something for you. It's inside."

Curiosity piqued, Lydia followed Joseph into the house. On the table lay a small package wrapped in soft deerskin. She unwrapped it carefully to reveal a miniature cradle board, exquisitely crafted and decorated with beadwork in patterns she recognized as Sarah Dove's distinctive style.

"It's beautiful," she breathed, running her fingers over the intricate beadwork. "But why would they send this?"

Joseph's expression held an intriguing mixture of amusement and tenderness. "According to Thomas, Sarah Dove had another dream. He was somewhat vague about the details, but it appears she believes we'll have need of it by next autumn."

Understanding dawned slowly as Lydia processed his meaning. "She dreamed...about a baby? Our baby?"

Joseph nodded, watching her reaction carefully. "So it seems."

"And how do you feel about that possibility?" Lydia asked, her heart quickening.

Joseph set his coffee cup aside and moved to take her hands in his. "I feel..." he paused, searching for the right words. "Terrified. Exhilarated. Humbled at the thought of creating a family together. But mostly grateful that whatever comes, we'll face it as one."

Lydia leaned into him, resting her head against his chest where she could hear the steady beating of his heart. "As one," she echoed softly.

Outside, the snow continued its gentle descent, blanketing the ranch in pristine white. Inside, warmth radiated from the hearth, where Joseph had built a fire to ward off the increasing chill. But the greatest warmth came from the certainty that had grown between them, a certainty born of choice and commitment, tested by challenge, and deepened through genuine partnership.

Lydia thought of the binding cord from their Blackfoot ceremony, now hanging in a place of honor beside the small wooden eagles Little Crow had carved. It seemed a perfect symbol for what they had found together, separate lives now purposefully intertwined, and stronger for the joining.

Joseph's arms tightened around her. "Weather's turning," he observed, glancing toward the window where the snowfall had intensified. "We should check on the livestock before dark."

"I'll help," Lydia offered immediately, already moving toward her coat and boots.

Joseph's smile held equal parts of love and admiration. "I know you will. That's who we are now, facing whatever comes together."

As they stepped out into the swirling snow, Lydia paused to take in the transformed landscape. The ranch buildings, the distant mountains, the vast sky above, all wore winter's first dress, beautiful and challenging at once. Like life itself, Montana offered no guarantees beyond the certainty of change, the promise of both hardship and beauty in equal measure.

But she would face it with Joseph beside her, their paths joined by choice and blessed by traditions that spanned different worlds. That knowledge settled deep in her heart, solid as the mountains on the horizon, enduring as the land beneath her feet, and as transformative as the journey that had brought her home.

Author's Note

D ear Reader,

Thank you so much for joining Lydia and Joseph on their journey through the rugged beauty of the Montana Territory. I hope their story of love, faith, and resilience beneath those wide, open skies touched your heart as much as it did mine while writing it.

As you may have noticed, *Beneath Montana Skies* includes interactions with the Blackfoot people—an Indigenous tribe with along, rich, and deeply rooted history in the American West. While I've done my best to portray these moments with respect and care, I also took a few creative liberties for the sake of the story, particularly in how Lydia and Joseph formed relationships within the tribe and were blessed by them before their Christian marriage.

These narrative choices were made with reverence, not to misrepresent, but to honor the spirit of cultural connection and community that can transcend boundaries.

That said, the real history of the Blackfoot Confederacy is profound, complex, and well worth exploring. I encourage you to dive

Leave A Review

I f you enjoyed this book, please consider leaving an honest review on Amazon

Visit Our Website:

www.vivianbelle.com

Visit Our Amazon Author Page HERE

Find Us On Social Media:

Facebook

Facebook Author Page

Instagram

deeper into their story—whether through books, museums, or online resources. Their traditions, struggles, and strength have played a significant role in shaping the history of the land we now call Montana.

Thank you for reading and for opening your heart to both fiction and history. And who knows? Maybe Lydia and Joseph aren't the last characters whose paths will cross with this beautiful, storied land...

With gratitude and happy trails,

Vivian Belle

* 9 7 8 1 9 6 6 0 9 3 2 0 6 *